THE HOUSE OF LIES

ANITA WALLER

Copyright © 2025 Anita Waller

The right of Anita Waller to be identified as the Author of the Work has been asserted by her in accordance with the Copyright, Designs and Patents Act 1988.

First published in 2025 by Bloodhound Books.

Apart from any use permitted under UK copyright law, this publication may only be reproduced, stored, or transmitted, in any form, or by any means, with prior permission in writing of the publisher or, in the case of reprographic production, in accordance with the terms of licences issued by the Copyright Licensing Agency.

All characters in this publication are fictitious and any resemblance to real persons, living or dead, is purely coincidental.

www.bloodhoundbooks.com

Print ISBN: 978-1-917705-23-3

*To Carol Flynn.
For her encouragement, friendship
and cakes.*

*There is no satisfaction in vengeance
unless the offender has time to realise who
it is that strikes him, and why retribution has come
upon him.*

— Arthur Conan Doyle

PROLOGUE
APRIL 1997

'You're absolutely sure he's the right man for you?' Malcolm Johnson asked his only daughter. He was trying unsuccessfully to dab at some stray tears that had magically appeared when he had experienced his first sight of her in her wedding gown.

'Oh, Dad, of course he's the right man for me. And to prove it I'll be marrying him in...' Jessica tilted her left wrist and glanced at the gold watch her father had given her the previous evening. 'Thirty-eight minutes. Now stop blubbering and help me get downstairs and into that car without falling over the hem, or even the train.'

He lifted her hand to his lips and gently kissed it. 'You are the absolute double of your mother, and she would have been so proud.'

'Don't make me cry, Dad, it's not a good look mascara running down my cheeks. She's been on my mind constantly for the last few weeks as we've been running round like headless chickens getting ready for a wedding, and it would have been my dearest wish that she be here for my big day, but that wasn't meant to be. I'm pretty sure everybody at the wedding will be thinking of her today.'

Malcolm opened the bedroom door and stepped back to allow her and the floaty, frothy vision of a dress to descend the stairs, where the driver of the limousine was waiting to settle her in the back seat. It wasn't an easy task, but eventually they were on their way, with Jessica feeling ever more anxious as they covered the short distance to the church.

She had had the ominous feeling that her dad knew... something. He had said at least three times over the past few weeks that she could still change her mind. He hadn't explained why he was making the ridiculous statement, and slowly it had pecked away at her brain.

But she was marrying the love of her life, and as they neared the church she was more convinced than ever that her dad was just being a normal dad, wanting the very best for his daughter when in his eyes there was no very best. But in her eyes that was the man she loved with all her heart, her Chris. Her own idea of the very best.

The bridesmaids were waiting as she pulled up outside the church. Jess glanced across immediately to her chief bridesmaid, Katie Ireland, and Katie gave a slight nod. This had been their jokingly agreed signal to say that Chris was waiting before the altar for her arrival by his side.

Jess breathed a huge sigh of relief and smiled brightly at the limousine driver as he held the door open for her. She stepped out, and like magic her father appeared at her side.

He tried to make light of how he was feeling. 'We can always get back in and head off home,' he said, looking deep into her eyes.

'Shall we?' she said, the grin lighting up her face.

'If only,' he muttered quietly, and held out his arm for her. 'Come on then, let's get on with the fun.'

Katie tidied the veil and train and stepped back as the bridal party prepared to enter the very full church.

The photographer waited for a moment, then began to take the photographs that would form the beginning of the album – the arrival of the bride, albeit nervously smiling.

Jess was stunningly beautiful, and she felt as though she was gliding rather than walking as she moved gracefully down the aisle to the organ music, supported by her father's arm until she reached Chris's side. Malcolm stepped to one side and sat on the front pew, watching as Katie helped to move the veil from Jess's face. Jess handed her bouquet to Katie, and finally looked into the deep blue eyes of the man she was about to promise to love and honour for the rest of her life. Not obey. That was a step too far, but the love and honour part was easy.

It went magnificently, and Mr and Mrs Harcourt exited onto the church steps to the sound of bells ringing all around the area. Confetti cascaded over them, and the photographer took what seemed like a million photographs before releasing everybody to the reception venue.

He sped off in his little car. He needed to be there first so that he could capture pictures of the happy couple arriving at the hotel, and as he drove away at the end of the evening he was keen to see the results of his few hours of work.

It had been a good wedding, including a stunning first dance to a Johnny Mathis number, 'My Love for You'. The couple had clearly practised it, and his camera had worked overtime.

So why did he feel some tension in the bride? And every time the groom left the room, why was he followed immediately by the bride's father? But for all of that, it had been a rattling good do, and the guests had enjoyed it, even if the bridal party had seemed a little off.

Jess and Chris left the next morning for a honeymoon on Crete, an idyllic two weeks that did much to dissolve any disquiet caused by her father.

The hotel was wonderful, the island all that they could have wished for, and they returned home with glowing tans, dozens of photographs and a desire to start married life away from the heat of the Cretan sun, to become a normal married couple.

Albeit, it would be as a couple who were to start their lives staying with Malcolm until they could move into their own home, which seemed to be taking for ever to finalise.

And Malcolm watched. And listened. Some twelve months earlier he had laughed off the first comment he had heard about Chris and one of the girls he worked with. But he had been unable to ignore something that happened on the two-day fishing trip they had both enjoyed, although neither of them won any prizes.

It had been a good day, the two of them being keen fishermen, and the overnight stay in a pub that catered for anglers had made the trip special.

But one a memory stayed with Malcolm. A girl standing outside Chris's bedroom door, tapping quietly. He had slipped back inside his own room, leaving his door slightly ajar.

'You're alone?' he had heard the girl whisper.

'Yep. Have to be up by seven to get breakfast, so we'll make the most of the hours we've got,' he heard Chris answer just as softly. But not softly enough.

And Malcolm had wondered how the hell he was going to tell Jess, and ultimately possibly lose her, because he didn't doubt Chris would come up with a cracking good reason for the high-heeled floosy to be outside his door. Malcolm could hear it now, some story of a late night snack being delivered. But that girl had carried nothing but a handbag...

And now he had to welcome both Chris and Jess into his

home for as long as they needed to be there, be polite to Chris, and possibly a little reserved towards Jess just in case he couldn't stop his thoughts from escalating into words.

Should he have said something before the wedding? It was too late now, and Malcolm suspected it wouldn't be too long before Jess realised maybe her new husband wasn't quite the catch she had initially thought.

Jess nodded. 'And thank you for informing me. It's a shock, but I have things to do. I have to get Josh and Adam here from Cornwall. I've already rung them to tell them to set off as soon as they can. They'll be here later today.'

'Can they just leave the pub at a moment's notice?'

'They can. They have a married couple working there as their main staff members, and they're moving in to take over while our boys need to be here for their dad.'

'And Malcolm? Is he feeling any better?'

'He's okay. Just feeling his age a bit, I suspect. He's seventy-eight, nearly seventy-nine now, and I think he's suddenly decided he needs to act his age. He's recently employed a gardener, because he simply did too much digging and it floored him. I feel sorry for the poor man he's set on because Dad will follow him round like a little dog, making sure he's doing everything right.'

'How long is it since your mum died?'

'Just over thirty years. She had a stroke and didn't recover. Dad never wanted anyone else, but in my heart – and I'm sure Mum would have wanted the same – I wish he had met someone else. He's a lovely man, my dad.'

Elsa flashed a quick smile. 'Always so polite. My first husband was a complete thug, and I got rid of him after a couple of years, but I was with him long enough for it to put me off ever having another partner. Maybe that's why your dad is still on his own – he was put off having someone else because he had perfection the first time around.'

'I'm sure you're right,' Jess agreed with a slight nod of her head. 'He gave our boys their inheritance early so that they could buy their pub – they were friends with the previous owner due to many after surf evenings spent in there. So they were the first to know when it went up for sale. We said we would help them get it, but Dad stepped in immediately, saying he had intended leaving a considerable financial settlement for Josh and Adam, because Chris and I would inherit his home. Everything was settled very quickly. They've increased takings since they started there a year ago, and apparently their surfboarding skills have increased exponentially!'

Jess didn't begrudge her boys their pub, but it had left her pretty much on her own dealing with Chris as he became increasingly unwell. One night, she had fallen into such a deep sleep that she missed him calling for her. After that, they decided to engage a carer, and that's when Elsa arrived.

The nurse smiled. 'Hard when they're so far away, isn't it?'

'They'll be here later to mentally support me, but I know it will be hard. I think they believed their father will live for ever, so now they've had to have it spelled out for them. Hence they're on their way back to Sheffield, probably still refusing to believe what's happening.'

Elsa reached across and gently touched Jess's hand. 'Your boys are no different to any other sons and daughters. No child thinks of their parents as being anything other than immortal, but later tonight they will see him and they'll know. It may be quicker than three days – he has had a bad day today. If you need to say your goodbyes, do it sooner rather than later.' She stood and walked towards the kitchen taking the now empty teacup with her. 'I'll go and check on him; you sit and rest.'

Jess gave a gentle nod and cradled her cup. Today was set to be the day she had promised herself many years ago. There would be no consequences now. She would say to Chris the words she had buried deep inside for twenty-seven years and would reveal her revenge for Chris's actions. Her time was here.

Chris's time, too, was here, but not for very long.

She finished her tea, stood and walked upstairs where she spent a minute retrieving one of the wedding pictures they hadn't considered suitable for their wedding album. She had kept it hidden for years in the pocket she had created in the back cover of her journal, the hefty book that knew all her secrets. It lived in an old bag in the bottom of her wardrobe, safe and secure as nobody knew of its existence.

It had simply been a picture of the guests swirling around the dance floor. Chris and Katie were standing a little too close and staring into each other's faces. Jess had been pictured dancing with her dad, and her back was to her new husband and her bridesmaid. She suspected that she had been held firmly in that position by the man who had truly loved her, Malcolm.

But she had known as soon as she saw the picture. Something had happened between Chris and her best friend, her chief bridesmaid. The woman who had been the keeper of all her secrets until the day the proofs came from the photographer. After that, Jess kept her at arm's length. No more late night conversations, giggles, night out plans. Her trust of Chris, and of Katie, died that day.

Jess opened up her journal to the entry she had made on the day she had realised *infidelity* wasn't just a word in a dictionary, it was a physical deed between her husband and her best friend.

She remembered the laughs and giggles between Katie and Chris, and their explanations: 'It's just something we're organising for the wedding! Stop asking questions, Jess.' And she had believed them.

The entry in her journal was becoming almost illegible, she had run her fingers across the words so many times.

> *I am certain C and K are seeing each other. I should have pushed Dad for answers. Can love die this quickly? I want to hurt him so badly. Chris, I swear to you, one day you will regret sleeping with her, I'll make you pay if it takes the rest of my life.*

And now that day was here. Her life, she felt, had been a life spent waiting for this moment. Chris had hurt her so badly, and he could have stopped it all by telling her the wedding was off, but he didn't. He married her, and still had Katie, her bridesmaid complicit in all the deception.

But Katie didn't matter. Only Chris. He had deceived her; he was the one married to her; Katie owed her nothing.

Jess stroked her words one more time, knowing she would never read them again. She had things to tell her dying husband that would make this the worst day of his life.

Over the ensuing years three more pictures had been added of Chris and Katie. She slipped all four photographs into her jeans pocket before replacing the journal in the bag, drawing the long zip across to secure it, and walking slowly back downstairs to destroy her husband.

Twenty-seven years had been a long time to live without being able to give love, but from the moment she had known for definite that Katie and Chris took every opportunity to be in bed together, she had switched off her love for the man she had married.

CHAPTER TWO

Jess waited until Elsa left the lounge before approaching her. 'I need some time with Chris,' she said quietly. 'Alone time. Take a couple of hours off. It's going to be hard for the next couple of days so if you need to do anything, do any shopping, take some time to do it now, while I can handle things.'

'You're sure?'

'I am. I need to discuss things with him, find out what he wants me to do for the boys, if anything, and at the moment there's a glimmer of life still in him. If I don't speak with him today, I'm sure the chance won't be there tomorrow. I don't want to wait until Josh and Adam get here because we have to discuss some financial stuff.'

'Then thank you, I will. If you need me while I'm out, ring me. I won't be more than a ten-minute drive away. I need to get a couple of birthday cards, and organise sending some flowers to my mum. She's just lost her best friend to a stroke, and is feeling pretty down, so flowers will help.'

'They always do.' Jess smiled.

Jess stood by the lounge window until she saw Elsa's car drive away. She reckoned she had two or three hours before their boys arrived. She turned her back to the window and looked across towards the hospital bed that had been her husband's home for the last few months.

'You're having visitors today,' she said softly as she moved to sit in the armchair that brought her level with his cancer-ridden body.

He frowned a little. 'They came this morning.' His voice cracked as he attempted to speak.

'That was your three wise men. Came to see if you fancied a round of golf. Good friends, Paul, Ollie and Daniel, I actually heard you laugh at one point. No, your visitors today are our sons, should be here in a couple of hours or so. Might be less than that if Josh is driving. Their rooms are ready, and I've taken one of my meat and potato pies out of the freezer, because I just know what they'll want for their evening meal.'

Chris half held up his hand. 'None for me.' His speech was definitely slurred.

Jess nodded. 'I know, Elsa will be back to sort out your needs. She's nipped into town for a bit, because I wanted to talk to you in private.'

Chris closed his eyes, as if the effort of keeping them open was just too much.

'You need to sleep?'

He nodded.

'Then let's see if we can wake you. I know, Chris. I've always known about you and Katie.'

His eyes opened. 'Katie?'

'Yes, Katie. My best friend, the one who was my support at our wedding, remember? I have a picture.' She held out the photograph she had hidden away for so long. 'You see, Chris, I never wanted to lose you, and more so when we had Josh, then Adam. And we've had a reasonably happy life. I don't think you ever suspected I stopped loving you soon after we married. I held my own feelings in check, cared for you, made a lovely home and brought up our children, our boys, to be happy, mature young men who will go far in this world. But I've had to carefully monitor you, and bide my time. I never trusted you, not for one minute of our twenty-seven years of being together.

'If I had gone first, you would have found a journal eventually, in the bottom of my wardrobe, that details everything I have done to pay you back, and everything I know. Because I do. Know things, I mean. It's a lengthy journal and a very comprehensive one. It tells everything you've done and everything I've done for the whole of our married life. You see, I know Katie wasn't the only dalliance you had. There were others. Katie was merely the first.'

Chris's eyes were not only open, they were fixed firmly on her face.

She picked up his water and guided the straw to his lips. 'You need a drink?'

He took the tiniest of sips then shook his head. She replaced the cup, and turned to him.

'So, shall we continue? At first I used to follow you, but after two years Katie and the poor fellow she married – can't even remember his name...'

'Jeremy,' Chris whispered.

'That's right! Jeremy. Well, when the two of them emigrated to Australia I thought it might be over and I could rest easy. You joined the golf club and teamed up eventually with Paul, Oliver and Daniel to make a regular foursome and life became calmer for me.

'No more listening to that cow Katie as she said how good her new feller was in bed, when I knew exactly who her feller was, and no more hearing her tell me where you two were meeting up that night, without revealing it was you she was seeing. I followed, Chris, I followed, and saw the two of you.'

She laid out the other three pictures and held them up so he could see them. 'It didn't even drop off when she met Jeremy. She screwed around with both of you. But then one night she told me Jeremy was taking over the Adelaide branch and she was going to go with him. You had one big meet-up in a swanky hotel in Newark two nights before she left, and I thought it was all over.' Jess tapped on the final photo.

Chris tried to speak. 'I didn't know...'

'You didn't know what, Chris? That I knew?'

'No idea,' he whispered.

'That's because I'm much smarter than you, Chris. But wait while you hear the rest of it. Because it's payback time. Payback for twenty-seven years of being treated like the little wifey at home who knows nothing, who had to put up with your conferences, your meeting clients – and you thought I didn't know what you were doing, because I had to stay at home to look after our boys.'

She studied his face. He looked like an eighty-year-old man; the cancer had taken everything from him, his joie de vivre, his looks, and now his life. A few more hours and he would be no more.

His eyes had closed once more, and she guessed he was trying to think, to work out what she meant by 'the rest of it'.

'Chris, open your eyes,' she said. He opened his left eye, waited a moment then opened his right one. He didn't speak.

'We had only been married six months when I realised I should walk away, but I still thought I could win you back. At that point I thought we could return to how we had been, so I kept trying, and you were smart enough to keep both of us happy. And then I became pregnant. That changed everything. I had to work things out for my benefit from that moment on, and simply bide my time, because I knew one day I would win. And that day is today.'

She waited to see if there was any reaction. He continued to stare at her.

'I knew then I wouldn't leave, because our baby needed a daddy as well as a mummy, and you loved Josh so much. Then Katie went off to Australia and I thought we would be okay. Adam's birth followed just over a year later, and my fate was sealed. But I couldn't get over your betrayal, Chris. I couldn't. There was no chance of forgive and forget, and when I reached the stage of following your car when you said you had arranged to meet Daniel, Paul and Ollie at the golf club, I knew I had to do something to settle my own mind. It's called revenge, I believe.'

She hesitated. 'I know you've known the three of them for a considerable number of years, but they're not like women. We talk about our sex lives, about what we like to do, about whether we fake it or don't even bother to pretend – but I'll bet your three best friends don't talk about anything like that, do they?'

Chris was shaking. She once more helped him have a sip of water, and laid him gently back onto his pillow.

She continued her chat with a conversational tone, and a smile on her face. 'They talked to me about it, Chris, about what they liked, about what they'd like me to do to them, and in the main I obliged. I wanted to be memorable, and if you happen to speak to any of them before the end, I'm sure they'll tell you I'm a cracker in bed. I think they have accepted they won't see you again, though.

'So all I can do to help you out is tell you your three friends have been totally loyal to you. Not one of them has spoken to the others, and they certainly haven't told you. All four of you think I'm the one and only. Apart from their wives of course,' she added with a slight laugh. 'I decided many years ago that if I survived you I would find some way to tell you what I had done, to pay you back in some small measure. If I didn't survive you, it's all detailed in my journal. There is just one thing you might want to think about – I fell in love. With one of your golfing friends. No names, no pack drill, okay!' She turned her head as she heard the sound of a car engine – she guessed Josh's Land Rover – pull onto the drive.

'Our boys are here. I know you won't repeat any of this because you're not really capable of much speech, but I'll tell them you've made it all up if you do mention any of it. This is just between me and you, Chris, just as our marriage should always have been between the two of us, and nobody else. But it wasn't, was it?' She straightened his covers, kissed his forehead and went out into the hall, slipping the photographs back into her pocket until she could replace them in her journal.

CHAPTER THREE

Josh and Adam walked in dragging suitcases behind them.

'We're here for as long as you need us, Mum,' Adam said, and pulled her into his arms. Josh took the suitcases upstairs to their rooms, and Jess made them a drink before checking whether their father was awake.

She left all three of them alone, and returned to the kitchen. Elsa had returned and was washing her hands before heading into the lounge.

'He's fine,' Jess said. 'Adam and Josh have only just arrived, so let's give them half an hour with him, then medication and suchlike can continue. He's only had sips of water while you've been out, but he looks greyer today than he did yesterday, don't you think?'

'I do. There's very little we can do now, Jess, his pain is under control but organs are starting to fail. He'll probably sleep most of the time from now on until he simply slips away. As there are three of you to watch for signs of change, I'll probably get a couple of hours sleep this afternoon then stay by his side all night. I'm relieved Josh and Adam got here in time to say their goodbyes.'

'Thank you, Elsa. You've been an absolute star through all of this. I couldn't have handled it without you.'

'Did you have your chat with him? Was he awake enough to understand everything?'

'Yes, he understood,' Jess said. 'He didn't speak much, but what he did say let me know he fully understood what I was saying.'

'Then the conversation he's having with his sons will probably ease the way for him as well. He's tired, Jess, tired of not being able to do anything. Tired of being dependent on drugs, tired of having no quality time with anyone. He's ready to go, Jess.'

'I know. He's been ill for so long, and I'm ready to let him go.'

They both looked up expectantly as they heard the lounge door opening. Josh and Adam joined them at the kitchen table, and both remained silent.

'He's asleep?' Elsa asked, standing to go to her patient.

'He is,' Josh replied. 'Does he sleep for long?'

'He may do this time,' Elsa said, trying to soften her words. 'He's very near the end, and ninety per cent of patients simply slip into a coma, then fade away completely. You can sit with him as much as you want, of course, although he may or may not realise you are there. I will be with him all night. I'm going to give his next dose of medication now, and then I'm going to take a nap. I may be needed during the night.'

Josh and Adam looked at each after she'd finished speaking, and Adam said a simple, 'No.' His mother knew he meant 'No, don't ever say anything so final, my dad isn't going to die.'

Jess wanted to take both of them into her arms, but she felt scared. They may be her babies, but those babies had somehow become adults with their own lives, a business to run; the distance in miles between Cornwall and South Yorkshire had created a familial distance as well.

Elsa left the kitchen and headed for the lounge. They listened for the closing of the door.

'It feels like being in limbo, doesn't it?' Jess said softly. 'When he does leave us he will be out of pain, all stress gone, but for us it will change everything. We'll have to learn how to live without his presence, and that's going to be so hard.'

The boys exchanged a glance. 'You'll be on your own, Mum. Will you cope?'

'I won't be given a choice. Financially I have no worries. Your father has worked with our solicitor and everything is settled in my name, with small bequests to you two. You obviously will share everything equally when I pass...'

The door leading from the back garden opened with its usual creak. Josh and Adam immediately stood and moved across the room.

'Granddad,' they said in unison.

Malcolm held open his arms. 'Good to see you, lads. Was it a good journey?'

Adam smiled. 'Scary. Josh drove.'

'You've seen your dad?'

'We have. He was awake when we arrived. Able to speak anyway. He asked me to get him some fresh water, and I could hear Josh and Dad chatting so I took my time. We spoke a bit more when I took the water in and then he drifted off. We'll go and sit with him again when he next surfaces enough to know it's us.' Adam's sadness was reflected in his voice.

Malcolm walked across and bent to kiss his daughter's head. 'Okay, sweetheart?'

'I am now our boys are here. And Chris knows they are, so he'll force himself to wake up.'

Malcolm made the effort to go and spend a few minutes

with the son-in-law he had never wanted in his life, although he would not have chosen this way of getting rid of him. Divorce would have been better, but he had soon realised Jess had forced herself to accept Chris's behaviour, although he wasn't sure that Chris had known that. But Malcolm had; he had seen the pain on her face at times, and he had known she was unhappy.

No, Malcolm was there for his daughter and grandsons. He left a sleeping Chris, turned in the doorway for a last look at him, and a frown crossed his face. The few words that had emanated from Chris when his father-in-law had spoken with him were the last ones he ever uttered.

The boys sat with him but Elsa kept checking constantly, and it was only when she went to get Jess that the realisation hit them that their father was in the last few hours of his life, and wouldn't be speaking again.

Two hours later they saw Elsa nod towards their mother, who was holding on to Chris's hand. Josh and Adam reached to clasp his other hand. It was cold, unresponsive, but he occasionally dragged out a shallow breath.

Elsa moved out of the room to make a phone call, returning almost immediately to say the doctor was on his way.

'Dad,' Josh said, but there was no response. He tried again. 'Dad...'

Elsa laid a gentle hand on each of the boys. 'He can't hear you. He's going to quietly slip away over the next few minutes.'

She left the room to answer the front door, returning a couple of minutes later with the doctor. And the end began immediately.

The next day was sunny, but nobody really registered that fact. Josh and Adam were both quiet, only coming to life when Jess spoke of a memory, a time when life had been so different with two parents; they spoke little to Jess and Malcolm, but chatted together about what would happen next.

Seeing their father's body being removed by the undertakers had been one activity too many, and they had sobbed alongside their mother, who finally had to accept she was no longer a wife, but a widow.

Elsa had packed the few items she had needed during the past few months of caring for Chris, cleaned out her bedroom and stored everything in her car.

When she walked through into the kitchen it was to see Jess, Josh and Adam sitting quietly round the table, and Malcolm washing up some mugs they had used earlier.

'You want a drink?' he asked Elsa, who shook her head.

'No thank you, Malcolm, I'm heading home now. Jess, I've notified everybody on the medical side, and they will be here to collect the bed within a couple of days. You don't need to do anything; they'll take the oxygen and everything else at the same time. I just want to repeat how sorry I am. Chris was a lovely man, and I couldn't have wished to work for a better family. I would like to attend the funeral if that's okay with you all?'

Jess stood and came round to the woman who had taken so much from her shoulders. 'Of course it's okay. I'll text you the details as soon as we have them. And thank you so much for the way you've cared for Chris, I'll never forget that.' She hugged Elsa, and watched as the woman left the kitchen.

Josh stood and followed her down the hall, then escorted her to her car before returning to join his family.

Malcolm went home conscious he was leaving Daisy, his Cavachon, a little too often, and promised Jess he would be back the following day. She walked down the garden path with him, and kissed his cheek. 'Thanks, Dad, for everything. And if you're coming over tomorrow, bring Daisy with you. We no longer have to worry about her chewing through oxygen pipes and suchlike, and she's not a dog that likes being alone.'

'I will,' he said. 'When I leave the house without her, she looks so forlorn. See you in the morning, sweetheart.'

Jess could hear Josh and Adam deep in conversation as she walked back down the hallway, and stopped for a moment. They suddenly felt estranged from her. At a time when she needed them the most, they were holding her at arm's length. Surely Chris hadn't been able to speak for long enough to tell them what she had spoken of...

She had timed her revenge to perfection. He wasn't capable of more than a few words, it exhausted him to think, never mind speak. But his hearing had been okay. And his eyes had been a little cloudy, but clear enough to register shock. She knew it had never occurred to him for one minute that his wife knew about his affair with Katie. But to hear from her own lips that she had slept with each of his three best friends was too much.

The revenge, the payback, she had planned for so many years was complete, yet she didn't feel any better for it. It would live on in her brain, and she patted her back pocket, checking that the pictures were still there. They needed replacing in her journal, then she would make decisions. That journal held too many details of her meetings with Chris's three golfing partners, and unless she wanted someone finding it after her own death, it had to go. She would have a bonfire one night in the future, she decided, and burn everything that related to her thoughts, wishes and dreams of the last twenty-seven years.

She knew that would take courage, but before her own death it would have to happen. She knew over the next few days she would be adding details of the last few days to it, because it was an automatic action – keep her journal accurate, keep it up to date.

She was tired but she wasn't convinced sleep would come.

Josh and Adam's conversation had died away. She guessed they had gone to their individual rooms, and she knew they needed time out just to think about Chris. To wonder how life would be without him.

She entered the lounge that had been a sick room for so many months, and felt quite shocked that the bed had been stripped, the bedding placed in a large white plastic bag and left on the mattress. In addition there was a brown paper bag that held all that was left of Chris's medication, and she emitted a deep sigh. Elsa had thought of everything, had ensured nobody in the family would have to deal with the mundane side of death. She had been the perfect choice, but Jess had known it from the start. She cared; it showed in every movement, every word. It would seem strange in the house without her there.

Jess quietly closed the lounge door behind her and climbed the stairs, heading up to her own room to change out of the clothes she had been wearing for two days. She needed a quick shower, then she would have to go into the office and make some phone calls, put arrangements in motion for the funeral, and place a notice in the local paper.

But first she had to tell Paul, Oliver and Daniel that their golfing partner was no more.

She slipped the four pictures out of her back pocket before adding her jeans to the laundry basket, opened her wardrobe door to lift out the bag containing her journal, and unzipped it. It was too light. She knew as soon as she picked it up that it was too light, but still she eased the zip open and ran her hand around the large bag's inner.

The journal wasn't there.

CHAPTER FOUR

Jess remembered catching her index fingernail in the zip as she had closed it after placing the book inside. This most precious book that told everything from her wedding day through to the entry she would shortly be adding about the death of her husband. A precious book above all others. She placed her bag on the bed, and stood.

She looked around her bedroom, so neat and tidy with very little out of place, feeling stressed. A quick glance in the en suite showed nothing unusual, certainly not a journal on the windowsill, or anywhere else for that matter.

Her mind had been somewhat distracted when she had replaced the book; could she have put it somewhere else by mistake? But she had squealed with the snag on her fingernail, and no matter how out of sorts she had felt, she would not have sought out a different bag to put it in; it had lived in the old brown leather one for over a quarter of a century. Until the previous day, nobody but herself had even known of its existence.

Nothing made sense. There had been nobody else in the house when she had told Chris about the book that catalogued their lives, including their affairs, and he certainly hadn't been capable of remembering all she had said, much less speaking about it. Within a few hours of their talk he had slipped away, so whatever he did take from their conversation was now gone for ever.

Jess headed back downstairs, unhappy, uneasy, and thinking hard about where she could possibly have put the book, considering that Chris's death, although unsettling, hadn't been unexpected. She was still performing in her normal logical fashion, and deep down she knew that the small tear in her fingernail proved she had placed it in her usual old bag.

So who had it now? The boys had never known of it, Chris had never known of it, and she didn't think Malcolm had known of it, although Malcolm had been the person who had bought her the journal all those years ago, and given it to her the night before her wedding day, along with the delicate gold watch she loved.

But Malcolm didn't know she had ever used the book.

The only other person in the house had been Elsa, and she definitely hadn't known of its existence. Unless...

Surely Chris hadn't been alert enough to tell his carer what his wife had told him? Or could he have told their boys?

Jess dismissed both ideas. Elsa had said she was sure Chris was into the last few hours of his life, and would simply fade away, his breathing slowly lessening until it stopped. And that had been exactly what had happened, and she had been with him until the doctor confirmed death.

She sat down on the small armchair that they had pushed into the bay window space and briefly closed her eyes. Although Chris was no longer there, the bed and everything he had needed was still there, and she prayed the van would arrive early the next day to remove it all. She needed normality, she needed to find her journal to tidy up her thoughts into the written word. She needed to record her thoughts about her ultimate revenge, and how it didn't feel so sweet now.

The intention had always been to tell Chris as she walked away from him to start a new life, it hadn't been to tell him as he passed on to the next life.

'What happens now?' Josh laid back on Adam's pillow as he asked the question.

'No idea really. We've had some time to get used to the idea that this would happen, but I'm assuming Mum and Granddad know what comes next. I know Mum wants us to go to the funeral place to discuss arrangements, but as to what arrangements she means, I'm clueless. And should we stay here until after the funeral?'

Josh shrugged. 'I suppose we should. There'll be a fair bit to do. She was in a state after she'd rung Dad's mates, wasn't she?'

'Not surprising really. Danny, Ollie and Paul were more like brothers to Dad, weren't they? And they've always gone to places as four couples. Been a good relationship, all round. For both of them.'

Josh heaved himself up off the pillow. 'What if...' He stopped speaking as the gentle tap on the bedroom door told them their mother was outside.

The door opened, and she popped her head around it. 'I'm going to make a hot drink, maybe a few sandwiches. We still need to eat even if we don't really want to. Any preference?'

'Anything will do, Mum,' Adam said. 'You okay?'

'So-so. It will all seem so final tomorrow, more real, when they take all the equipment away. Erm... I've mislaid a book, well, a journal really. It's one I write in, keep my life on track with, that sort of stuff. Have either of you seen it?' She measured an approximate size with her hands, and demonstrated the thickness with her thumb and forefinger.

'You've mislaid a book that size?'

She nodded. 'I always keep it in a certain place, been there for around twenty-seven years, and now it isn't. I can only put my forgetfulness down to what's happened during the past week because everything intensified all at once, but I can't for the life of me find it.'

'Leave it till tomorrow,' Adam said. 'The lounge will need a thorough sorting, hoovering and suchlike, so we'll check there first. Don't worry, it doesn't have legs, it can't have left of its own accord. We'll find it.'

Jess still looked troubled, but nodded. 'Come down in ten minutes or so, I'm not doing much, but I think my headache is down to not having had food for a couple of days. I'll do tea and coffee, but if you want something stronger, you know where it is.'

She closed the door behind her, leaving Josh and Adam to stare at it. 'She'll make herself ill.' Josh frowned at the thought.

'She will. We can't stay away from the pub forever, but we have to make sure she's okay. Let's go eat.'

Malcolm and Daisy walked up the road, a long walk made longer by neighbours stopping to ask if Jess was okay. He repeated the same words to almost everyone, finally reaching his daughter's home with a truly skittish dog bouncing around on tippytoes, thanks to the frequent stops she had been forced to endure.

He walked around to the back garden, checked the garden gate was secure and let Daisy off the lead. She tore around like a whirling dervish, and he smiled. He left her running riot and entered through the back door.

Jess, Josh and Adam were sitting around the table, ham sandwiches in the centre, mugs of hot drinks in front of them.

Jess stood. 'Drink, Dad?'

'Coffee, please, Jess.'

'Sit down. Help yourself to food. We're never going to eat that pile but...' She waved her hand in the air, dismissing her own words.

'Thank you. I'm not eating either, so I'm assuming you three haven't been?'

'Granddad, you seen a thick journal sort of book around the place?' Adam looked at Malcolm; his grandfather didn't look well.

'Don't think so. You lost one?'

'Mum has. Don't worry about it, it'll turn up.'

Jess placed a cup of coffee in front of her father. 'It's the journal you gave me the night before Chris and I got married.'

'Really?' Surprise was etched on Malcolm's face. 'You used it?'

'Always. It's used for loads of stuff – passwords, our bank accounts if we need to swap money around, that sort of thing. It's like a memo book just for me, but everything goes in it – how I felt when I had the boys, the devastation when they told us Chris's cancer was terminal, it's all in there. I update it about once a week, so it'll turn up at some point.'

Malcolm felt inordinately pleased that Jess had used the book. It had been a most unusual purchase. Everybody used diaries, but he had been to a new stationery shop specifically to pick up a notebook for himself and had seen the ornately tooled leather book with *Journal* written across the front.

The interior was special – it didn't have dates. You filled in your own date for the day you needed to make an entry. He knew of his daughter's love for stationery, and it had been a last-minute wedding gift just for her. He realised he had never once heard her say she had used it, so felt a small frisson of pleasure at the knowledge that she had used it, and as recently as the day before.

'Do you need help to look for your journal?' he asked.

Jess shook her head. 'It can't be far away. I keep it in a special bag I've always used for it, and I must simply have put it down while I dealt with something else, and I'm sure it will turn up in the most unexpected place.'

They ate very few of the sandwiches; Jess cleared everything away, loaded the dishwasher and they moved into the small lounge that was more of a library than anything else. It didn't have a television but it did have beautifully crafted bookshelves. The furniture maker had done a magnificent job and the wood, a dark, dark oak, glowed in whatever light happened to be coming into the room through the bay windows. Lamplight in the evenings caused the richness to glow with an even darker hue, and the deep red lounge suite blended in cohesively; it was most definitely a room much-favoured by all the family, and any visitors.

'Love this room the most,' Malcolm said as he sat on the sofa by the side of Adam. 'It's much cosier than the other lounge; and Chris kept some wonderful whiskies in here.'

'It's my favourite, too. Dad loved it as well. He always tutted at us if we needed him, and he was in here. We used to invent stuff we wanted him for, just to annoy him, get him away from his books.' Adam paused. 'I'd give anything to be able to annoy him one more time.'

'He was ready to go, Adam. I chatted with him last week, but not for long. He was simply too tired. The drugs took away most of his pain, but they took everything else about him. Yes, he was ready to leave us.'

Jess moved across to the drinks cabinet. 'We should have a whisky, raise a glass to our man, because he sure would appreciate us doing that. He was definitely a whisky man. Any preferences?'

Malcolm laughed. 'Any will do for me, they're all special.'

Jess poured out four drinks and handed them round. The cut glass whisky tumblers twinkled as they raised them in appreciation of the rich amber contents.

Malcolm spoke. 'To Chris, husband, father and son-in-law. And hoarder of fine whiskies. God speed, Chris, with love.'

CHAPTER FIVE

It was some four weeks after the funeral that three men sat at their normal table in the bar of the golf club, whiskies in front of them. Paul Browne, Oliver Newton and Daniel Rubens raised their glasses.

'To Chris,' Paul said, and they all echoed the words before draining the glasses.

'It seems really odd now he's gone, don't you think?' Daniel said thoughtfully. 'I know he hasn't played a round for some time, but while he was alive he was still part of us, our foursome. Just a non-playing member. But now it's final. Now we're three.'

'He had a good send-off,' Oliver said, closing his eyes for a moment. 'Plenty of people there. You think it's because he was so young? I don't mean young young, so to speak, I mean he wasn't old. He's actually the first friend I've lost, and I'm struggling to get my head around it. Fifty-one, he was just a year older than me. God only knows how Jess is coping, I'll maybe pop round and see if there's anything any of us can do.'

'The boys have gone back to Devon now,' Paul joined in. 'She's in that great big house on her own, although I know her dad lives close by. I chatted to him at the funeral, interesting man, knowledgeable about all sorts of things. Known him a long time, but never talked at length with him before. They're very close, him and Jess. He lost his wife about thirty years ago, he was saying, and I think Jess is very supportive of him.' He waved towards the bar, held up three fingers, and turned back to his friends. 'Let's make an afternoon of it. Take advantage of Naomi volunteering to pick us up.'

'She's a star, your wife.' Oliver grinned at his friend. 'I don't think Denise would have volunteered.'

'Naomi didn't volunteer. I bribed her with a promise of a meal at the Vicarage if she'd pick us up and deliver us to our respective homes. She made me make the booking before she said yes. I'm henpecked, really.'

His two friends both laughed. 'Join the club,' Daniel said. 'I once accused Andi of ruling me with a rod of iron, and the consequences of that statement weren't good. I just keep quiet now, makes for a much easier life. Funny how she never says anything about the four – three – of us meeting up twice a week though. Is golf an acceptable thing?'

Ollie shrugged. 'Must be. Denise just goes along with it as a fact of life. I suppose because we've done it for so long. And it's a man thing. Or in our case it's a man thing.'

'We're going to miss him, Chris I mean. He was the one who always laughed, didn't take anything too seriously. So what do we do? Look for somebody to replace him, or just play as a threesome?' Daniel looked pensive.

'For what it's worth,' Ollie said, 'I think we don't actively look for a new fourth member, we just play as a threesome. If somebody actually asks to join us, or we get a new member join the club, we can discuss it further, but I'm quite happy to continue as a threesome. We've been playing like that for a few months now.'

Daniel and Paul nodded in agreement. 'That makes sense.

Losing Chris is going to take some getting over, so let's take some time out. Not from golf, but from changing anything. That okay?' Paul looked at the other two, and thumbs were raised. He went on. 'And we'll keep a watching brief on Jess – and on Malcolm, because he's not getting any younger – just like Chris asked us to do.'

Jess patted her knee and Daisy jumped up, always keen to be stroked. With Malcolm away for a couple of days on a fishing break, the little dog had arrived at Jess's home with her own packed suitcase and her own bed.

She stroked Daisy's head, and with almost a sigh she settled down into Jess's lap, dropped her head for a slight snooze and awaited further instructions. Jess also closed her eyes; the silence of the house at night was almost too much now the boys had returned to their pub. She was drifting in and out of slumber when she heard the car engine.

She knew it so well, the purr of the Porsche Carrera, and instantly she moved, waking Daisy from her fitful nap before heading to the front door. She was opening it before Ollie had chance to ring the doorbell.

Neither said a word. He stepped into the hallway, closed the door carefully behind him and took her in his arms. 'Are you alone?'

'I am. Dad's dog is here for a couple of days, but as far as human beings are concerned, I'm alone.' She smiled up into his face and he bent and kissed her, enveloping her into his warmth.

'It's so good to see you again,' she breathed into his chest. 'It's been too long. You can stay for a bit?'

'I can. I'm the designated checker-up to make sure you're not struggling.' He smiled. 'That okay?'

'It is, but you don't need to check on me. I'm a strong woman, Ollie, as you well know, and I'm coping fine. Yes, it's odd, but everything went back to the hospital pretty quickly. We got the decorators in to do some remedial work in the lounge; and I have everything back in place. I must confess to using the library most of the time, but eventually I'll stop seeing Chris in the other one every time I walk through the door. I'm reading a lot, not eating much – but enough – and the boys ring me most nights so you can report back to Daniel and Paul that all I need is time.'

'And me?'

The question came out of the blue, and Jess stiffened. Then she leaned against him. 'And you. I hoped the months of caring for Chris and having my freedom truly stopped would cure me of you, but I heard the Porsche's engine and my stomach did a somersault.'

He tilted her head towards him. 'So it's the car that you're after?'

'No, it's definitely the driver. The car is just something that goes perfectly with the owner.' She smiled. 'It's so good to see you again, just the two of us.'

'I was nervous,' he admitted. 'I did think I might not be welcome any more, it's been so long...'

'Ollie,' she said carefully, 'I don't say *I love you* without very careful thought. The last man I said it to was Chris, nearly thirty years ago. No matter what happens or doesn't happen between us, I love you. You're a very special man.' She grinned at him. 'And you've got a Carrera that I desire. Coffee?'

He laughed. 'Oh my God, Jess, I've missed you so much. And yes please, to the coffee. The last time I told you I loved you was the day you told me the terminal diagnosis for Chris, and I deliberately haven't mentioned anything further because it wouldn't have been fair. You had enough to handle, so I backed away. I turned myself into Chris's golfing partner along with Daniel and Paul, but never for a minute did I stop loving you and remembering what we had.' He took a deep breath, as if scared of revealing too much of how he was feeling.

'Whatever happens now, we take it very slowly. Denise and I already lead very separate lives, and Elle is in her final year at uni, but has already decided she wants to stay in Newcastle, so we're buying her a flat there.' He paused, staring at the woman who was simply looking at him, knowing she was wondering what was coming next.

'We can't be open about our relationship, I accept that, and I accept it for as long as it takes. Josh and Adam would be horrified if they knew we had anything between us. Their father has only just passed, so we have to have patience, if that's what you want.' He watched as relief flashed across her face.

Jess stood and pulled him close, before kissing him. 'I'll make us a coffee.'

Afterwards, Jess walked down the driveway and waited as Oliver sank into the driver's seat. They spoke softly, and he said he would ring her that night after Denise had left to go to her book group. He put down the window, and she gently closed the door, remarking that it sounded just like a VW.

He laughed. 'Amazing piece of marketing for VW, that was. But I can assure you this sounds like a Porsche, not a VW.' He reached out of the window to grasp her hand. 'I love you, Jess. Ring if you need anything, and I'll report to the other two that you're doing well, but I'll keep in contact with you. That okay?'

'It is. It makes me feel better that you all care, if I'm honest. I don't feel so alone now. Now go! We really do have to be careful.'

He nodded, put the car into drive and she waited until his brake lights flashed at her, as he reached the end of the road. She couldn't help the smile that was plastered on her face.

Daisy wagged her tail as Jess re-entered her home, and wagged it even harder as Jess put on a jacket and picked up the dog lead.

'Come on, Daisy. Let's go to the park.' She checked she had poop bags in her pocket, then opened the front door. She needed to think, and a nice long stroll with Daisy was just the thing that felt right.

It occurred to her that although the little dog was not big enough to attack any intruders, having Daisy around the house automatically created a sense of security in her own home. Maybe she should get a dog?

She could at least discuss it with her dad, who she knew would be delighted to help her find the right one. It might even give him some peace of mind, because she knew he worried about her being on her own in such a large property.

Ten minutes later they entered the park gates, Daisy now walking sedately by Jess's side. She had sniffed every lamppost, every roadside tree, every car tyre on their journey, but on the path through the park there was nothing that required her sniffing skills.

Jess sat on a bench and allowed her thoughts to roam. Daisy was underneath the bench, and soon began to snore, so Jess remained as still as she could. Ollie was on her mind. She had truly fallen for him, even though her flirting with him had originally been part of her revenge plan.

She hadn't anticipated Chris becoming ill. She had planned for a revenge that would happen when the boys were gone and leading independent lives. She had waited more than twenty-five years for her revenge, intending to let Chris know she was aware of his affairs, particularly with Katie.

And then cancer blighted their lives.

She had entered the fleeting passionate moments with Daniel and Paul into her journal, and they remained in her memory as interesting episodes for telling Chris when the time was right to hurt him as much as he had hurt her. But she couldn't cast Ollie aside.

She had known that when she told Chris about Oliver Newton, it would be to tell him it was no fleeting affair.

The terminal diagnosis had been a shock. 'He won't reach fifty-two,' the consultant told her. She almost decided not to continue with her plans for retribution. Her duties in bringing up their children were virtually at an end, and she was preparing to go, to follow her own dreams, preferably with Ollie. But the speed of Chris's deterioration changed her thoughts. It wouldn't be an easy death, and they had been together a long time. She was teetering on the point of a decision to burn her journal and forget her plan.

Until the night Chris asked her to let Katie know. And she reinstated the plan.

CHAPTER SIX

Josh turned his back so that Adam could lower the zip on his wet suit, then he did the same for his brother.

'Cracking dip,' Adam said, and bent down to pick up his surfboard. 'We'd best get back; we said we'd only be an hour or so, but we've been a bit longer.'

'Waves were good today; you have to grab them when you can. It seems ages since we did this. It's not the same without Dad falling off his board all the time though, is it?'

Adam sucked in his breath. 'He'd have loved it today. He was never too keen when the waves were high, but he might even have stayed on longer in these waves. I miss him.'

'Me too, especially at times like this, but we've seen him in some awful pain at times, and he couldn't have continued, he just couldn't.'

Adam could sense almost desperation in Josh's words and he paused. 'Hey, I do understand you know. We have to let it go, he's at peace now, with no more pain. It's really the fact that he was so young to be taken from us that hurts the most. If it had been Granddad who went, yes I would have been devastated, but I could have accepted it more.' He leaned on his board and looked around. 'Dad'll always be here with us, here on this particular beach. I think that's how Mum is handling it, that he'll always be with her in that house.'

Josh remained quiet. 'You think?' he said when he finally spoke. He picked up his board once again. 'Come on, let's get back to the day job; somebody needs to serve some customers.'

They strapped the boards on top of Josh's Land Rover, and Josh exited the beach car park slowly, before putting his foot down once they were on the road. Adam had given up saying anything about his brother's driving, now accepting that yes, Josh went far too fast, but he could handle it.

Josh glanced across at Adam and smiled. His eyes were closed. And his hands weren't gripping the sides of the passenger seat. Progress indeed.

Several customers spoke to both men as they walked through the bar before heading upstairs to change into something more appropriate than wet suits for working downstairs.

When they eventually arrived looking infinitely more civilised, it was to hear that stocks were low on several items, so Josh said he would do the wholesalers run the following day.

'You hear that?' Adam said to the drinkers sitting at the bar. 'Go easy on the crisps. There's a world shortage, but we're dealing with it.'

It was a good end to their day, and both Josh and Adam felt it had been a day on which they had needed, not just to enjoy the board time, but also to feel at one with Chris again. He had been the one to insist they started swimming lessons before they could even walk. He'd also insisted on so many holidays in Devon and Cornwall – holidays where their love of surfboarding had developed.

They locked the doors after the last of the staff had left for home, and headed upstairs to their flat.

'You want a drink?' Josh asked.

'Only a milk,' Adam replied. 'I feel knackered. I'll have a small glass of milk, then I'm off to bed. Good waves today, but they kill the back and legs.'

'I'll get it. And have a lie-in tomorrow. I'll be off out early, get some jobs done like the wholesalers, but it doesn't take two of us. And you can do the evening shift tomorrow with me. Neil's covering till six so no need for us at all during the day, really. We're not that busy. And if there's a problem, we do have phones.'

'Okay. I'll have a couple of paracetamols with my milk, get rid of this headache.'

Josh opened the fridge, poured the two glasses of milk, and delved into the everything drawer for the tablets. He carried them through to the lounge, where Adam's eyes were already closed.

'Here,' he said quietly, and handed over the tablets. 'These are our last two, so I'll pick some up while I'm out and about tomorrow. Get them down you, and go to bed. Not feeling ill, are you?'

Adam shook his head. 'No, just tired. Threw myself about like a lunatic in that water today, and I think I'm paying for it now.' He swallowed the painkillers and washed them down with the milk before standing to leave the room. 'Thanks for this,' he waved the glass, 'and I'll see you at some point tomorrow. If we're fully covered for staff, don't rush back. The customers can wait for their crisps till tomorrow night.' He smiled as he left the room, as did Josh.

The next morning, Josh left a note for Adam to say he would ring later. He hadn't been able to sleep so was making an early start by going to the wholesalers. The day was gloomily overcast, and he felt relieved they had headed for the beach the previous day, when the sunshine had lifted their spirits marginally. Today would have definitely crushed them underfoot.

His first stop was to fill up with fuel, and he grabbed a coffee to take with him. Even at that early hour he bumped into a couple of his customers, so it took fifteen minutes before he was back in the driver's seat and heading for the huge wholesalers.

Two hours later his car was fully loaded, his stomach had managed to accommodate yet another coffee and a bacon sandwich, and he drove out of the car park and headed for the beach.

Josh had almost a full day to kill, and he needed to think about what he was going to do.

Adam didn't surface until midday. He made himself a drink, and crawled back into bed, switched on his television to see if anything dramatic had happened in the world, then switched it off again when it became clear it was all about politics, politics and more politics.

He opened his Kindle, read his latest purchase for half an hour, then gave up. He needed food.

The fridge looked a little sparse, and he hoped Josh would think about stocking it up while he was out doing what Josh did best, being alone. He'd never been any different, always preferring his own company to that of a group, and it had worried both Jess and Chris, but Josh was Josh, and nothing would change him.

Adam, on the other hand, was the gregarious one, always chatty, happy to help anyone, to simply be with anyone.

He picked up his phone to ring his brother, but then

thought better of it. He had sensed the previous day that Josh was feeling a little overwhelmed, and he suspected the early morning start he'd mentioned in his note was exactly what Josh needed – maybe a few hours sat on a cliff top somewhere, just thinking, possibly reading, taking time out to simply be Josh.

Adam made himself a hot chocolate, did a quick trip downstairs to check everything was as it should be, and was a little disconcerted to see only three customers.

Neil moved the length of the bar to stand by his boss. 'Don't panic, this is the first time I've stopped since we opened. We had two mini-buses in, it's definitely been lively. They left about ten minutes ago, so I'm quite relieved that there's only three customers in at the moment.' The outside door swung open, and three ladies walked in.

'Six,' he said, and moved down the bar towards his new customers. 'Okay, ladies, what can I get for you?'

Adam grinned, and left Neil to it, knowing that any number of customers would be dealt with efficiently and accurately.

He headed back upstairs still carrying his hot chocolate, and turned up the heating thermostat slightly. It wasn't simply a miserable-looking day; it was decidedly chilly. Autumn was definitely heading towards winter.

He rang Josh, but there was no answer. He guessed he was driving, so didn't try again. Josh would see the missed call when he stopped, and contact Adam.

And Adam knew he didn't have to speak to his brother; it was just a need to be in touch.

He finished his hot chocolate and rinsed out the cup before stashing it in the dishwasher, then switched on the machine. There had to be easily three days of dishes, and this was his contribution to that day's housework, he reckoned.

Should he get the vacuum out? He talked himself out of

that, and went back downstairs to check the pub hadn't suddenly got busy after Neil's influx of three ladies. It hadn't.

Neil was wiping down tables ready for the evening crowd which always made up for any lack of numbers during the day. 'You want something, Adam?'

Adam shook his head. 'No, just wanted to check you hadn't got a coach party in. Everything okay?'

'It's fine. Look, go back upstairs and relax. You and Josh have had a rough few weeks, and you have staff who can do everything here. You need to recover. We're all going to miss your dad, but you two will miss him most of all and you have to heal. So go upstairs, put the TV on, read a book, do a jigsaw. Whatever, but you're not on duty till six o'clock tonight. Okay?'

Neil's words brought a smile to Adam's face. 'You telling me off?'

'Too bloody right I am. Josh has disappeared for the day, he's done what was needed, and now you have to do the same.' He spun Adam around, and gave him a gentle push in the back. 'Vamoose,' he said. 'You're not currently required.'

And Adam laughed. A genuine laugh. *I haven't done that in a long time,* he thought. 'Thanks, Neil. I'll go and see if we've actually got a jigsaw, but if not I'll read.' He shook his head. 'A jigsaw? Do people still do jigsaws?'

Neil heard him say it. 'I'll bring you one in tomorrow,' he called. 'And yes, people still do jigsaws.'

Adam read. At least, he read until his Kindle said he only had ten per cent of charge left, and then he stopped. He rubbed his eyes which were in some danger of closing, and decided to jump in the shower, change his jeans for some smarter wear, and get ready for his evening shift. He still hadn't heard from Josh, but knew he would be okay. It was simply what Josh did, spend time thinking and being alone.

Josh, of course, rang while Adam was in the shower and he

didn't hear it, but by the time he had finished and got dressed for the evening session, his brother was back at the pub.

'Hi, bro,' he called as he climbed the stairs. 'You okay? You didn't answer your phone.'

Adam shook his head in exasperation. He reached the top of the stairs at the same time as Josh. 'I didn't answer my phone? Where were you when I was ringing you?'

'Polzeath.'

'Polzeath? Without me?'

'I didn't surf. Just sat and looked at the sea most of the time. It helped. I've thought a lot of things through, and I think we should talk to Mum and maybe Granddad as well about them coming to live with us. Well, not exactly at the pub, we haven't got room, but to move down to Devon. We can't help them if they're in Sheffield and we're down here. Not easily anyway. You think Mum will go for it?'

Adam laughed. 'Not an earthly. And you can be the one that mentions it.'

CHAPTER SEVEN

Sunday morning found Jess feeling a little out of sorts. Daisy had now gone home with Malcolm, and she hadn't mentioned her thoughts about getting a dog of her own, just in case he whisked her off to the nearest dog pound to see which one would suit her best. She needed to give such a huge decision much more thought.

She took out the notebook that had become her temporary journal until her real one resurfaced, and began to write down how she was feeling. She wasn't missing Chris, and that was the hardest thing to write. Her love had died on the day she had confirmation he was seeing Katie, but she couldn't dismiss all of their twenty-seven years as a waste of time.

They had co-existed comfortably enough, once she had realised she had to switch off her love. They had produced their sons; Chris had been an excellent father if a rubbish husband, and they had lived a good life. It simply hadn't been what she had envisaged on their wedding day. She had wanted a lifetime of love; Chris had other ideas.

Her thoughts were jumbled, and in the end she gave up and placed the notebook carefully on the top shelf of the second bookcase unit, slipping it in between *Salem's Lot* and *Misery*. Stephen King would be the guardian of her words until she found her real journal.

Her doorbell signalled she had a visitor standing on the front doorstep and she peeped around the curtain to see who it was. She was surprised, yet pleased, to see Elsa, and quickly left the library to welcome her.

Jess smiled as she opened the door. 'It's lovely to see you,' were her first words.

'And you,' Elsa said, with an answering smile. 'You were all on my mind last night, so I thought I'd pop round and just say hello.'

'Well, come in! I was just going to put on some coffee, might even find a piece of cake.'

Elsa followed Jess through to the kitchen, and sat down. 'So, how are you doing?'

'We're okay. Getting used to our new normal. The boys are back in Devon and I try not to miss them, but I do. They've asked Dad and me – and Daisy – to go down and stay for a month over Christmas and the new year. They obviously can't come here, it's their busiest period, but I can go help them. I've promised to think about it, but I'm not sure I'm ready for such a massive change. It would be, because they know how much I love Christmas here. And Dad's health isn't great, so I'll give it a lot of consideration before I say one way or the other. It's only October, I've plenty of time.'

Jess switched on the coffee machine, and cut two slices of chocolate cake. 'If you don't swallow this, it's not fattening,' she said, and placed a plate each in front of them. She sat down and reached across to touch Elsa's hand. 'Thank you for coming.'

'No problem. I missed you, I missed the family. I was here for five months, and when you get to know somebody as well as I got to know all of you, it's a wrench to leave. I'm on annual leave for a couple of weeks, so I thought it might be okay to call round. We're not encouraged to re-visit once our patients have passed, but...'

Jess laughed. 'But you're on annual leave and technically not employed.'

'That's right. I knew you'd understand. So you're doing okay?'

'Honestly? I think I'm doing very well. I have a brilliant solicitor and all the legalities of the house being entirely in my name, bank account changes, that sort of thing, is now done, and I've an appointment for next week to tidy up my will.'

'You'll stay here?'

Jess shrugged. 'It's my home. I couldn't give up my library easily, but I must admit the house does feel huge when I'm rattling around in it at night and I'm on my own. I didn't notice it when Josh and Adam were here, but as soon as they went back it really hit me. I'll not be thinking about moving for at least a year. I've decided to give myself time to settle into the place as the sole occupier, and if I find I'm struggling after that year, then I'll put it on the market. Who knows what will happen in that year.'

'Who knows,' Elsa echoed. 'You think you might move down to be near your boys?'

'Devon is beautiful...'

'But it's not the Peak District,' Elsa finished the sentence for her, and laughed.

'It's not, and I know I'd be swapping what I have on my doorstep for a doorstep into the sea, I'm not sure that would be what I want.'

She stood to get their coffees, and Elsa smiled her thanks.

Jess continued to voice her thoughts. 'And Josh and Adam have made their own lives. I feel as though I would be burdening them not only with me, but also with Dad. It's not fair, they're building a business. Just suppose I became ill; it would take them away from their lives, and it does become all-consuming, caring for someone you love who is desperately ill. It's funny, but I would never have thought like this before...'

'Before Chris,' Elsa said gently. 'I was very fond of him, you know. He was intelligent, witty when he wasn't in pain, and he apologised all the time for being such a trouble to me, but he wasn't. A trouble, I mean.' She took her fork and broke off a piece of cake. 'How many calories in this piece?' she asked, smiling at Jess, before continuing.

'Some of my clients can be really nasty, especially when they get a time limit put on their life, but Chris didn't react like that. He accepted it, frequently asked me to support you as well as him, but that's what we do, as carers. We support the family. And Chris had such a lovely one. I think about you all, most days.' Elsa paused for a moment as she watched for any signs of distress in Jess.

'I know Josh and Adam took it hard, but they didn't really see Chris when the pain was bad, when he was moaning even in his sleep. They didn't see the incremental increases in dosage that we had to make. We had given Chris a pain-free end, and that's what they saw. A different father to the one they grew up with, but not one who cried out in pain. You saw every stage, Jess, and took it all on the chin. I can't tell you how much I admired you.'

Jess had no words. She knew Elsa wouldn't be speaking in this way if she had been aware of the last conversation she and Chris had shared, but Elsa also wouldn't have known the background to their lives that had led up to her finally letting Chris know what she had concealed for all of their married life.

They finished their cake and coffee, and Jess suggested they head to the lounge. She wanted to show Elsa the large room first, where she had spent so much of her time with Chris, and she opened the door. 'It's changed a bit in here,' she said.

Elsa looked around. 'Wow. It's beautiful. You're a real homemaker, Jess. So different to how it looked last time I was here.'

'I rarely come in here,' Jess said slowly. 'When I do, I see Chris in that bed.'

'It will pass,' Elsa replied. 'All my clients say the same, but eventually the room will return to you. It's early days, Jess. Don't beat yourself up about it, but don't avoid coming in here. The more you open that lounge door, the more the room will stop being what you're still perceiving it to be.'

They walked across the hallway into the library, and Elsa sighed. 'But this room is spectacular.'

'I know, and strangely enough Chris spent so much of his time in here. We have always been big readers, as you can probably tell, yet I don't feel his presence in here as I do across the hallway. He kept his stock of whisky in that bar unit, and would have one most nights. But being in here doesn't affect me or make me miss him even more.'

'That's because this is your room. It's your happy place. Book love is a powerful thing, isn't it?'

'It is. Towards the end, when Chris couldn't even hold a book, I read to him until he drifted off to sleep. And before you ask, I didn't read him any of the Stephen King books; I stuck to his favourite genre, because he always enjoyed a good spy thriller. Those times were special for both of us. Sit down, Elsa, let's enjoy a bit of the ambience in here, away from the temptations of chocolate cake.'

Almost an hour passed in pleasant conversation, and the two women agreed a trip out to Bakewell one day would be a very welcome interlude during Elsa's annual leave period. They could combine it with a shopping expedition while in the market town, and it all would make their lives infinitely brighter.

Elsa left, and Jess returned to the library. The house felt ridiculously quiet; it had always been a noisy house with two young boys, very close in age, growing up in it together. Their relationship with Chris had also been noisy, because he had been a hands-on parent who joined in their games, built dens from blankets and dining chairs, became the Sheriff of Nottingham to their Robin Hood and Little John roles. And now there was nothing.

'Alexa, play piano music,' she instructed the little ball speaker. The music washed over her, and she picked up her book. It was Icelandic noir, her current favourite genre, and she became immersed in snow so heavy and claustrophobic, she couldn't help but marvel at the writing skills of the author.

Reykjavik had been a place they had spoken of visiting when Chris felt a little better, but Chris hadn't got better. The initial pain hadn't been a pulled muscle or a trapped nerve; the MRI scan had revealed a much worse diagnosis. Jess placed a bookmark in the book and leaned back her head.

One day, she promised herself, *one day I will go and see just how magical this place really is.* Her eyes closed briefly, and it was the book falling from her lap with a thud that made them open again.

'Come on, Jess Harcourt; only ninety-year-old women have nanny naps. Get up and do something.' Her voice sounded firm enough, but the willingness to move was a little absent.

She picked up the book, and replaced it on the side table, ready for her evening reading time. Then she stood, stretched her arms to encourage energy into her body, and left the security of her comfort room. She needed to strip the boys' beds, then put in a wash load to have everything clean and ready to put back on for their next, as yet unplanned, visit.

They had left their rooms remarkably tidy – clearly living away from home had taught them more about tidiness than she had ever managed to instil in them when they lived in this home.

She started in Josh's room, stripped the bed then quickly sprayed some polish around before dusting the furniture. She gathered up the bedding to take it downstairs to the utility room when she felt her mobile phone ring in her back pocket.

She dumped the laundry on the stairs and removed the phone as quickly as she could. Andi.

'Hi, Jess. Just a quickie. First, are you okay?'

'I am, thanks. And you?' Jess felt puzzled. Although Andi was Daniel's wife, they had never been particularly close.

'I'm okay. Tell me, have you seen or heard from Daniel since yesterday morning? He seems to have disappeared.'

CHAPTER EIGHT

Jess sat on the stairs and stared at her phone. Disappeared? Daniel? The quiet one of the remaining three golfers. She hadn't seen or heard from him, she told Andi, but she could hear the worry in the other woman's voice. Andi had explained she was ringing around everyone, because he hadn't been in touch. She was now going to report him missing to the police.

Jess knew Daniel had taken Chris's death hard, had been unable to comprehend they could do nothing to save such a fit man from the cancer that was eating away at him; he had made it very clear just how incomprehensible to him it was.

Had he simply gone away for a few days for a break? If that was the case – and it was a strong possibility – why hadn't he told Andi?

She knew they didn't particularly get on, and that their partnership and life was treated pretty much as a convenience. They shared a house because it was easier than selling up; neither had another partner, yet it seemed Andi was concerned enough to report him missing after just one day.

Bringing up Daniel's number on her phone seemed the logical thing to do, yet she hesitated when it came to actually ringing him. Although he had been close to Chris, physically he had been closer to her. She had never told him he was only part of her revenge plan, and he was part one. Paul had been part two. Part three, Oliver, had effectively dismissed parts one and two from her life as lovers.

She clicked off his number. It would be better if she rang Andi later to see if there was news. It would be a difficult conversation to have with Andi if Daniel responded to her call. She knew if he saw her name come up on his screen, he would answer. Hadn't Chris asked him to look after her? And according to Oliver, it seemed they were taking Chris's request seriously.

She slipped her phone back in her pocket and continued on her mission to set the first wash load in motion. Then she headed back upstairs to repeat her actions in Adam's room, which again was noticeably tidier than it had ever been when he'd lived at home. The fact brought a smile to her face.

She was on the point of returning to her book, glass of water in hand, when the phone pealed out once again. Oliver. Her heart skipped a beat at the sight of his name, and she answered quickly.

'You've heard Daniel seems to be missing?'

'I have. Andi rang. She seemed worried, but he only went yesterday. You think she's worrying because something may have happened to him? I thought maybe he had somewhere better to be, because they don't exactly share a life anymore do they?'

'No, they don't, but I still don't think he would just take off without telling her where he was going. I'm going to have a drive round, head up to the golf course, anywhere I think he might be. Want to come?'

Her heart jumped. 'You're not taking Denise?'

'She took herself off to Newcastle this morning for a few days with Elle. I'll be there in twenty minutes.'

Jess slid into the passenger seat of the Carrera, and fastened her seat belt. 'Still not heard anything?'

Ollie shook his head. 'No, and it's so out of character. Apparently Andi went grocery shopping yesterday afternoon. He was there when she left, he asked her to bring a trifle of all things, so he wasn't planning on leaving obviously. I wouldn't leave if there was trifle in the house. When she came back with the shopping she hit her horn to get him to come out and help her, then noticed his car wasn't there. He hadn't left a note or anything. She rang him, but no answer. I've covered for you being here with me by telling her I rang you this morning to check you were okay, and you said you were feeling a bit lonely, so I'm picking you up to help me look for Daniel. Andi said to say thank you.'

'Tangled webs and all that,' Jess said quietly. 'So where do we start?'

'We'll go up by his workplace, see if his car is there. If it isn't, we can drop down the road to the golf course. Just keep a look out for that bright blue Mercedes. It stands out so we should spot it if it's stashed somewhere. You think maybe he has another woman?'

'Not really,' Jess said, frowning. 'I actually think he would tell Andi, because the divorce gave them a pretty open relationship. They'd sell the house and split the proceeds if it ever came to them separating properly. And I think he would tell you and Paul.'

Ollie sighed. 'Exactly what I thought. So where the bloody hell is he? I'm more than concerned, because this isn't like him. He's not thoughtless; he knows Andi will be worrying, he knows we will be worrying. And presumably his phone has run out of charge because when you ring it now it goes to voicemail. Okay, this long grey building here that says Rubens Tech Services on it is his place. In theory, nobody should be here other than Daniel because it's Sunday and only he works weekends, not his staff. But it looks as if there are no cars at all, and certainly not a blue Mercedes.'

'What else does he do in his life apart from his garden, his work and golf?'

Ollie thought for a moment. 'I don't think he does anything. They have no kids, his garden is so tidy it needs little doing to it, and that leaves us with golf. But he went missing yesterday, so he's not just nipped up to the golf club for a shandy, has he? And he doesn't drink when he's driving. Let's go see if his car is anywhere around there.'

They turned around and drove back down the hill, both of them silent. Both uneasy. Ollie reached across and grasped Jess's hand. 'We'll find him, don't worry. Losing Chris hit all three of us hard, you know. Maybe Daniel just needs some time out to come to terms with the senselessness of it all. You understand that, don't you?'

She nodded. 'I do. But I saw Chris's quality of life, and he simply didn't have one, not at the end. His pain was manageable, but only because of the morphine, and that took away everything else about him. It was a relief when he left me, because only then did I know he was at peace.'

They reached the crossroads and turned right to head towards the golf club. Everything suddenly came to a standstill. They could see the flashing blue lights of a police car blocking the road and any access to the golf club, and further up the road was a second police car similarly employed to stop traffic approaching from the opposite direction.

Cars in front of the Carrera were turning round in the middle of the small road, so they could head back the way they had come from in the first place, and Ollie and Jess locked eyes.

'He's here, isn't he?' Jess said, the quiver in her voice obvious. 'What has he done?'

'I don't know. Look, I'm going to turn around and escape whatever is happening here, then I have somebody I can ring and ask what the hell is going on. Hang on five minutes and we'll know more.'

'Jack? It's Oliver. Listen, we're trying to get to the golf course, but the road is closed from both ends. I'm a bit concerned the closure is connected to why we're trying to get there. Can you tell me anything without telling me anything? You know it will go no further.'

He listened carefully to what the voice at the other end of the line was saying, then simply said, 'Daniel Rubens. SWFC tattoo on right arm.'

He listened some more, then finished by thanking the contact. He took a deep breath before pulling Jess towards him. 'I'm sorry, a body has been found on the golf course, and from the description it sounds like Daniel. That tattoo told me it was him.'

'And that's reliable information?'

'Chief superintendent. It's reliable.'

'Oh my God. Why? Why would he do this? He had a good life, a healthy business... why, Ollie?'

'He didn't do it, Jess. We can't repeat any of this to anyone, you heard me guarantee that. It seems his throat has been cut.'

There was silence from Jess's side of the car as she struggled to take in the information imparted from the contact on the other end of the phone.

Finally, her face devoid of all colour, she spoke. 'You're absolutely sure?'

'Yes. I'm going to drive you home. I need to go and see Andi. Will you be okay on your own? Or do you want to risk the wrath of Zeus descending on us when Andi tells Denise you were in the car with me?'

'No, we can't risk anything. Take me home, I'll be fine. Don't tell Andi I was with you; just say I changed my mind about going and you decided to drive to the golf course to see if he was there. I... I don't know how to process this.'

'Okay, I'm currently a free agent as Denise is in Newcastle, so not answerable to anybody about anything. I'll drop you off. Get yourself a brandy or something, you've had a shock. I'll go see Andi, but I'll need to tread carefully in case she doesn't know yet. It's not my place to tell her, and I can't compromise my contact by telling her. But she will know pretty quickly as she's reported him as missing. I can tell her about the police cars blocking the road outside the golf club, which will give her a bit of a heads-up for what's to come. You think this is sensible?'

Jess brushed away a tear. 'I have no idea. I would never have thought this would be the outcome of our search, never in a million years. Just take me home, Ollie, and do what you have to do. Ring me later and let me know what's happening, will you?'

'I will, my love.' He put the car into drive and drove to Jess's home, where she let herself into the front door. She turned to wave at him, and he pulled away, once again flashing his brake lights as he left her.

She stood in the hallway feeling at a loss. She didn't know what to do; her mind felt numb.

She hung her jacket in the cloakroom, swapped shoes for slippers, and went to put on the kettle. Brandy had seemed like a good idea, but a cup of tea sounded an even better one.

Ten minutes later she was in the library, a pot of tea ready to be poured into her cup. Her mind was running riot. Although the word hadn't been said, it seemed Daniel had been murdered. Who on earth would want to murder such a man? Gentle, considerate, a good employer... why? Why kill him?

She poured out her tea, and picked it up for her first warming sip. She needed some comfort, yet she had nobody she could contact, not until the death had become public knowledge. And suddenly she was crying. Daniel had been her lover, albeit a secret one, and while she hadn't loved him, she had cared deeply. And now he was gone. She felt incredibly alone, lost in her thoughts, remembering the tattoo on his arm where she had finger-traced the outline of the owl, the letters SWFC, all transferred later that evening via her pen to the missing journal.

She moved across to the Stephen King shelf and removed her substitute journal. She sat at the desk and opened it, beginning to tell the story of her day.

And the sad end.

CHAPTER NINE

There was a police car outside Andi and Daniel's home, and Ollie guessed they were here to impart bad news, not just to check if he had arrived home yet. He sat in his car for a moment, then got out and walked across to the policeman standing outside Andi's door.

'You're a friend, sir?'

'I am. Oliver Newton. Okay to go in?'

'Give me a minute, I need to check. Has Mrs Rubens been in touch with you?'

'Earlier today. I've actually been up to the golf course to see if I could see his car, but I couldn't get near because it's all closed off. Police cars all over the area, so I thought I would head here. My guesses seem to be accurate.'

The constable gave a brief nod, and headed inside, leaving Oliver to stand on the doorstep, staring at the work of art that was the garden of Andi and Daniel. Even with the summer flowering almost finished, the autumn plants were working hard at producing colour, and he knew Daniel would have been delighted with the results of their creativity. *Daniel.* He felt sick at the thought of entering the house and dealing with the second death of their quartet in only a few weeks.

He turned as the PC opened the front door. 'It's okay, sir, you can go in.'

Andi was sitting on the sofa, a glass of water on the coffee table in front of her. She looked ashen. She stood as he entered the room, and walked across to him. He put his arms around her and held her tightly.

'I'm here to help,' he whispered. 'I went to the golf course, but it was all closed off. Two and two have obviously made four...?'

'They've found his body. I don't know what to do...'

'Come and sit down before you fall down.' He led her back to the sofa and sat by her side, handing her the glass of water.

'Mr Newton?' There was a man and a woman in the room, the woman in a smart grey trouser suit, the man in a navy suit and clearly in charge.

'I am. Close friend of Andi and Daniel. I've been to the golf course, but couldn't get even as far as the car park to check if his car was there.'

'I'm DI William Stewart, and my colleague is DS Claire Landon. Claire will ask you a few questions before you go, just to see if you know of any reason for Mr Rubens to be at the golf course yesterday.'

'Yesterday?' Ollie was puzzled.

'The attending doctor at the scene believes Mr Rubens died between four and eight yesterday afternoon. There will be a more accurate time frame when the post-mortem is carried out. No attempt was made to hide the body, it's only as the weather has uplifted slightly and people decided on a quick round of golf, that he has been found.'

Andi stifled a sob. 'I'm having trouble understanding this. Daniel didn't have an enemy in the world. And the only people he goes to the golf club with are you three... two,' she added, as her memory kicked in.

DS Claire Landon was taking notes of everything that was being said, and she looked at Ollie. 'Can you elaborate on that, Mr Newton?'

'I can. There were four of us who have played golf together a minimum of twice a week for several years. Myself, Daniel, Paul Browne and Christopher Harcourt. Chris passed away a few weeks ago, and now Daniel has gone. Chris died of natural causes, before you ask. Cancer.'

'And you didn't go to the golf course yesterday?'

'No. We generally stick to Tuesdays and Thursdays, occasionally switching to a Friday if anything crops up to stop any one of us playing. We take it pretty seriously as a commitment.'

'Thank you. If you can give me Paul Browne's address?'

Ollie removed his diary from his inside pocket, flipped to the back pages and read out the details. 'I'll warn him you're coming, because as far as I know he doesn't even know Daniel is missing.'

'I spoke to him,' Andi confirmed. 'I rang all of you, even Jess, this morning. He hadn't seen or heard from him.'

DI Will Stewart looked at the tall man on the sofa. 'Can you think of anyone, man or woman, who would want to hurt Daniel?'

Ollie shook his head. 'Absolutely not. Chris was our comedian, I'm the mediator, Paul is the teacher, the quiet one, and Daniel was the...' he hesitated, 'the nice one.'

The detective turned his attention to Andi. 'Have there been any problems at work that you know of?'

Andi sighed. 'I wouldn't really know. Although Daniel is my ex-husband, we live totally separate lives. We share this house because it's convenient. Neither of us wanted another partner, we just didn't want each other, but that means I know very little of what happens in his life. I imagine Ollie knows more than I do.'

Ollie jumped in. 'He hasn't said anything about any issues at work. He's a brilliant employer, or so I've been told, and people don't tend to leave him once they start to work for him.'

'He had a laptop here?'

Andi nodded. 'Yes, in his study. He keeps lots of files relating to work in there as well.'

'I'm getting someone to come out from our forensics team to go through his office.' DI Stewart took out his phone and tapped a brief text message into it. 'He'll leave you a receipt for anything he takes, but that will include his laptop. Daniel's phone was with him when he was found. We'll be charging that up as soon as we get it back to the station. I'll also be allocating a family liaison officer to you. She will keep you informed of any progression in the case, and you'll also have her phone number to contact her if she isn't here. So, just to be clear: you didn't know where Daniel was going to yesterday?'

Andi shook her head. 'No, I heard his car go, but we don't tell each other what we're doing really, unless we're not going to be home later. It's a sort of unwritten rule that we need to know if we're not returning home, because we have hefty security on the place, and it goes on around ten at night during the week, as we both work. Weekends it's around eleven, but even so, we always know what to do about locking up. Daniel said nothing about staying out, which is why I started ringing around our friends this morning. He just doesn't do this.' She was beginning to sound quite distraught.

'Andi,' Ollie said gently, 'can I get somebody here to be with you? You shouldn't be on your own.'

'I've rung Mum. She was shopping at Meadowhall, but she's heading home to pick up some stuff then coming to stay. I'll be okay, Ollie. It's just been such a shock. I can't begin to understand why anybody would want to hurt Daniel in any way, never mind kill him.'

And she cried. Long drawn-out sobs that she had no control over, and Ollie grabbed a box of tissues, thrusting them towards her. 'I'll stay till your mum gets here.'

The two police officers stood. 'We need to go back to the crime scene. The FLO will be here within a couple of hours, and these are our numbers if you need to call us.' They both placed their cards on the coffee table. 'The forensics man, he's called Rob Senior, will be here shortly. He'll just go to the office and get on with his job. We're sorry for your loss, Mrs Rubens, and we will need you to formally identify your husband's body, but I'll be in touch about that.'

Ollie escorted Will and Claire to the door, and thanked them. 'I'm going to leave our PC here for a while, because he'll keep any random journalists away, but he'll only be here until about six. Unless he says there's a problem, of course.' He handed Ollie his card. 'Just in case you have anything to add,' he said.

Ollie nodded, watching as their car pulled away from the roadside. He remained on the doorstep after spotting a vehicle slowing down as it approached Andi's home. It proved to contain Rob Senior, so he led him into where Andi was lying with her head resting on the back of the sofa, her eyes closed.

She opened them as Ollie spoke. 'Andi, this is forensics, Rob Senior. I'll take him up to Daniel's office, I'll only be a minute.'

She didn't speak, simply held up a hand in acknowledgement.

'I understand I'm to collect a laptop, Mrs Rubens. Do you by any chance know your husband's password to access it?'

She pulled her handbag towards her and took out a small

notebook. She tore a page out and wrote the password down, then passed it to Rob.

Rob looked around the office. So neat, even the paperwork on the desk was stacked tidily. He put on gloves, and went to sit at the desk. The laptop was closed so he opened it. It immediately asked for a password.

'I'mfedup!2022,' he said aloud, as he read from the small piece of paper. He put it in his wallet, knowing it would be needed again once he had the laptop back at his own desk.

The screen opened up once he clicked enter. He did a very quick scroll through emails, and then closed it. It would be scoured thoroughly once back at headquarters, he just needed to be sure that nothing in current emails was pertinent to the death of Daniel Rubens.

He switched on his camera and began to video the entire office, and although he saw nothing amiss in this first sweep, he knew it would be scrutinised carefully within the next few hours, so he was careful to get into every nook and cranny.

Once the filming was complete, he turned to the desk itself. It was clearly an antique, in immaculate condition. Highly polished mahogany, it emitted a glorious glow in the late afternoon light. With one large and two smaller drawers down each side, and a central drawer across the leg gap, it wasn't only magnificent to look at, it was wonderful to sit at. The chair was a dark brown leather, comfortable in the extreme.

The top right-hand drawer was locked. He accessed the others with no difficulty, but had to go downstairs to speak with Andi about the key to the locked drawer.

She looked puzzled. 'I don't have one. I imagine it must be on his car keys, which are presumably with him.'

'Okay, it's no problem. I'll request his keys from his belongings. I'm sorry, but it does mean I'll have to come back. I'll ring you before I do. Is that okay?'

'Of course. You got into his laptop?'

'I did, I briefly looked at his emails. Nothing that looked out of place on that initial check, but it will be a much closer look when I get it back to my desk.'

'I'm just glad he hadn't changed his password. He started to use that one when we decided to go our own separate ways.'

She seemed to crumple as she spoke, and Rob thanked her and went back upstairs. Her friend seemed to be coping with her quite well, and he'd still got work to do in the office.

CHAPTER TEN

Ollie left Andi in the more than capable hands of her mother and the FLO, who turned up two minutes after Sheila Peters' arrival from her aborted Meadowhall trip. Three women all speaking at once and making cups of tea was enough for Ollie to say he had to go. 'But ring me immediately if you need anything, Andi,' he said as he left.

He took a moment to say goodbye to the PC who was standing watch by the front door, ready to deal with any intrusive reporters. 'She'll be okay,' he said. 'She has female support now,' he said.

'You Daniel's friend?'

'I am. We've just lost another close friend to cancer, and now this. I seem to be supporting a lot of grieving ladies at the moment.'

'I'm sure they appreciate it,' the young PC said, and waved as Ollie climbed into the Porsche. Jon Farmer didn't feel envious in any way; why should he? He had a Toyota Aygo...

Ollie pulled up outside Jess's home, and she opened the door before he'd even set foot on the path. 'Dad's here,' she said quietly, and he gave a brief nod to say he understood. Daisy gave a tentative bark of warning while wagging her tail enthusiastically, and Ollie bent down to rub her ears. 'Don't go all brave on me, Daisy, I just don't believe that bark.'

He followed Jess into the library and leaned over to shake the hand of Malcolm. 'Sad day, Malcolm,' he said. 'I take it Jess has told you as much as she knows?'

'She has. She said you might call round to tell us what the hell is going on.'

'I can't tell you much. Andi now has her mum with her, and the police have sorted out a family liaison officer for her. Plus there's a smart young PC outside her door, although he's just there until 6pm. Andi's in a bit of a state as you can imagine, and I've told her to ring me if she needs anything.'

'Is there a cause of death yet?' Malcolm sounded frail.

'Nothing that will be official until after the post-mortem, but it does appear to be a knife crime. And they seem to be treating it as murder rather than self-inflicted. I just...' he hesitated. 'I just can't see anybody hating Daniel enough to kill him.'

'That's exactly what I said to Dad. He's not got a nasty bone in his body. Ollie, you need to ring Paul. He's hearing rumours about it, and rang me to see if I knew anything. I said I thought you were with Andi, and if I saw you I'd ask you to ring him.'

'I will. I'm going straight home from here to have a huge brandy, so I'll ring him when I've sorted myself out. Everything felt quite harrowing while I was with Andi. She's devastated by it. I know they weren't together anymore, but they still lived in the same house, and she's bewildered by it all, as we are. Why Daniel? He's such a nice feller, good business head, and I've no idea what will happen with that business now. I suppose his second-in-command can manage at the moment, but the beating heart of it all was Daniel.'

'I'll ring Andi in the morning,' Jess said. 'See if she needs anything, even if it's just a cup of tea. Thank you for popping round to let me know, Ollie. I haven't rung the boys yet, but I will. They know their father's golfing group so well, and they'll be gutted by this.'

Ollie stood. 'I'll ring as soon as I know any more. Malcolm, do you want a lift home?'

Malcolm grinned. 'Much as I would love a lift in that car, I'm staying here tonight. My daughter insisted; said me and Daisy need looking after.'

'Huh,' Jess joined in. 'He's nearly eighty, and when he arrived after walking over this afternoon, he was wobbling all over the place. His blood pressure was way too low. He's in the spare room tonight, and he'll be at the doctor's surgery tomorrow. Daisy can pretty much decide for herself where she's going to sleep.'

Jess went with Ollie to the door, planted a swift kiss on his lips, and said she would ring him after Malcolm was settled in bed.

He nodded, gave her a return kiss and opened the door. 'Bye, Malcolm,' he called, and walked down the path.

It occurred to Jess that suddenly her world was turning upside down; 2024 was proving to be a strange year. At this time in 2023 there had been no hint that her life was about to implode. She resisted the urge to follow Ollie down the path and kiss him properly, instead just waved as he drove away, waiting for his taillights to flash as he reached the end of the road.

Jess checked Malcolm's blood pressure one last time, before he headed off to bed with a glass of milk and a blanket for Daisy.

She had been really concerned when he had wobbled his way into her home, though he kept insisting he was fine. She didn't listen, and booked him into the doctors. He was far from fine.

Ollie rang just after eleven, and she settled down to a chat with the man she had never envisaged falling in love with – her idea had been to count him as a notch in her journal for her to ultimately tell Chris about. Which was exactly what Paul and Daniel had been. Pleasant interludes. But Ollie had been so much more.

He had truly cared for her, had been so supportive when the terminal diagnosis had been issued for Chris, and had put their meetings on hold until whenever.

Whenever had arrived, and Jess had no idea where it would lead. The situation with Ollie's marriage wasn't clear cut, as Daniel's had been, and she knew she would have to have patience.

She and Ollie talked for an hour about all sorts of things – their relationship, making time for each other, and about Daniel. Neither of them could understand why the brutal death had happened to their friend.

After saying goodnight to Ollie, Jess went upstairs and listened outside her father's bedroom door. After a couple of minutes of trying to decide whether to go in or not, she heard bed springs creak as he moved.

Relief surged through her; she had been truly worried at the definite wobble he had shown, and she was determined he would go to see a doctor, whether he wanted to or not.

Her own room felt chilly, but she didn't mind. She was a winter person, liked the feel of thicker pyjamas when the weather took on a colder aspect, and she climbed into bed, snuggling down quickly.

She couldn't get Daniel out of her mind, and as she drifted off to sleep it was his face that haunted her dreams.

By Monday morning Daniel's murder had made the newspapers. Andi took a call from Jess first thing.

'I'm coping, Jess, thanks. Look, I can't talk long, the chap from forensics is returning within the hour to open a drawer of Daniel's desk that he couldn't get into last time because it was locked.'

'I won't keep you then. But if there's anything...'

Andi suddenly felt defeated – and though she was grateful for the offer of help, she had no idea what to ask for. 'I don't know what to do. Everything's suddenly not right, and why would anybody want to kill Daniel? He was a nice man, wouldn't harm anybody. Mum stayed here last night, but after Rob – the man from forensics – has been today to unlock the desk we're going to stay at hers for a few days, just until they've found the person who did this.'

'I don't blame you,' Jess replied. 'If I can do anything, just give me a ring. I'm so sorry this has happened, Andi. I couldn't sleep last night, Daniel was so much on my mind. It must have been so much worse for you.'

Andi realised the other woman was talking for the sake of it, so she thanked her for her offer of help and said goodbye.

Rob Senior arrived at just before ten o'clock, and left by five past ten, mission accomplished. The drawer key had indeed been on Daniel's car and house keys. The contents of the drawer – financial paperwork and a small notebook – were removed and a receipt left with Andi.

'Everything will be returned to you once the case is finished,' he explained. 'I've left my contact details on your husband's desk, just in case you come across anything that seems strange, like an email that's not right, anything like that. We are keeping the car keys because the car is going to be taken into our auto facility for a full forensic sweep.'

Andi nodded. 'You have my phone number if you need me. If you have to come back here for anything, I won't be here for a few days, I'm staying at my mum's, but I can return here if you need to get back in. In fact, as you have his keys, you have my permission to return if you need to, while I'm away. The alarm code is 6831.'

He thanked her for her cooperation; she watched him drive away, gave a huge sigh and re-entered her home to finish packing her bag. Two days, and her life had been completely turned upside down, and not in a good way.

'I'm ready, Mum,' she said, and the two women climbed into their cars for the short journey. Andi breathed a sigh of relief. Her home was no longer her sanctuary, she didn't want to be in it at all at the moment. Maybe she would feel differently once the shock had dissipated, but for now she felt as though she'd rather be in a tent than in her own comfortable home.

Rob logged the contents of the desk drawer in as evidence, and glanced quickly through the financial documents. It seemed they were Daniel Rubens' personal bank statements, and they showed a healthy balance in each account. Rob decided he must be in the wrong job; his finances looked nothing like this.

He made sure the statements were in order, and put them back into the evidence bag before picking up the small notebook. He suspected this would prove to be a little book of business contacts, and therefore worthy of deeper investigation, but as he began to delve into it he realised it wasn't contacts at all: it was clandestine meetings with someone. Someone Daniel referred to as X, which wasn't helpful in any way.

The notations stopped halfway through the book, so the logical conclusion was that the love story was over. And it was very clearly a love story, most definitely in Daniel's mind. He had made notes when A was away with her job, and Rob assumed that was his live-in partner, Andi. He obviously didn't want Andi to know he was seeing X, so did this mean that Daniel's wife knew X?

Far too many exes here, he grumbled. *X is an ex, A is an ex. I need some clarification. Or somebody does.*

He gathered everything up and went upstairs to the Major Crimes office. He was surprised to find DI Will Stewart there.

'Got a minute?'

'I have. We've got dozens of beat bobbies combing every blade of grass on the golf links, and I should be there cheering them on. You have something for me? Like the weapon that everybody is searching for on the golf course?'

Rob slid out the small notebook from its protective bag. 'No weapon, but I've got this. He had a lover, did Daniel. No idea if it's a man or a woman, but it's called X.'

Will opened the small blue book, and glanced inside. Rob waited. Finally Will raised his head. 'It's a woman. Feels like a woman. I'll head out to the hotel that's mentioned, find out if he booked in under his own name, or if X booked it.'

'I've to log this into evidence, but there's not that many pages. You want me to photocopy them before I hand it in?'

'You're a star. Yes, please. I'd like more time to study it. There might just be a little bit of something...'

CHAPTER ELEVEN

'If Mum says she doesn't want us chasing up to Sheffield, does she mean she doesn't want us chasing up to Sheffield, or does she mean "I'll make up your beds?"' Adam sounded stressed.

'Well she's clearly upset by Daniel's death, but I think she made a point of ringing us about it because she knew we'd see it on the news. And she did say she didn't want us going up, not until the funeral anyway. I propose we take her at her word in this instance.' Josh gave a slight nod, as if agreeing with his own thoughts.

Adam still didn't look convinced. 'I'll ring her later, sound her out. If anything's changed and she does want us there, I'll go home. It doesn't need both of us.'

'I quite liked Daniel,' Josh mused.

'Maybe we only know one side of him. Have you ever thought he might use his tech business for importing drugs, or taking contracts out on people?'

Josh looked at Adam. 'No, I can't ever say I thought that of him. Did you?'

'Well, no, but...'

'There's no *well no* but about it, numpty. We've known

Daniel about fifteen years, maybe more, and he hardly drinks alcohol, never mind dabbles in drugs. He has upset somebody, hasn't he? But it's the usual stuff in this place that we should be considering. In fact, we shouldn't even be thinking about happenings in Sheffield, we've enough on our plate with this Halloween thing we're putting on. I haven't time to be investigating murders as well. Have you?'

Adam grinned. 'Not really. I'll ring Mum later and ask her if she wants to come and stay here for a bit. Her and Granddad.'

The granddad in question was finally sitting in the library of his very patient daughter, nursing a cup of tea and listening for the second time to the explanation of how he should be taking his blood pressure three times a day for the next week, writing it all down and returning to the doctors the following Monday.

'Are you listening, Dad?'

'Of course I am.'

'But do you understand how important it is?'

'Of course I do.'

'You're being glib.'

'I've never been called glib before.'

'Dad!'

'Sorry.' Malcolm tried to look contrite.

'Okay, you and Daisy have to stay here for the week, because I can't trust you to do this properly.'

'I'll need some clothes.'

'I'll pop round and get anything you need.' She smiled at him. 'Stop arguing. You can go home once we've completed this week-long thing with the BP monitor, and have been back to the doctors next Monday. You scared me with all this wobbling about. What if you fell and couldn't get back up?'

Malcolm almost managed to look contrite. 'I know. I'm being illogical. It just isn't a good feeling to know I'm getting older and can't be trusted to remember to take my blood pressure readings for a week.'

'Treat it like a week's holiday. And I'll enjoy taking care of you.'

Malcolm reached out to grasp her hand. 'I apologise for turning into a cantankerous old fool. And thank you, you're a good girl.'

'I am,' she admonished, 'and don't you forget it.'

Jess was surprised to see Paul's name on the screen of her phone, and she left her dad sleeping on the sofa while she went into the kitchen to take the call. 'Paul? You okay?'

'Better for speaking to you. I miss our chats.'

She laughed. 'I'm sorry, but we agreed it was over…'

'I know. It's just this with Daniel. I don't know how to handle it at all, and I'm always the sensible one. The police were here this morning, just after eight, to talk to us both. I had to ring school and tell them I would be in later, but they told me to stay home, to look after Naomi. She hasn't taken it too well; she had a soft spot for Daniel, thought Andi treated him badly. The twins are talking of heading home to be with us, but they've only just gone back to uni for this term, so hopefully we've convinced them to stay in Manchester.'

'They can't do anything to help,' said Jess. 'I've told my boys not to come home until we know it's time for the funeral. Try saying that to them, it might work. I haven't spoken to the police yet, but I suspect they'll be here at some point. Did they have any clue about anything to do with his death?'

'Kind of. They found a little book, just a notebook they said, so no dates in it, but it seems as if Daniel had met somebody. Did you know about it?'

Jess felt herself go cold, and she involuntarily shivered.

'Somebody else? No, neither he nor Andi have ever mentioned anything about it. Does she have a name?'

'Not according to DI Stewart. Daniel refers to her as X, apparently.'

'He needed to keep her secret then.'

'Seems like it.' There was stress in Paul's voice. 'But for heaven's sake, who would want to kill Daniel?'

'I must have said that a dozen times since yesterday. Surely it wasn't this X person?'

'No idea. It just seems so sad that our golf foursome is suddenly down to two, and it's happened so quickly. We hadn't got over losing Chris, and now Daniel has gone. Look, I'll get off. Thank you for talking to me, Jess, I just needed to hear your voice again, I think. I miss you.'

'Take care, Paul. And keep it in mind that nobody knows yet why Daniel was targeted. Just be aware.'

'You think I'm in danger?' He sounded shocked.

'Not really, I just think it will pay to be on your guard.'

They disconnected, and Jess walked across towards the patio doors. She stared out at the garden, marshalling her thoughts. Could Paul and Ollie possibly be in danger?

Then she realised how ridiculous it sounded – their connection was golf. Had they beat some other team? Had they moved somebody's golf ball to make it a more difficult shot? Could golf be that cutthroat?

Cut. Throat.

She opened the patio doors, stepped out onto the decking and took deep breaths. Her thoughts were now starting to sound stupid, and despite everything she wished she could talk everything over with her sensible one, with Chris. But you can't expect a sensible conversation with an urnful of ashes.

She walked towards the left-hand side of the back garden, to where the rose garden was. The plants were fading, and Chris's request had been that his ashes be scattered in the rose garden when the plants were really flourishing in June time. She would do that, her last act for him.

She picked a deep red rose that wasn't quite fully open, and took it indoors. Standing it in a small glass of water, she carried it through to the library where the urn now stood, awaiting disposal of its contents.

'An October rose for you, Chris,' she said, then added, 'RIP.'

Malcolm turned and the pain in his neck woke him instantly. He groaned, realising having five minutes with his eyes closed on the sofa had maybe been a bad idea. He rubbed his neck, and sat up.

His book had fallen on the floor, and he had no idea where his place was. *Note to oneself,* he thought, *use a damn bookmark in future.*

The door opened quietly, and Jess poked her head around it. 'You're awake! It's time for a bp check. You feel better for that little nap?'

'Not really. I can't move my head now.'

'If you feel tired, Dad, you should go to bed. This sofa is more for sitting on than sleeping; no wonder your neck is stiff. Right, let's get this check done and we can discuss what we're going to eat.'

He held out his arm and she placed the cuff around it. The little machine buzzed as it did what it was supposed to do, and she pursed her lips. 'It's a little low. The tablets won't have kicked in much though, so we'll see how we go as the week progresses.'

She removed the cuff and placed the machine in the drawer.

'If I'm not in at the time it should be checked, that's where we'll keep it.'

He looked at her. 'Yeah, right. Like I'm going to remember to do it.'

She raised her eyes to the ceiling. 'Oh, Lord, give me strength. Dad, this is really important. Morning, mid-afternoon and bedtime. Same times every day. Of course, I could always ask Elsa to help with your care...'

'Don't you damn well dare,' he responded. 'I'm not old. Okay, I'll remember.'

Jess smiled. *Sorted.*

It came as something of a surprise when Elsa arrived that evening bearing flowers. 'I heard about Daniel,' she said, handing them over to Jess. 'I knew you'd be upset. I won't stay long, just wanted you to know I'm thinking about you and your wider family and friends. They'll miss him.'

'You're a very welcome visitor. I threatened to send for you this afternoon to look after my dad. Hearing your name sorted it all...'

'Really? Am I that scary? And what's he done that he needs me to bully him?'

'The doctor has put him on a week-long check of blood pressure readings, three every day. I can't get through to him how important it is. I've made him stay here for the week, but it also means I daren't go out unless I can trust him to do the check. Hence your name was mentioned, and that scared him just enough to promise he would do it.'

Elsa laughed. 'That's what I like to hear, terrified patients who do what I say. Doesn't happen very often, I must say. I'm usually too soft with them.'

'He's in the library. Come and say hello, he'll think I've asked you to call.'

Jess opened the door and the two women walked into the room. Malcolm put down his book, accidentally closing it yet again without the bookmark.

'Hi, Malcolm.'

'Elsa,' he croaked. 'Honestly, I'm not ill. I don't need looking after...'

'Well it's a good job I'm here delivering flowers then, isn't it?' She grinned at him and he visibly relaxed. 'I wanted to say how sorry I am that one of your friends has died. I know Chris was very close to his golfing pals, and as a group they spent a lot of time together. I met all of them through caring for Chris, and liked all of them very much.'

'We'll miss Daniel,' Malcolm said quietly. He reached out to stroke Daisy and she jumped up onto his knee. 'Normal deaths caused by our bodies having stuff wrong with them is acceptable. Not good, but acceptable and understandable. But to die because somebody else decided you should is so wrong. It must have been a dreadful death for him.'

Elsa sat down at Jess's insistence, and she reached across to take Malcolm's hand. 'Don't dwell on it, Malcolm. Concentrate on getting this blood pressure stuff sorted with the right medication. That's the most important thing at the moment.'

He groaned, and Daisy lifted her head. 'I've got two of you nagging at me now. When that chart thing goes back to the doctors next week, I promise it will be the most perfect chart they've ever seen in that surgery.'

'Too right it will,' Jess said. 'I've set an alarm on your phone for three times every day, at the same time every day. There'll be no escaping it, Dad. We will make you better.'

CHAPTER TWELVE

Tuesday started early for the Major Crimes Team. Uniformed constables were still searching every part of the cordoned-off golf course, and three detectives from the team had joined them.

DC Freya Newbould had been left behind to work her way through the entire internet if necessary (DI Stewart's words, not hers), to come up with a comprehensive picture and life for the victim, and to ring him if anything significant showed up. Freya liked a quiet office, and had breathed a sigh of relief when the last of her colleagues clattered downstairs.

DI Will Stewart and DS Claire Landon pulled up outside Jess's home, and stared at the house.

'Wow,' Claire said. 'This puts my second-floor flat to shame. I knew it would be nice because of the area, but crikey, this is more than nice. It's... magnificent.'

'Okay, here's the story just to refresh our brains. This was Christopher and Jessica Harcourt's home, until a few weeks ago when the husband passed away. Natural causes, some form of cancer, so Oliver Newton told me. So we need to tread carefully, it will still be very raw. I'll start the chat. Jump in when I start to flounder, or if I miss anything.'

'Will do. I'll take notes; you use your charm. Get her talking.'

'And don't forget the kid gloves,' he reminded her. 'This lady is probably still very much grieving for her own husband, and now she's lost a close friend as well.'

They walked up the path, and Jess opened the door. 'I saw your car and guessed you must be the detectives.' She glanced briefly at their ID, and ushered them through to the library. 'This is our favourite room, but it's also our comfiest,' she said with a smile. 'My father is staying with me for a few days, so he may join us, or he may not. I don't think he's actually awake yet.'

'No problem; it's you we're here to see,' Will said. 'And may we both extend our commiserations on the loss of your husband. We do appreciate it was fairly recent, and now we're here to speak with you about the death of a close friend. It can't be an easy time, and we'll keep it as brief as we can. Claire will be taking notes.'

'Thank you. I was learning to live with the knowledge that I won't be seeing Chris again, but hearing about Daniel has created a huge cloud over me. I know it's different – Chris had an aggressive form of cancer that he knew was terminal, and in the end he was ready to leave us, but Daniel? He was a lovely, polite man who wouldn't hurt anyone. Ask his workforce, they'll all say the same thing about him.'

Will said, 'Two of our team are there today. Our forensic people went in yesterday, removed his tech stuff so we can rule out money issues being the reason behind his death, but there seems to be nothing that would cause anybody to want to kill him. He has fourteen full-time employees apart from himself working there as well, so we're interviewing all of them. Just one little comment may lead us off on an entirely different tangent.'

'You knew Daniel and Andrea well?' Claire asked.

'Yes, we've known them for years. When I first met Daniel it was on a day when I went to pick Chris up from the golf club. They had just formed a foursome, and I believe it was only the second time they had played together. Daniel was the first to come and shake my hand, and offer to get me a coffee. Very polite. I chatted with him, mainly about work – his work. He had two employees at that time, and was looking to take a receptionist on who would handle the secretarial side as well. From that point on his business grew and grew, to what it is today. He was still with Andi then of course, but they drifted apart. I suspect because he was always at work.'

'Did Daniel meet anyone else?'

Jess didn't hesitate. 'Not to my knowledge. And of course, neither did Andi. I always said that if Daniel had been able to delegate some of the work he did, they would still be together, because neither of them moved on. They still shared a home, although not a life. Their home was their baby really, as I'm sure you've probably realised. They're both gardeners, and everything was immaculate. No children, so immaculate inside as well. An immaculate sort of life that fell apart.'

'So if I said we believed he had met someone else, you would be surprised?'

There was a momentary silence from Jess. 'Met somebody else? I would be... gobsmacked is the word I'm looking for. Do Oliver and Paul know? I'm certain Chris didn't, he would have told me because he would have been delighted. He didn't think Andi was right for Daniel anyway. She was never very friendly, unlike Naomi and Denise, Paul and Oliver's wives. It was really odd when we were together as a group, because it was a sort of unwritten rule that the three wives who had children didn't talk about them, because none of us knew whether it was a choice with her not to have them, or whether she couldn't have babies.'

'You have a family?'

'I do. I still have a dad, Malcolm Johnson. My mum died

many years ago. And we had two sons, quite close together, who now have a business. They own a pub just outside Torquay, in Devon. Josh is twenty-four, Adam twenty-three. They were here when Chris died, stayed until after the funeral, and then went back home.'

Jess felt she was talking too much, but didn't know how to stop. That the police suspected Daniel had, at some point, been seeing someone had come as a great shock to her. Had Daniel repeated what she had done? Made notes in a notebook? He couldn't have used her name, or DI Stewart would have mentioned it.

She decided to shut up, use as few words as possible if they still needed to question her, and get rid of them as quickly as she could. She most definitely did not want Oliver to find out she had slept with Paul and Daniel, as well as him. As it stood, only Chris had known the extent of her adultery, and he'd only known it for half a day.

She waited for them to continue. Will looked at Claire. 'You have all you need?'

'I do. Ready when you are, sir.'

They stood and Jess escorted them to the front door. 'Thank you for your time, Mrs Harcourt,' Will said. 'And once again, our deepest condolences on the death of your husband, and also your friend, Daniel Rubens.' He handed her his card. 'If anything else comes to mind, please give me a call.'

She nodded, and watched as they walked down the front path. She was back inside the house before Will had even started the car.

Will sat at his desk, deep in thought. He removed the photocopies of the little blue book now locked safely away, and began to read through it all again. Not one entry was dated, and he realised he could hardly go to the named hotel and ask for information, when he didn't even know when Daniel and X had visited. The notes were sparse – X *today* was the normal entry. X *today Premier Inn* was the undated entry that really would have been a massive help with the addition of a date. X *Sherwood Forest* was another entry. Then X *over*. There was nothing after that chilling entry. He had locked his little love book away in the top drawer of his desk, and Will wondered if he took it out occasionally to look at it, and reminisce about what he had lost. And possibly wondered why.

Claire popped her head around his door. 'No weapon found anywhere on the golf course, boss. They're opening it up again now. Any further thoughts on Jessica Harcourt?'

'Attractive woman. Does that count?'

'Nope. Could she be a killer?'

'Could she be X?'

Claire looked shocked. 'Surely not. She's been caring for a very poorly husband for several months, so I can't see that scenario. Can you?'

Will shrugged. 'Dunno. Maybe I'm clutching at straws. Maybe X is somebody from work, that would make more sense. Okay, preliminaries are over, let's get out there and start digging, and we'll take a look at his company first.'

'Freya's been ferreting around online for any information she can gather on the two remaining members of the golfing four, and it seems they're absolute angels. Both married to original partners, both have kids who are now grown up, never been in trouble with the law apart from a speeding fine in Oliver Newton's case, but it was ten years ago.'

'Can't see a murder charge following on from a speeding fine,' he muttered.

'Hardly. Wonder if they've gone into work.'

'Let's make this our mission for the afternoon, to speak to Oliver Newton and Paul Browne. With an e. I know I've done a preliminary interview with both of them, but it was very brief, and I think they need to know we haven't dismissed them from the case. Browne is a teacher, isn't he?'

'He is. Maybe not a wise move to interview him at work. The kids will have him pegged as a murderer at the very least before they can add two and two together.' Claire couldn't help the smile that creased her face.

'What does he teach. And where?'

'He's head of maths, at Belthorpe Boys' Academy.'

'The private school? Never been there, so let's go find out if it's good enough to send our own sons to.'

'I haven't got any sons, and neither have you,' Claire pointed out.

'Might have one day.'

She gave in. 'Okay, Sherlock. I'll ring the school and check he's actually in work today.'

They pulled up outside the huge gates that prevented entry to the school without the express permission of the receptionist who worked the electronic buttons.

After holding up warrant cards they were allowed to enter, and Claire parked the car in the large area in front of the impressive heavy oak entrance doors. They had to repeat their names into a small speaker, and finally entered the hallway of the prestigious and expensive academy.

'Well I'm definitely sending my boy here,' Claire said quietly. 'This is awesome. I just can't give birth to him until I'm at least chief constable. I don't even want to think what the fees could be.'

The receptionist walked towards them. 'Welcome to Belthorpe Boys' Academy,' she said, without any hint of a smile. 'We have had to ask Mr Browne to leave his class, but he'll be here in a moment. If you'd like to follow me, I'll take you to our interview room.'

The interview room proved to be nothing like the interview room back at the station. Oak-lined walls, portraits of old boys of the school, and furniture fit to grace any room in Chatsworth House.

They took seats side by side at the beautiful, highly polished table and by the time Paul Browne appeared, they felt completely daunted and overwhelmed.

Paul shook both their hands. 'They've put you in here to make you feel intimidated, to teach you that you can't pull teachers out of their classes.'

Will laughed. 'It's worked. But on the plus side, we've both decided if we ever have sons they'll be coming here. Did yours attend this school?'

'They did. And before you ask, I didn't get special rates. I have a ridiculously well-off mother and father, as does Naomi, and each set of grandparents paid for one of the twins to attend here. It's much easier for me now they're in uni, believe me.'

'They're studying maths?'

'They are. I don't think they'll teach the subject though, they're much smarter than me. I reckon in ten years they'll have the most prestigious accountancy firm in the north, and I will hopefully be retired and travelling the world with my wife.' He laughed. 'That's our current plan, anyway, but it was kind of a similar plan to what Daniel wanted within the next ten years or so, and look what's happened to him.'

CHAPTER THIRTEEN

Claire switched on the engine, and leaned forward to enter the postcode for Oliver's address.

'Thoughts?' Will asked.

'I definitely need that chief constable job. Is there a girls' academy that's anything like this?'

'I suppose there must be, but I'm damned if I know. I like Paul Browne, don't see him as having anything to do with the death of his friend, but he's still in the disbelief stage that this could have happened to Daniel Rubens. I hope that doesn't make him vulnerable. Off guard.'

'You don't think Daniel Rubens' death is a one-off?' There was a note of puzzlement in Claire's voice.

'We can't rule anything out, at least until we get a motive. If everybody is saying what a nice bloke Daniel was, why is he dead, and in such a horrific fashion? He's definitely upset somebody. And he has two really close friends, so I believe they have to be on their guard, but I need to say that without saying that. Know what I mean?'

She nodded. 'I do. You think they won't think like that all on their own?'

'I'm sure they won't. A woman might, but not a big butch feller. I tried to spell it out to Paul Browne, but I'm not sure he listened. Right, let's go and find Oliver Newton. Do we know what he does to earn a penny or two?'

'GardenScene.'

Will's head spun around. 'I didn't know that. How come you know it?'

'I talked to Freya. You should have a chat with her sometime, she's pretty smart. It seems he started working at a garden centre straight out of school. Bought it when the owner retired five years later, renamed it GardenScene, and now he has six scattered at various places in Yorkshire. Freya has the full list if you need it.'

'My God, everybody knows GardenScene. It's huge.'

'And it's clearly bought him a Porsche Carrera. Freya said no scandal or anything, just a hardworking man who's now sitting back a little and enjoying what he's worked for. Wife is Denise, daughter is Elle. According to Facebook, Elle's at Newcastle University.'

'These four men were destined for each other, weren't they? Decent blokes, one wife marriages, kids at uni. The only exception really was Daniel, but even he had stayed with Andrea. They divorced, but still lived in the same house.'

Claire pulled away from the kerb and glanced at the satnav. 'We're not too far from where he lives. Fancy a coffee first?'

'You paying?'

She shook her head. 'No, I'm saving up for school fees.'

He tutted, took out his wallet and passed her his credit card. 'Drive-through, or inside?'

'Drive-through. We can sit in the car park and drink it, watching the world go by. That okay with you?'

'It is. And you can fill me in on anything else Freya has discovered that I don't seem to know.'

'She said the full report will be in your inbox by the time we get back to the station. That probably means it's there now. She's pretty smart at anything she does on the internet.'

Will closed his eyes briefly. 'GardenScene,' he said slowly. 'Who would have thought?'

Claire laughed, and indicated to enter the Costa drive-through. 'It's really going to bug you, isn't it? And he probably paid cash for the Porsche.' She wound down the window. 'Two large lattes, please.' They moved on to the next window and she waved the credit card over the machine before handing it back to its rightful owner.

'I think I've just drained your bank account,' she said.

'Probably,' he responded. 'They do sell their lattes in a smaller size, you know.'

'I know.' Her reply was just a little too cheerful. 'That's the size I would have bought if I'd been paying. Thank you, boss, I do appreciate a large latte.'

He shook his head as she passed the cardboard tray over for him to hold. He wasn't sure, but he thought he was being bullied.

Denise Newton opened the door and stared at two people she didn't know.

'Can I help you?'

They spoke their names and held up warrant cards as proof. Finally she smiled. 'I'm sorry, I'm not normally so snappy, I'm just worried to death since Daniel's murder. Did you want me, or Ollie?'

'Both of you, really,' Will said. 'Is your husband here?'

'He will be in about ten minutes. He had to go to Harrogate; we're having a bit of a revamp at our garden centre there to make it more disability accessible, and decisions needed to be made. He never needs an excuse to drive that car, so off he's gone. He left about an hour ago, so shouldn't be much longer. Can I get you a drink while we wait for him?'

'No, we're good, thanks,' Will said. 'We've just called in at the Costa, had bucket-size lattes.'

'Then come through to the lounge. You can sit and admire the jungle we live in, while we wait for him.'

The room was essentially green. So many plants, so many sizes, so relaxing just to sit and stare.

'Oh my Lord,' Claire said, her eyes wide. 'This would be my idea of heaven. I have plants, but not on this scale. Mind you, my lounge is about a quarter of the size of this one, and I can't fit any more in.'

'Some of these are Ollie's experiments – he cross pollinates and every so often I'll find a plant that wasn't there the day before. It will be one of Ollie's trials. I've grown used to it, but some of them turn into great triffids; that's when I draw the line.'

'You've been together a long time?'

'Yes, we met at the garden centre that became the first GardenScene after Ollie bought it. I started work there about a year after he did, and we became really close, really fast. We were engaged and planning our wedding when the owner of the garden centre decided he'd had enough. We begged and borrowed to get the buying price together, and put the wedding on hold for a further three years. I wouldn't change any of it. Since then we've acquired a further five centres, all run very smoothly by the right people. As a result, Ollie no longer has a set working day or days, he basically swans through life playing golf, nipping out to oversee something at one of the centres, or he potters in our own garden. We have our own lives, yet we also have a shared one, best of all worlds.'

All three sat down eventually, although Claire was the last

one to do so. She was fascinated by the variety of plants in the room, and knew on her next day off she could very easily find herself in a GardenScene garden centre.

It seemed like only seconds later when Oliver arrived. He bent to kiss his wife's head, and shook the hands of the detectives. 'Do you have anything concrete yet?'

'We don't. Whoever killed your friend took the knife away with them. It has taken two days of intense police searching to cover the entire course, but there is nothing. He didn't say anything to his wife about where he was going, but it seems he rarely did tell her anything since their marital split. According to CCTV at the golf club, he was the only occupant of his car when it arrived. He walked into the bar, had a glass of lemonade, then said goodbye to the barman. There is nothing after that. He didn't return to his car, and it remained in the car park overnight, but nothing much was significant about that because cars are frequently left there overnight by any members who decide to have a drink.'

'So he walked onto the course?' Oliver frowned as he tried to make sense of Daniel's actions. 'Why would he do that? Did he have his clubs with him?'

'He did. Did he normally keep them in the car whether he was planning on using them or not?'

'They were always in the boot. He sometimes liked to go up to the practice field on days when we hadn't made plans to meet up. He said he found it easier to think about work issues there. I wonder if he intended going to the practice field. It had been raining and he was perhaps seeing how wet the ground was.'

'You're clutching at straws,' Denise said. 'When has wet grass ever put you lot off? It doesn't. For what it's worth, I think he'd decided to have a quiet hour on his own. His clubs were with him, and he'd only had a glass of lemonade. In other words, he intended driving home. Over to you now, DI Stewart.'

'And I think you could possibly be correct, Mrs Newton. Want a job?' Will smiled at the chatty woman who had entertained them so charmingly while they waited for Oliver's arrival.

'No thanks,' she said, 'I've got one. Have you seen the number of plants I have to water every day?'

'Mr Newton,' Claire said, 'when was the last time you either spoke with, or saw, Daniel Rubens?'

Ollie closed his eyes for a moment. 'We had a very quick game of golf on the Thursday. You're still saying he died on the Saturday?'

Will joined in the conversation. 'Yes, slightly revised time of death according to an email I received earlier. It's now been put between 2pm and 6pm. The barman thought it was about 1.30pm when Mr Rubens left the bar, but he couldn't be any more accurate than that. The car arrived in the car park at 1.03pm.' He kept his eyes on Ollie.

Ollie's face creased into a frown. 'So whoever killed him could have been here and waiting for him for some time. They clearly didn't arrive together, but why on earth would he arrange to meet someone he didn't know? My thinking is going towards someone he did know. Somebody from work? Or was he targeted by mistake?'

Will gave a gentle nod. 'We will be going into Daniel's workplace and speaking to everyone there. If there is someone holding a grudge, it will be mentioned by somebody, I'm sure. He was a much-loved boss, so I understand.'

Oliver reacted almost angrily. 'He was. They'll all miss him. The chap who will be running the whole shebang now is someone called Graham Marstead. Good friend of Daniel's, and Daniel totally trusted him to keep everything running smoothly. They've been together since Daniel opened the business on that site.'

Will stood, and Claire followed. 'Thank you for your cooperation. Oliver, if you think of anything, no matter how small, give me a ring. And it goes without saying that you need to take care. We still have no idea why Daniel was killed, so we feel that as his closest friends, both you and Paul Browne need to be extra vigilant.'

Shock was etched on Denise's face. 'My God, I'm going to lock Ollie in the garage until you come here and tell me who has killed Daniel, and that you've got him under lock and key.'

'That's a good idea, Mrs Newton,' Will said, with a smile.

Oliver groaned. 'Don't say that to her, she'll never let me out of here again.'

'Well, at least you'll be safe,' Will countered. 'Seriously though, all joking aside, I do want you to be aware of your surroundings, of who is there, and don't go out alone. Just take precautions, and I'm sure you'll be fine.'

CHAPTER FOURTEEN

Wednesday morning delivered a day of autumnal disaster across the entire city – thick fog that blanketed the skies, and swirled around across the pavements and roads. Jess stood at her window after drawing back the library curtains and stared out. She could envisage where her gate was, but wasn't convinced she could actually see it. Today would be a day to stay in, to crank up the heating, and to read.

She could see a glimmer of lights of headlights piercing the fog, and as the vehicle stopped outside her home she leaned forward to work out what it was. A Land Rover.

She smiled. Her boys. She left the library and went to unlock the front door, removing the security chain that was still in place.

'Josh!' She held out arms and he stepped inside, returning the hug.

'Just me, Mum.'

'But why? I'm okay, and it's such a long way to come up here.'

'I woke up at three, couldn't even read myself back to sleep, so I left a note for Adam, said I was coming here for a couple of hours. I know he'll think I'm crazy, but I just wanted to check you were okay, especially with having Granddad to look after as well now.'

'Well you certainly chose the wrong day,' she said with a laugh. 'Visibility's a bit limited.'

'Tell me about it. And the more northerly I went, the worse it got. There was none of this when I left Devon.'

'You stopped for breakfast?'

Josh shook his head. 'No, I guessed you'd have bacon in. And by the time I was considering breakfast, the fog was getting thicker. I just kept going.'

'No problem. Bacon and tomato sandwiches. Coffee?'

He sighed. 'Welcome home, Josh. That sounds like heaven.'

Malcolm joined them in the kitchen, the smell of bacon having drifted into his room as well as the added confirmation that someone was here. Daisy was scratching at the door to be set free.

They chatted about Daniel, with Jess saying as much as she knew of the murder of their close friend.

'But he was so quiet,' Josh said. 'Worked hard at improving his golf until he surpassed the other three, so Dad said. Just a nice bloke. Clever as well, so I understand.'

'Well I think anybody who understands a computer is clever,' Jess said, 'but you're right, he was super-smart. He never spoke about his work; it's only because your dad used to ask him questions if he needed tech help that I realised who Daniel was. Mind you, that doesn't mean much. It took me for ever to find out Oliver was GardenScene. I knew Paul was a teacher at the swish academy place, that cropped up accidentally one day. But mainly the men were golfing friends, and I'm sure that was something primary with them.'

Josh finished his second bacon sandwich, and leaned back on his chair. 'Mum, that was superb.'

'I'm pleased you enjoyed it. Dad? You want another one?'

'No thanks, when you reach my age, Jess, you know your limits.' He smiled at his daughter. 'Your mum used to like a bacon sandwich, and I never did, but as I've got older I can appreciate the delights of one.'

'So you're finally growing up?'

'Maybe. I'm grown up enough to know that we'll not be taking Daisy out for a walk today, unless this lot clears up pretty fast. She can go for a chase around the back garden.'

'Are you staying overnight, Josh?' Jess asked her son, who was rubbing Daisy's head.

'No, we've a brewery delivery at seven tomorrow morning. I just felt I should pop up for a few hours, because you might not be telling us everything when you say you're okay.'

'I am okay, I promise you. Losing Daniel, and the manner of his death, has been hard, but not as hard as losing your dad. You've actually made my day, arriving unexpectedly.'

'I'll take Daisy for a few minutes' walk,' he said. 'Granddad, do you need anything from your house? I thought I'd just go and check everything was okay.'

'Good lad. The cupboard at the side of the cooker is where I keep packets of treats for Daisy. A couple of sachets would be helpful, I think she's having withdrawal symptoms.'

Daisy bounced her way around to the home she felt sure was her real one, and Josh actually felt as if he was fighting his way through the thick, drifting swirls of all-enveloping fog. It was a truly uncomfortable walk and he felt relieved to arrive at the front door of his grandfather's home. He did a thorough check of the entire house before returning downstairs to clip on Daisy's lead for the return journey.

The fog wasn't lifting; Josh actually felt it was getting heavier, and he was glad to be back with Jess and Malcolm. 'It's horrible out there. Mum, don't go out. Do you need me to go shopping for you before I head home?'

Jess shook her head. 'No thanks, Josh. That's what oversize freezers are for. Bad weather, freezer visit. But you'll take care? And you'll ring me as soon as you're home?'

'I will. Just remember it will take me longer than normal, unless this starts to lift. I can't remember a pea-souper as bad as this before.'

'Well, when you do get home, reassure Adam I'm okay. We may come down to you for a few days at Christmas through to the new year. But don't worry, I'll book Dad and myself into a hotel. I know you've not organised all your rooms upstairs yet.'

Josh laughed. 'We keep putting it off. Even with the two of us, it's hard work and long hours running a pub. It's really why I'm here, we've decided we need a full day a week off, separately. Doing nothing to do with the pub. Today is my full day. Adam's taking Friday this week, unless he changes his mind. It feels good to escape, yet I'm looking forward to the brewery delivery tomorrow, and doing the general cleaning of pipes and suchlike.'

'You didn't make a mistake in buying the pub then?'

'Definitely not. It's given us a good income, and it's doing so much better than when we took it over. We have plans to live off premises eventually, and turn the entire upstairs into letting rooms, but that's future plans.'

They had a pleasant couple of hours simply talking, and when Josh drove away on his journey back to Devon just after three o'clock, he went armed with a flask of coffee and sandwiches in case he suddenly decided he was starving.

Jess went out to the car with him, and waited until he wound down his window. 'Thank you for caring enough to come,' she said, 'but please don't forget to let me know you're home safe. This hasn't lifted all day, and I'll be worrying until I hear from you. And slow down!' she said, knowing his penchant for speed. She hugged him through the window, and he kissed her cheek.

'Love you, Mum. Love to Granddad as well,' Josh said, and pulled away from the kerb with a wave. She watched for as far as she could see given there had been no lifting of the fog, then walked back into the house. How that boy could lighten her life.

She sent the second text message of the day to Oliver, telling him Josh had now left on his return journey to Devon, and ended it with 'love you'.

His response was three heart emojis and a 'love you too'.

Oliver had spent most of the day at GardenScene at Leeds, his biggest acquisition by far, and one that he was looking at expanding even further. It had a well-respected coffee shop, but there was a patch of land that he felt could accommodate a restaurant, and he had been meeting with architects and other people who knew far more than he did about building restaurants.

Denise took a passing interest in the business, offering advice and thoughts when he asked for them, but rarely volunteering any input. It had been so different when they had first met at the original GardenScene – they had a goal, to have their own garden centre and plant nursery one day, and for ten years or so that was good. And then it wasn't good.

With Elle now living in Newcastle, he suspected it wouldn't be long before Denise moved into a flat there; she seemed to like the place so much more than Sheffield. And Elle was talking about staying there instead of coming back to the city of her birth following the end of her course.

Oliver wasn't devastated by the thought of a split in their marriage, but he didn't like the idea of Elle staying in Newcastle. He had talked it through with Jess, who had tried to explain how difficult it was when children left home.

'The essential thing to do,' she had said, 'is to let Elle know how much she is loved. That will always bring her back home to Sheffield when she needs comfort and solace.'

'You'll get used to their rare visits, and appreciate them all the more for it. And I lost two of mine to Devon!' Oliver remembered her words with clarity, and hoped she was right.

He wondered why Josh had visited in possibly the worst driving conditions for twenty years, but switched his mind back to the sheaf of papers the architect was handing over.

'Think about it all, Oliver, it's definitely feasible, if it's what you really want. And obviously we're happy to take on the job, but a restaurant is a lot more responsibility than a coffee shop. I'll leave you to read through everything, and give you a call next Wednesday?'

'That's fine. Thank you for everything today.' They shook hands, and he watched as the two men walked back to their car. It had been a good day, but he really wanted to discuss it with Jess.

And now he had to drive back in this blessed fog, not a pleasant prospect. He checked his watch, saw it was half past two and headed towards the coffee shop. A latte and a doughnut would just about see him through until he reached home tonight, and could ferret around in the freezer for anything that seemed edible.

One day, and he knew it would come eventually, he would be able to ring Jess and suggest they go out for a meal, spend time together, develop the blossoming relationship. He needed her.

It was a custard doughnut. He wished he'd asked for two, after realising he hadn't actually eaten anything since the previous evening, and then it had only been beans on toast.

'You'll fade away, Ollie,' he said, using a napkin to wipe any stray custard from his face. The young girl clearing tables smiled at him. 'You need anything else, Mr Newton?'

He hesitated. 'Would I be classed as greedy if I had a second doughnut?'

'No. Definitely not. That's what doughnuts are for, to encourage you to have a second one.'

He smiled at her. 'Then I might manage one, please.'

She disappeared to the counter, and returned with the bun. 'Apparently we're not supposed to charge you. I didn't know that earlier. So this one's free.'

He laughed out loud. 'I think you'll find I actually pay for it in the beginning, but thank you anyway.' He glanced at her name badge. 'And don't worry, Lara, I realised you didn't know, and I wouldn't have said anything. I'll enjoy it all the more now that it's free.'

She blushed and left him to enjoy the utter gluttony of his second doughnut, and he reflected on the success of all the coffee shops. Right staff, he decided. And definitely the best food. The doughnuts were superb, as was the coffee. He was leaning all the more towards thoughts of the new restaurant.

He needed to talk to... Jess.

CHAPTER FIFTEEN

Paul rubbed his eyes, and decided enough was enough. It had been a long day; he was marking test papers where it was obvious fifty per cent of the class hadn't understood one word of what he had said; he'd had a long staff meeting, and now he needed food. He needed to go home. Thoughts of the slow cooker containing a pork stew for his evening meal spurred him on. He gathered up the papers still to be marked, pushed them into his briefcase just in case he could find enough energy at home to complete them, and took a glance around the classroom, before closing and locking the door behind him.

Naomi was staying at her mum's – they were out with her sister at the theatre. Hence the slow cooker meal for whenever he arrived home from school.

He rather felt it would be a nice evening; he was rarely on his own. The only drawback, of course, was the marking...

He reached the school's large front door without seeing another soul, waved his pass at the sensor and waited for the click as the door unlocked. He opened the door and was shocked to see the fog hadn't lifted in any way from the awful journey to school some nine hours earlier. He listened for the locking mechanism to engage and headed over to his invisible car. It gradually became more visible as he approached it, and he clicked his fob to unlock the boot lid.

It swung up slowly, and he leaned forward to place his briefcase and his shoulder bag inside, moving his sports bag out of the way. He felt the pain in his back, and it took his breath away. But then he couldn't get his breath back.

The second pain in his back saw him tumbling forward and he tried to turn but although he didn't know it, he was already much too late for restarting his life.

Exsanguination was fast and dramatic, with most of his life blood mixing in with the assorted bags now underneath him in the boot of the car. He was dead before the boot lid was slammed down on him.

Naomi thoroughly enjoyed the performance, although trying to remember the last time she had been to the theatre with Paul had proved impossible. Football matches yes, theatre performances no.

The three ladies left the Crucible Theatre and became immediately embroiled in fog once again. 'This is awful,' Naomi said. 'I know we said we'd catch the tram home, but it's quite a walk when we get off the tram, and in this lot? I think not. Come on, we'll take a taxi and drop Caro off first, then go on to yours, Mum.'

'Good thinking,' Caroline said, shivering as she pulled her jacket tightly around her. 'It's so cold, as well.'

Five minutes later they were in a black cab, heading home, slowly. The driver apologised. Said it had been a hell of a day with the fog, and his eyes felt red raw. He was taking no chances, and they quickly reassured him. 'Take as long as you need. We're not in a rush.'

Caro left them, and the driver waited until she was in her front door before setting off to take his two remaining passengers to the next address.

Anne Brigham handed over a twenty-pound note with a feeling of relief, and she and her daughter headed up the path. They waved at the driver who was clearly making sure they were home safely. He pulled away with a wave of his hand, and they walked into the warmth of Anne's home.

'Hot chocolate?'

Naomi nodded. 'Please, Mum. It's a hot chocolate sort of night, isn't it? This damn fog hasn't lifted at all. Paul rang me this morning to tell me he'd arrived safely at school, but I must confess I was still in bed, hadn't realised how bad it was. Anyway he advised against going out until it began to lift, but it hasn't.' She glanced at her watch. 'I should ring him, but he might have gone to bed. He doesn't stay up late during the week... no, I'll ring him in the morning.'

'Go and sit in the lounge, sweetheart. I'll make our drinks, but just give Caro a ring, will you? Tell her we're inside now.'

Naomi took out her phone, and sent a swift text to Paul, saying 'Night, sweetheart. Love you xxx', then rang Caroline. They chatted for a couple of minutes, then she disconnected, checking to see if Paul had replied. There was nothing, so she assumed he had gone to bed.

The chocolate was truly delicious. They watched a little bit of television, chatted for a few minutes about Daniel's death, and then both headed upstairs to bed.

It occurred to Naomi how lonely her mum must be now that

her dad was no longer with them, and she resolved to make more time for her, starting with the coming weekend. They could maybe have a couple of hours at Meadowhall or something. She'd talk to her about it before leaving for home the following day.

The morning dawned clear and bright. No sun, that hadn't surfaced, but the fog had lifted. It would make the headlines in *The Star*, the awful day of fog, but it would fade away in everyone's memories before much longer. When the snow came it would be much more memorable, and last for a longer time.

Naomi was woken by Anne bringing her a cup of tea, and she sat on the edge of the bed and chatted to her daughter, enjoying the moment. You never stopped loving your child when they became an adult, but things changed. And sometimes Anne just wanted to put her arms round either Naomi or Caro, and hug them, tell them she loved them. Bringing Naomi a cup of tea to wake her up was the next best thing.

'I was thinking,' Naomi began, 'would you fancy a trip to Meadowhall this weekend? Spend a bit of money? I'll drive.'

'Sounds good to me. Which day?'

'Sunday? Just in case I end up in some football ground on Saturday.'

Anne laughed. 'You don't fool me, Naomi Browne. You love the matches just as much as Paul does. I've seen you screaming at the TV screen trying to get somebody to shoot.'

Naomi grinned. 'Don't tell Paul that. He thinks I do it under sufferance. It's strange how we always end up in the Sheffield Wednesday shop, and he always buys me something. It's called bribery. He thinks I need bribing to go, but I honestly enjoy it so much. And it gets him away from lesson plans and suchlike, that time we spend at any of the football grounds we go to.' She picked up her phone. 'He hasn't texted. Hope he hasn't slept in; he'll not be popular at school.'

They finished their drinks, and Naomi slipped out of bed. 'I'll have a shower, then head off home. It's been a slow week in the second-hand clothing market, but I've a couple of orders to post out, and I couldn't do them yesterday with all that fog. So Meadowhall on Sunday? Pick you up about eleven?'

'That will be lovely, and I'll treat us to lunch.'

Naomi smiled. 'That makes it even better. Think Caro will want to come?'

'It's more will bossy boots let her come, isn't it?'

Caro's controlling husband was dismissed from their conversation with a humph sound. 'I'll ring her, see if I can persuade her. And now that fog's lifted I think I'll walk home.'

Naomi pursed her lips. 'Please do ask her. She'll dump him one day, and then she'll be able to be Caro again. I was a bit surprised she came last night, but I didn't say anything. Perhaps she's fighting back.'

'Thanks for the tea, Mum. A quick shower and I'll be on my way. Leave Caro to me. So Sunday is our day, okay?'

The secretary at Belthorpe was starting to feel a little irritated, despite it being so out of character that Paul Browne hadn't arrived at school. She had now rung him three times, and received no response. She checked his file, and rang his wife.

'Mrs Browne? Is Paul okay? He's not in school yet, and we're a little concerned because I can't get an answer when I ring him.'

'Not in school?' Naomi was a little breathless. The fog might have gone but it was quite cold. 'I stayed at my mum's last night so I've not seen him since yesterday morning. Look, I'm almost home now, be about five minutes. He may be ill. I'll get back to you when I've spoken to him.'

'Thank you, I hope everything's okay.'

Suddenly Naomi felt sick. She hadn't heard from him since his text the previous day warning her about the fog. She broke into a jog, running the rest of the way home, feeling more uneasy with every step.

Her own car was there, but there was no sign of Paul's. She entered their home, shouting his name and heading straight upstairs. He must be ill, she felt, but if he was, where was his car? How had he got home? And the house smelt delicious from the flavours emanating from the slow cooker stew pot that had clearly not been turned off.

The house was cold but what was far worse was that she could sense it was empty.

She rang the school. She could hear the panic in her own voice as she explained to the woman who had initially contacted her that Paul wasn't home, but neither was his car. And he had used his car to drive to school the previous day.

'Look, don't panic, Mrs Browne,' the secretary tried to soothe the scared caller, 'I didn't think to check for his car. I assumed he must be ill, but I'll go and look. I know where he parks it, round by the large bin store. I'll ring you back when I've had a look.'

Naomi sat on the bottom stair clutching her phone. The air around her felt oppressive, and she didn't know what to do. In just a short fifteen minutes her life seemed to have disintegrated, and she prayed for her phone to ring and for the school to be telling her Paul was having to do some repairs to the car because it had stopped working.

She felt stupid for even thinking along those lines. They simply didn't have cars that stopped working; Paul saw to that. The worst problem they had ever had to contend with was a flat tyre. And a flat tyre wouldn't have kept him away overnight; she was beginning to realise he hadn't been in the house since he left for work the previous day.

Where the hell was he? Would he have just taken off for Manchester to be with the twins? Had something happened to one of them? But she would have been the first one he contacted if that had been the case. In fact, if there was a problem with the boys, she would have been their first phone call, not Paul.

She checked her phone, and suddenly it rang. Belthorpe.

'Yes? Have you found his car?'

'Mrs Browne, can you come to the school?' The secretary's voice was muted, as if she was trying to speak without anyone else hearing her.

'Of course I can. What's wrong? Is Paul all right?' Huge waves of anxiety crashed over Naomi. Of course Paul wasn't all right if the school wanted her to go.

'I don't know, but come quickly. The police have just arrived, and you should be here. The gates will be open. We're expecting more vehicles. My name's Christa. Ask for me if I don't see you first. And drive carefully, Mrs Browne.'

'Naomi. I'm Naomi. I'm leaving home right now, I drive a silver Audi. Look out for me.'

CHAPTER SIXTEEN

Naomi drove fast and not particularly carefully. She knew it took Paul around twenty minutes to reach work; she did it in fifteen.

She pulled up with a screech at the school gates – they were open, but a police car was blocking the entrance. She hit her horn twice, hard. The police constable standing by the gates walked over to her.

'Can I help?'

'My name is Naomi Browne, and something is wrong with my husband, or so I've been led to believe.'

'One second, Mrs Browne. I'll get them to move the car.'

He walked across to the vehicle containing just a driver, then came back to her. 'I'll get in your passenger seat, Mrs Browne, then nobody else will try to stop you. If you head up the drive and park in the visitors car park your car won't be in the way. Then I'll take you around to DI Stewart.'

'DI Stewart?' She looked across at the PC as he climbed into her car. She pulled forward as the other car moved and put her foot down to go up the drive.

'Slowly, Mrs Browne, this is a school with a maximum speed of ten miles per hour on school grounds.'

'Sorry,' she said. 'I'm so scared... isn't DI Stewart the one leading the investigation into Daniel Rubens murder?'

'You've met him?'

'I have. He came to talk to us a couple of days ago. My husband is a close friend of Daniel.' Slowly realisation came. 'Why is DI Stewart here in connection with my husband?'

'I'm sorry, I don't really know anything. I'm just here to deliver you to the right parking area. There's a lady called Christa looking for you.' He pointed to the front door of the school. 'That's her on the steps.'

She jumped out of her car and ran, leaving the constable to close her doors. He watched as the two women met up, then headed back down the driveway to the gates.

'Christa?'

'Yes, Naomi. Do you want to come inside where it's a bit warmer?'

'No. Where is my husband's car?'

Christa put her arm around the shoulder of the clearly frightened woman. 'DI Stewart will be here in a moment. I've told him you're in my office.'

Naomi started to shiver. 'Could I have a glass of water, please?'

'Of course. I'm going to lock the door until DI Stewart arrives, so there'll only be the two of us until then. We've had to ask parents to collect their children, and they all seem to gravitate towards this office. I don't want them here at the moment.'

She directed Naomi to a small armchair, and fetched her a beaker of water from the water fountain. As she handed it to her there was a tap at the door, and Christa turned to release the lock. DI Stewart walked straight over to the woman he instantly recognised.

'Tell me what's going on,' Naomi demanded. 'Nobody's saying anything, but I do remember you're part of the Major Crimes Team, so whatever this is, it's serious.'

'Your husband drives a white Civic? Personalised number plate PLB...' Will glanced down at his notes and Naomi finished it off for him.

'1966. It is the year of his birth and the year we won the World Cup,' she said quietly.

Will gave a brief nod. 'I'm truly sorry to have to tell you this, but we have found your husband deceased inside it.'

Initially Naomi couldn't speak. She looked everywhere but at Will, but then stood. 'Take me to him,' she said.

'Not yet,' he said gently. 'We're removing him from the car without disturbing any forensic evidence, but I promise you will see his face before we take him to our pathologist.'

'He just died?' she asked, almost in a whisper. 'He just sat in his car and died?'

There was a moment of hesitation. 'No, this lady,' he gestured towards Christa, 'went outside to look for your husband's car. She found it in what I understand is his usual parking space, but noticed what she thought was blood on the bumper, quite a lot of it. She immediately rang the police because, as she explained, you hadn't seen Mr Browne since yesterday morning. We were here very quickly after her call, because we realised there were many children in the vicinity. We forced the boot lid open because we had no keys, and found your husband inside the boot.'

Naomi felt as if the room was going around and around. She tried to stand, but she didn't know why. Where was she going to go?

Christa held her firmly. 'Deep breaths, Naomi, deep breaths.'

Naomi looked at Will. 'He's been stabbed? Like Daniel?'

'At the moment we know very little, and until there has been a post-mortem I can tell you nothing because it would be speculation. The amount of blood in the bottom of the boot indicates a knife was used, but I'm not a pathologist. However, I promise you that when I do know, I will tell you.'

'And doesn't anything show on CCTV?'

'We've only been here half an hour or so, and haven't had chance to check on everything, but we will. However, it seems your husband always tucked his car in the corner round by the bins, so just how much will be on camera we can't tell.'

'Why? Why Paul? He was such an easy-going man, I've never known him fall out with anyone. What could have caused such hatred in someone that they would want to stab him to death? Take him away from me and the boys? Oh God, our boys. I need to bring them home.'

'Where are they?'

'Manchester University.'

'We can have them collected, if you need that.'

She shook her head. 'They have their cars, but maybe I should just tell them I need them to come home. They've just gone through everything with losing Chris Harcourt, a man they looked on almost as an uncle, so they'll maybe just assume we have some news of a similar nature. If I tell them the truth they'll not be thinking about rules of the road, will they?'

Will tried to put himself in the woman's shoes, and realised he wouldn't have a clue how to handle what she was having to deal with. So simple – Manchester wasn't a million miles away, just a quick trip over the Pennines on possibly the worst road in the United Kingdom, and with her boys knowing something was wrong. He didn't have a clue how he would tell the twins, if he was in the situation Naomi Browne now found herself in.

'I repeat,' he said gently, almost willing her to agree with his suggestion, 'we can collect the boys for you. This will involve telling them what has happened. I'm so sorry, Naomi, I don't know how you're going to deal with this.'

She shook her head. 'They're going to need their cars while they're here. Give me some time to decide how to deal with this. Can I see Paul yet?'

Will stood. 'I'll go and see, but this can't be rushed. We need to be forensically careful, to avoid losing any fingerprints and suchlike.'

Suddenly the tears she had been holding on to erupted, and began to stream down her face. 'Why?' she sobbed. 'Why Paul? He wouldn't hurt anybody, went out of his way to be a useful member of society, not a nasty bone in him.'

'I'll see what I can find out,' Will said, leaving Christa and Claire to comfort the stricken woman. And they still hadn't solved the problem of how to get her boys home from Manchester safely...

Paul Browne's body had been safely removed from the boot of the car, and the police auto rescue vehicle was just pulling up close by the Civic, ready for taking it away for forensic examination as soon as the forensic tent was removed.

The pathologist looked at Will and nodded. 'Yes, she can see him for one minute, then I'm taking him. This is a nasty one, Will. And although I need to do more tests for it to be conclusive, I'm pretty sure the same knife was used to kill this poor man as was used on Daniel Rubens.'

'I wouldn't be surprised,' Will replied. 'There's a connection

– as in best mates type of connection. I'll go and bring Mrs Browne across.'

'We'll leave the tent up till she's off the premises, she doesn't need to see all the blood.'

Naomi stared down at the still, silent face of her husband, and drew in her breath. 'He looks so peaceful,' she said.

'I promise you we'll find who did this,' DI Will Stewart said. 'And we'll take care of him for now. The pathologist needs to take him as soon as possible. Let's go back to the school office and decide how you want to sort getting your boys home.'

She reached out a hand as if to touch Paul's face, and Will gently stopped her. 'I'm sorry, you can't touch.'

Her tear-stained face lifted towards the policeman, and she turned and walked away, unable to say anything.

Christa walked alongside her, and led her back inside the school. 'I think it's time to call your boys,' she said gently. 'And is there anyone else you need to call?'

'My mum. I've only just left her. I stayed at hers overnight after a theatre outing. And my sister. Oh God, I don't know what to do. I'd best contact the university, explain what's happened. They can get Alex and Harry out of lectures so I can speak to them, I suppose. I simply don't know how to handle this at all. My head's spinning.'

In the end everything happened very smoothly. Alex and Harry were taken out of lectures, where they facetimed their mother to be given the news about their father. It was agreed they would return home immediately, although Naomi extracted several promises from both of them that they wouldn't exceed any speed limits, have respect for the Woodhead Pass and all its vagaries, and definitely no communications via mobile phone during the journey.

Her mother and Caroline were with her within half an hour of Naomi's return to her home. The three women huddled in a group in the hallway, before Anne took over making hot drinks for her daughters.

Caroline and Naomi sat side by side in the lounge, and Caro reached across to take Naomi's hand. In all her life she had never seen her sister look lost, but it was more than that. She was bereft. She had met Paul, had loved Paul, and that was it. Her husband and her boys were her life, and now one had been cruelly taken away.

'Have you told anyone?' Caro asked her sister gently.

Naomi shook her head. 'No, just the boys and you two. I feel as if it's going to make it real if I start telling people, but I have to tell Oliver soon because it's Thursday, and they meet up for golf Thursday afternoon. Paul doesn't...' she hesitated, '... didn't have lessons Thursday afternoons, which was why they liked to play on that day. Now everybody has gone, there's only Oliver left.'

'Do you want me to ring him?'

'Would you? I'm not sure I'll be coherent enough. I'll be glad when the boys get here, but on the other hand I want them to take their time.'

'Stop worrying about them. They're very capable drivers, and they'll have left straight away. Shouldn't be too long before they're home, and that will take a lot of the stress away. I'll go ring Oliver now if you pass me your phone. I don't have his number.'

Caro took the phone and disappeared into the kitchen, waited until Anne had carried the tray of drinks through to the lounge, then rang the last remaining member of the golfing group of four. She had only met Oliver a couple of times, and she knew this was going to be a truly difficult phone call.

CHAPTER SEVENTEEN

After Caro had finished speaking there was utter silence.

'Oliver? You there?'

'I am.' His voice sounded strange. 'What the hell is going on, Caroline?'

'I have no idea. I'm about to ring Jess to tell her, but I honestly don't know what I'm telling her.'

'I have to go round to see Jess this morning. We're supposed to collectively be keeping an eye on her as per Chris's wishes, but she's also looking after Malcolm at the moment so I thought I'd pop round this morning, see if she needs anything, so if you want, I can tell her. I'll go now before something lands on Facebook.'

'That would be a blessing. I can't tell you much because we don't know much, but he was in his car boot overnight according to what Naomi has managed to tell me. I suppose when the police come round to see us we'll find out more. The boys are due home from Manchester anytime, but in the meantime Mum and I are here for as long as she needs us. She's distraught, Oliver.'

'I can imagine. Okay, I'm going to grab my coat and go

straight round to speak with Jess and Malcolm now. If you do hear anything further, ring me, will you? I am utterly confused at the moment. Three of the four of us, gone just like that. In a matter of weeks.'

'I will. Tell Jess we'll keep her informed. I know everybody is still dealing with the loss of Daniel...'

'Thank you for letting me know, Caroline. Tell Naomi she's in my thoughts and she only needs to ring if she needs anything.'

After chatting for a couple more minutes, they disconnected and Caro sat and stared at the phone. It was too much. Too much to take in. And did Oliver not even think he could be in danger if somebody was targeting the group of golfers for some reason? Hadn't that occurred to him? Because it had occurred to her.

Alex and Harry arrived within a minute of each other, having followed their mother's instructions to the letter to shadow each other across the Pennines. Fresh tears flowed following their homecoming, so great was her relief at their safe arrival.

Naomi tried to explain what had happened to their father, but the amount she knew was negligible. 'We'll know more when DI Stewart gets here. He promised he would keep us fully informed, but first he needs to know himself.'

'I'm having trouble believing it,' Alex said, his normally confident voice now cracking with emotion. 'Dad was such a lovely man, never hurt anybody, so why? It just seems so wrong. Did they get the wrong person, do you think?'

Harry, the logical one of the twins, seemed to be deep in thought. 'It's linked to Daniel's death, isn't it? It can't be a coincidence that they've both died because a knife was used, they've got to be connected. Which means somebody is tailing them deliberately. They're not random deaths because somebody was in the wrong place at the wrong time. That's what we kind of thought with Daniel, but I'm not thinking that now, and I bet the police aren't thinking that either.' He brushed away a tear as he finished speaking. 'Why our dad? He never hurt anybody.'

Naomi stood and pulled them both close to her. 'Go and settle into your rooms, boys, you've had a stressful journey. If the police call today I'll give you a shout, but take some time out now.'

They grabbed cans of Coke out of the fridge and picked up their hastily packed bags from the hall floor as they headed upstairs.

'What do we do?' Alex asked as they arrived on the landing.

Harry pushed open his door. 'God knows. Mum's in bits, as are Nan and Aunty Caro. Should we drive over to the school? Would they let us in?'

'I can't imagine we'd even get through the gates. All the kids will have been collected by parents. They wouldn't have pupils there with a murder in the car park, and Dad will have been taken for post-mortem now. No, my feeling is we wait here. Sooner or later the police will arrive, and we can ask any questions then. Let's reconnect our phones to the doorbell camera, and we can see any comings and goings.'

Harry nodded. 'Smart thinking, Alex. I'm going to plug my laptop in, just in case I need to take it anywhere. I want to see if there's anything on the internet about Daniel's death, maybe give Andi a ring.' He paused. 'Why have our lives suddenly become such a load of shit?'

Alex smiled at his brother, younger by three whole minutes.

'Say it like it is, baby brother. Don't mince words. Go and get unpacked, we're home for some time, I reckon.'

Jess heard Ollie pull up, and went to the door with a smile on her face. She was alone; Malcolm had decided to go to his own home for a couple of hours, check out the garden, water his houseplants, and sit in his own lounge for a change, promising to pick up a fresh sourdough loaf for them on the way back. He had, of course, been accompanied by Daisy, and Jess had picked up her Kindle, relishing the moments of peace. Until the Carrera drew up outside.

'Come in,' she said softly, 'it's so good to see you.'

He pulled her into his arms and kissed her slowly. Then he said, 'Where's Malcolm?'

She laughed. 'Bit late to ask that, but he's gone home for a couple of hours. I think he regards it as the great escape, but he's watering plants and suchlike, so welcome to my father- and dog-free environment!'

'Come in here,' Ollie said, and guided her into the library.

Curiosity was written all over her face. 'What's wrong? Is it news about Daniel's killer?'

'Possibly' he said, 'but just hear me out. I don't know a lot, but this is what I've learned from Caroline.'

'Naomi's sister Caroline?'

He nodded. 'She rang me. It appears we have lost a third member of our foursome.'

'Paul? No, tell me that's wrong.'

'It's not wrong. I can only tell you what Caro told me, because I won't push my luck by ringing a certain contact again, but it seems Paul didn't go home last night after finishing school. Naomi didn't know because she went to the theatre with Caro and their mum, then stayed overnight at her mum's. This morning the school contacted her because Paul hadn't arrived at work. Naomi couldn't help because she hadn't heard from him or seen him either. The secretary found his car in the car park with blood down the bumper and underneath in a pool. Whatever happened obviously happened under cover of all that blessed fog, but when the police turned up they had to force the boot open. He was inside, and he had been stabbed. That's as much as I know, and they're at home waiting for the police to give them more information.'

Jess's face had become paler with every word. 'Paul? Dead? That lovely quiet man, gone? What had he done to hurt anyone? Oh my God, Ollie, is somebody picking you all off one at a time? And why?'

'Hey, don't talk like that, I'm not going anywhere. And I promise to be permanently on my guard until the police come up with answers. If killing us is the plan, it's not going to work, I can assure you. But like you, I've no idea why. It's almost as if losing Chris was the catalyst for what's happening now.'

Jess shivered. 'And presumably we don't know anything of what the police are thinking or doing?'

'Not yet, but I believe DI Stewart is supposed to be visiting Naomi this afternoon. Naomi, of course, went to the school, but although they allowed her to confirm it was Paul, that's as much as she knows. However, it is a stabbing, so they'll be linking it to Daniel's death. Especially if they can match the wounds to the same knife that caused them.'

'I want my dad here,' she said. 'I'm scared, he's not strong enough now to defend himself. Can you drop me off at his house, please, Ollie, and I'll walk back with him and Daisy?'

'I don't think your dad will be on this killer's radar; it's got to be something to do with the golf, but I'll do better than that. You ring him, tell him I'm on my way to pick up him and Daisy, and

I'll bring him back here. He wants a ride in the Carrera, doesn't he?'

Jess smiled. 'It's his main topic of conversation. Men and boy's toys. I'll never understand it.'

'Says the woman with a rather smart Lexus.'

She snuggled underneath his shoulder. 'Let's have five minutes of peace, and then I'll give him a ring, tell him to get ready for you to pick him up.'

Christa began the job of emailing all parents, advising them that school would be closed the following day, Friday, but would reopen as normal on Monday morning. All of the parents had complied at some speed earlier that day when the death on the premises had been mentioned – no pupils were left in school beyond half past eleven. She added thanks for their prompt response to the request that they collect their children, and said that full details would be disclosed as soon as they knew of any further information.

She read it through one final time and emailed it to the entire group, before leaning back in her chair and closing her eyes. She could still see, in her mind, the blood on the car, the puddle underneath it, and was instantly reminded of the sickness that had overwhelmed her.

Naomi had handled it remarkably well until the ramifications hit her. Her two boys, not in Sheffield but over the hills in Manchester, and having to travel on a particularly dangerous road while feeling deeply upset by the reason for being homeward bound. Christa felt much admiration for the older woman, but wouldn't want to be in her shoes over the next few weeks. A speedy clear-up on behalf of that rather dishy DI Stewart would be most welcome, she was sure.

She had gone through the CCTV tapes at the DI's request, but there had been nothing. Except fog. Because Paul Browne had always parked his car out of football shooting range, and round the corner near the bin. It was some distance from the school building and its security cameras, none of which had penetrated the density of the fog that had created havoc all day long.

They could tell Paul had exited the building just after five, presumably to go home, because his fob had been used to unlock the door, so the assumption was that he was attacked as he reached his car.

Christa gave a deep sigh, put on her coat and went to the head's office, where she said goodnight to Kenneth Lanstead. He looked worn out, and he thanked her for all the work she had done.

'All the parents have been notified we're closed tomorrow,' she confirmed, 'so if you need me to sit in on any meetings tomorrow, just let me know. I'm sure we'll have to organise some counselling for the boys; they're going to miss Paul. He was a bit of a favourite.'

Kenneth smiled at her. 'Thank you. We'll sort it first thing. We'll need it in place by Monday, I fear. See you in the morning, Christa, and well done. You're right of course, he was definitely a bit of a favourite, and we're going to miss him.'

CHAPTER EIGHTEEN

It was a chilly Friday morning when Will entered the briefing room, deep in thought. He had spent some considerable time the previous evening on the phone with Oliver Newton, in the hope it would put the one remaining member of the foursome on his guard, but it seemed Oliver had added two and two together, and he was already fully aware there was a problem.

Everyone looked up as he crossed to the whiteboard area – somebody had now added a picture of Paul Browne to that of Daniel Rubens, but off to one side there was a picture of Christopher Harcourt.

He stared at it for a moment then turned to face the room. 'I don't know who's done the board update, but well done for adding Mr Harcourt's picture. We know he died of natural causes, but his death was the first of three, all close friends. There may be no connection between his death and theirs, but instinct says there's a link somewhere on this board.'

There was a general shuffling as people stopped talking and settled down to listen. 'So, we have an early post-mortem report. It confirms what we suspected – that the knife used to murder Paul Browne is the same knife that was used to slash Daniel

Rubens' throat. I spoke with Oliver Newton last night, the only remaining member of the four-man golf team, and tried to put him on his guard, but he was already there. A smart man. We had a lengthy chat, but he has explained that he can't hide himself away. He has three huge meetings concerning a new development at one of his garden centres over the next seven days, and he can't put things on hold just on the off-chance somebody might want to stab him. I understood what he was saying, but I did point out that his new development meant bugger-all to anybody if he was dead.'

He waited for a moment, then tapped on Chris's picture. 'This is linked, I am sure of it. I have no idea why, so I want our resident tech department to really forage around on the internet and see what comes up.'

DC Freya Newbould heaved a sigh and held up her hand. 'That will be me then, boss.'

Will smiled at her. 'Thank you for volunteering, Freya. You're a star.'

He looked around at the faces in front of him; some he didn't know. 'Thank you to anybody here who's been seconded, welcome to our team. The ones who are in Major Crimes are the ones wearing their own clothes, so if you're new to the case, you know who to ask for information.'

There was a general nodding of heads. 'So, to continue with the PM report, death occurred between 4 and 6pm on Wednesday evening. To set that in your minds, it was the day of all that fog.' He looked around the room, checking everybody was following his words. 'That certainly helped the killer.'

He gathered his thoughts for a moment before continuing. 'It appears Browne was killed as he bent over the car boot to place his stuff inside, which has ultimately proved to be his laptop and his briefcase. There was also a sports bag in the boot, which contained anything he might need for his golfing.

'He was stabbed twice in his back, accurately it seems. The first stab would have done the job, the second was a just-in-case stab.' Again Will paused, making sure everybody was absorbing the facts. 'This could indicate, in view of the one slash needed to kill Daniel Rubens, that the killer is medically trained, but don't be guided by that; it could just as easily be a hefty individual who could handle an extremely sharp knife. We don't believe he would have seen his killer, as he was bundled immediately into the boot. The killer didn't stay around to clean anything up. It was Browne's blood on the car, and also underneath it and inside the boot. We are awaiting toxicology results.'

He looked around the room. 'Any questions?'

Just for a moment there was silence. Then a uniformed PC waved a hand in the air. 'Why? Do we have any idea why? PC Ian Davis, sir.'

'Good question, PC Davis. We have absolutely no idea why. There is the obvious link of a golfing foursome that ties them together, but they all seem to lead pretty clean-cut lives. I'm not sure what Christopher Harcourt did, but Daniel Rubens owned a tech support company; Paul Browne was head of maths at a very prestigious fee-paying school, Belthorpe Academy, and Oliver Newton, the only surviving member of the group, is GardenScene. He owns all of them, five or six at the last count. As far as we are aware, nothing in their lives could lead to what has happened.

'There is one thing that is nagging away at me, and it's a little notebook. It was found in the home office of Daniel Rubens, and appears to annotate his meetings, clandestine no doubt, with somebody he calls X. It's undated, and we don't even know if it's a man or a woman. Daniel still shared a home with his ex-wife, but they had divorced. Which leads me to think that maybe X is still married, and I'm guessing it's a woman. If this is a clue to these murders, I have no idea how it helps us.'

'Thank you, sir,' Ian Davis said.

Will smiled. 'And can I ask you all to drop the *sir* bit? I'm boss, when we're working a case, I'm only *sir* if we happen to run over the chief constable or something. Okay?'

There was a chorus of 'yes, sirs' from the uniformed lads, and everybody laughed.

'Right, let's get on. Freya, you know what to do?'

'Already on it, boss.'

He hadn't really needed to ask. 'Okay, I want at least six uniforms doing door to door near the school entrance. Whoever killed Paul Browne got into the school grounds somehow – and it's a locked main gate. There must be some other way that pupils enter and leave, that is left open in case of dental visits, doctor appointments and such things.'

He waited a moment for everyone to absorb what he was saying. 'The school is closed today, but I think staff will be there if you need to go through the main gates for anything. I want neighbours in the locality to think if they saw anybody they didn't know hanging around the school entrance. The police didn't turn up till the day after, so you can use that to jog their memories for the right day. The day of the fog.'

He turned slightly to face a small group. 'My team, you know what you're doing, so let's crack on. Claire, we're heading out to talk to the wives today, see if their brains have come more into gear now. They may have remembered something that they didn't think about earlier.'

The room was cleared within a couple of minutes, and Will headed back to his own office. He sat deep in thought, waiting for Claire to follow him. She was their organisational expert, and would be filling the uniformed officers in on statements if they were needed, and making notes of any houses visited where nobody answered the knock on the door.

Eventually Claire joined him, smiling. 'Nice bunch of lads we've been given. Keen as mustard. So, what are we doing?'

'I want to go back to the first one to be murdered, Daniel Rubens. I think he's the key to it all, because of this X person. Maybe his wife knows something, but she simply hasn't been asked the question. We should go ask it?'

'We should. What question?'

'Who the hell was your ex-husband screwing on the side?'

They were thwarted in their interview of Andi Rubens by her absence from home. It had seemed a good idea to take her by surprise and just turn up unexpectedly; a quick call to her mobile phone revealed she was at her mother's home for a few days because her mother had two dogs who required feeding and watering. So did they want to divert to Huddersfield to see her?

An agreement was reached that she would return home for a couple of hours the following day, and DI Stewart and DS Landon would be there for eleven o'clock.

Will looked at the disconnected phone and sighed. 'It's bloody Saturday tomorrow.'

She nodded. 'Working again, are we?'

'I promise we'll just do that one interview then we're done. I wasn't thinking what day it was today when I made the phone call.' He gave another deep sigh. 'It's been a hell of a week, hasn't it?'

Claire concurred. 'And it's not over yet. Oliver Newton. He's been put on his guard?'

'I spoke to him at length last night, but he can't come up with anything that would lead us to finding who is doing this. I didn't mention X to Oliver, just in case it meant something to him. I didn't want him turning into an avenger, and going after X himself. That'd complicate matters even further.'

'So now what?'

'We're not too far from the Harcourt home, so let's shoot over there, speak to Jessica Harcourt and see what we shall see.'

'My mum used to say that. It was when she wanted to shut me up, when I was wanting something. She'd say, "let's see what we shall see," and I used to pretend I knew what she was talking about.'

He laughed. 'Never really thought about what it meant. Think I picked it up from my dad. My wife has all sorts of odd little sayings that I hear coming from my daughter's mouth occasionally.'

'Wife? You have a wife?'

'Not so you'd notice. She took our little one and left me about six years ago. Technically she's now an ex-wife, and although I have some contact with Carly, our daughter, it's only minimal. They live in France with the feller she left me for.'

'And that's why you're pretty fluent in French, isn't it?'

He grinned. 'Got it in one. I figured Carly would become bilingual, with the emphasis on French, so I have French lessons. We face time, and she laughs at my accent a lot, but we converse mainly in French. It's not the life I thought we would have when the pregnancy was announced, but it's the life I have.'

Claire sat for a moment, not sure how to respond. 'I'm so sorry,' she said at last.

He reached forward and started the car. 'Don't be, it's all water under the bridge, and I'm well over losing my wife to a Frenchman. And when Carly is old enough to travel the world under her own steam, I shall make it very clear she has a home in England any time she wants it.'

They drove over to Jess's home, and followed the Carrera down the road, parking up just behind it. They watched as

Oliver got out of the driver's seat, and Malcolm and Daisy out of the passenger side.

Oliver and Malcolm waited until the two police officers joined them, and then went up the garden path towards the front door. Jess opened it. 'We having a party then?' she asked, staring around at everyone.

'We just wanted a little chat, and it's absolutely fine if Mr Johnson and Mr Newton are here. We're all aware of what's happening, and maybe we can share ideas as to why all of this is affecting you and your friends so badly.'

Jess turned and walked down the hall. 'Go in the library,' she called over her shoulder, 'I'll bring tea, coffee and biscuits.'

Claire and Will grinned at each other. This was a bit of an improvement on their previous call, where they hadn't even obtained an entry into the house; this one provided drinks and snacks!

CHAPTER NINETEEN

'Is my daughter in danger?' Malcolm asked, after sitting quietly, listening to the backwards and forwards chat between the police officers and Jess and Oliver.

'I don't believe so,' Will said. 'What is troublesome is the death of Christopher, because that seems to have been the catalyst for what has followed. He was the first one to die, albeit of natural causes, and we're actively looking for a link between the three deaths.'

'So Ollie is in danger as well?' Jess asked.

'I believe so, but we have discussed it and he feels he can handle it.'

'Ollie?' Jess said, staring at him.

'Jess, whether I'm in danger or not, I can't stop carrying on with my life just because some maniac has taken a dislike to us.'

'It's more than a dislike,' Claire said quietly. 'The killer is picking you off one at a time, and for some reason it's followed on from a perfectly normal death to cancer. Jess, you must have had long talks with your husband before he passed. Did he ever intimate you might have a problem after his death, or he'd had one before it?'

'Nothing that caused me to worry. We mainly talked through our finances, because Chris was quite savvy with money, and he wanted to make sure our boys were looked after.'

'Oliver,' Will said, turning to the man he felt was their biggest problem, 'when did you last see Chris?'

'All three of us came to see him on his last day, although we weren't aware he was so close. He was still fairly coherent, responded if any of us asked him a question. He talked about his amazing carer, Elsa, but he said he had gone beyond having food, was basically living on sips of water. All of us actually thanked Elsa as we left, but she more or less shrugged it off, said it was only what any caring human being would do. We knew it was the last time we would see him because as we left, Jess told us she had sent for the boys, and they were on their way from Devon.'

'And you, Jess? Did you manage to speak with him?'

'I did. I sent Elsa out – if I remember correctly she wanted to send some flowers to her mum, so she nipped down to the florists. I asked her not to rush back, because she had said she didn't think Chris would get through until the morning, which meant she would be on duty all night. I wanted some time with Chris while he was still able to hear me, just to clarify something about the boys, and it was a very precious time. He nodded rather than speaking, but when Josh and Adam arrived he seemed to perk up a bit. I left them alone with him for about half an hour, then Elsa returned, shooed the boys out of the room so she could give Chris his pain relief. I could hear a little bit of talk between the two of them, but not much. Dad also had five minutes with him. That was actually the last time I heard Chris speak, I believe, because he fell asleep, and slowly slipped away from us.'

'An awful time,' Will said. 'I'm so sorry for your loss. He was still a relatively young man. So did Elsa have a room here?'

'Yes, the lounge held a hospital bed for Chris when he could no longer climb stairs, and right next to it, we have what used to be a toy room when the boys were small. We threw out all the toys and turned it into a bedroom for Elsa. She was with us for about five months, and was a godsend. She helped me get through it all just as much as she helped Chris.'

'Would you have an address for Elsa?'

'I would,' Jess confirmed, and wrote her friend's name and address, plus phone number, on a piece of paper. 'She's possibly helping some other family with end-of-life care at the moment, so be aware of that when you contact her. I will say she never expressed any concerns about any conversations she had with Chris. She's a very professional lady and I'm sure she would have said if she felt Chris had something on his mind.'

'Thank you, we'll be careful,' Will said. 'We have three officers at Daniel Rubens' company today, talking to his staff and taking statements. I'll be looking through it all tonight just in case somebody comes up with something that's significant, but it strikes me that Mr Rubens was a very quiet, very personal sort of man, so I'm not expecting a lot from the visit. Please don't worry, Jess, our calling here today was simply to see if anything had jogged any thoughts following the death of Paul Browne so soon after Daniel Rubens' death.'

'I know this is going to sound stupid,' Jess said, 'but I feel as if I'm losing my guardian angels. I know Chris, on that last day, made Ollie, Daniel and Paul promise to keep an eye on me, to make sure I was supported if I needed repairs to the house and suchlike, but suddenly my backup system has been decimated.' She reached across and grasped Oliver's hand for a few seconds. 'I'm scared for Ollie. Who the hell has taken the other two, and how will you keep Ollie safe?'

'We can't force anybody to accept protection,' Will said, 'but I did have a long conversation with Oliver about the situation.

I'm not going to say he listened to me, but he is at least aware of our concerns.'

Oliver gave his slow, gentle smile. 'I can handle myself,' he said. 'Don't worry about me.'

Malcolm remained quiet. A heavy blanket of unease seemed to be settling over him. He stood and shook the hands of the two officers as they got up to leave. 'Thank you for keeping us informed, although I realise you have little to tell us at the moment. Wasn't there CCTV at the school?'

'There was, but it's just like looking at a grey cloud for the relevant time frame. Paul had parked his car too far away for the camera to get anything but swirls of fog. But I promise you, Mr Johnson, we will find who did this to both of your friends, because somebody will slip up and give us information that only the killer would have.'

Malcolm nodded and said, simply, 'I know.'

'Okay,' said Ollie once the detectives had left. 'I'm going to head home. Denise is on her way home from Newcastle. She's got a book group meeting at the library tonight. There's nothing you need me to do before I leave, is there, Jess?'

'No, we're fine thanks. Just take care, Ollie. You heard what those two said, and they're clearly concerned for your safety. As we are.'

Malcolm nodded, entirely in agreement with what his daughter was saying.

Jess walked outside with Oliver, and once again chatted through the car window to him. 'I'm really scared by what's happening, Ollie. Take care, won't you?'

'Well, they've actually managed to rattle me, so I will be extra careful until they come and tell us they've got him or her. I promise.'

Jess looked up as she heard a car horn, and saw a Land Rover passing. For a few seconds she thought it was Josh, but then realised that the hand that was waving at her actually belonged to Elsa; she waved back enthusiastically, then stepped back as Ollie pulled away from the kerb, following the Land Rover down the road.

She headed back indoors after watching for the taillight flash from the Porsche, waited ten minutes then rang Elsa. 'Lovely to see you, albeit driving past my front door,' she said.

'I was taking some medication to a patient, so I didn't have time to stop. I've got the weekend off if you want to meet up for a coffee or something?'

'That would be lovely. Costa on the retail park?'

'Wherever. Coffee is coffee. I'll come and pick you up, then we only have to park one vehicle.'

'I thought your car was Josh's when you hooted this afternoon. He never considered having a Land Rover until he saw yours, you know. You're a bad influence on my turbo-charged son.'

Elsa laughed. 'I know. He was fascinated by mine, so I told him where I'd got it from. The rest is now history. Are they okay, our boys?'

'They are, Josh came up to see me that day when it was really foggy, but now we're back to phone calls and text messages until one of them arrives for food.'

'And how's Malcolm?'

'He's okay. Hasn't missed one blood pressure check, and we go back to the doctors on Monday to see if everything is okay. If it is, he can go back home.'

'Right, I'd best get off. What time tomorrow?'

'Half ten? Does that suit you?'

'Certainly does. Take care, Jess, and love to Malcolm.'

They disconnected and Jess sat and stared at her phone. The woman had been an absolute godsend to her and her family, taking on the difficult shifts with Chris, handling all his medication needs, and being a rock. And turning into a friend.

Her phone vibrated, reminding her that Malcolm needed a blood pressure check. She waited, and then heard her father shout that he would see to it. She smiled. Finally, she could trust him to do the check when his alarm went off. Knowing he would make regular checks, she could now let him return home. She considered his training to be complete. If only she could train Daisy not to dig up her flower beds, all would be well temporarily in her world.

It would all be a lot better if she could find her journal, still missing and still missed.

Oliver drove home, his thoughts anywhere but on the road. He had enjoyed the solitude of their home that had followed Denise's escape to Newcastle for a few days, and wished he could be more enthusiastic about her return. It seemed to him that the magic of their early married life had drifted away; as he had become more successful and they had welcomed Elle into their family, they had divided. He had taken on more and more of the work involved in growing their business empire, and Denise had become, first and foremost, a mother.

He pulled into the garage, leaving plenty of room for Denise to park her own car at the side of his. It had been a bit of a luxury over the last few days to just swing his car in without having to think about how it was parked, and he grinned. He knew Denise would grumble it was a tight squeeze anyway, because she always did, but the garage was plenty big enough for two cars.

Leaving the garage open, he went through the door into the kitchen. He grabbed a water from the fridge, and drank most of it in one gulp. His thoughts drifted not only to the afternoon he had spent at Jess's house, but also to the conversation with Will Stewart the previous night. Was he dismissing everything foolishly? Was he in danger? Was he putting Denise in danger by his own cavalier attitude?

Caution, he told himself. *Stop being so cocky, and check everything is secure.* He headed upstairs, locked every window, then did the same downstairs. He only found one small bathroom window unlocked.

He heard Denise's car arrive, and she drove straight into her parking spot. He went back through the kitchen and into garage, and kissed her gently on the lips. 'Welcome home. Good journey?'

'It was, considering it's Friday. I think there's something wrong with the car's electrics though. Can we book it in, get it checked over?'

'I'll do it. Take the Carrera tonight; I don't want you breaking down in the middle of nowhere.'

Shock was etched on her face. 'My God, I can't wait to see Annmarie's face when I turn up at the library in a Porsche.'

CHAPTER TWENTY

Neither Ollie nor Denise felt hungry so they settled on cheeseburgers. After booking her car in for an electrics check on Saturday morning, Oliver filled her in on all that had happened since her departure for Newcastle. They spoke amicably, as old friends.

She licked the tomato sauce from her fingers, and sat back. 'Thank you, Ollie, that was lovely. Can I speak with you now?'

He nodded without saying anything. 'I have found a flat in Newcastle with two bedrooms, for Elle and myself. Elle wants to stay in Newcastle when she finishes this final year. She doesn't want to come back to Sheffield except to visit you. Eventually I will buy a property, but for now, we have this beautiful little flat overlooking the Tyne, and I will be packing up and moving there next week.'

'Do I get any say in this?' His marriage was imploding, his daughter was planning a future on Tyneside and his calmness was taking him by surprise. It was, he realised, because Jess filled his thoughts.

'Not really, and I think you've known for quite some time this was coming. We've simply drifted away from each other, haven't we? And I've realised I need a different style of living now. Elle will be pleased that I've told you, because she thinks you're going to be hurt by it and she said I had to tell you as soon as I could. I told her you wouldn't be. You aren't even surprised, never mind hurt. And you won't lose Elle: she'll still Facetime you twice a week, but now everything is out in the open.'

'I'm not hurt,' Ollie spoke quietly, 'but I am sad. We've been together a long time, built a really successful business together because of our love of plants. But I did recognise your life had drifted off in another direction. Is there someone else?'

Denise laughed. 'Not on my side.'

Ollie chose to stop that discussion. 'Do you want me to take you to the library tonight? You'll have your own car back tomorrow, but I don't mind taking you. I can sit at the back of the room and read.'

'Not likely. When do I get the chance to drive the Porsche? And I promise not to dent it.'

'Thanks,' he grinned, 'that's good of you.'

She stood. 'I'm going to have a quick shower and change my clothes, then I'll be getting off. If you can pull the car out of the garage and point it in the right direction so I don't reverse into the stone wall, it would be a help,' she said, trying to hide her laughter.

'If there's a danger of that, I will.'

It was already dark when he reversed out of the garage, and manoeuvred so the car could be driven forwards easily. He left it on the driveway, locked it and stroked it gently. 'Take care of her,' he said, 'and don't let her go too fast.'

He returned to the kitchen and sat at the table. He needed room to spread out the papers he had brought home concerning the proposed restaurant. It was by no means a done deal, he needed to be sure it would work financially, as well as being aesthetically pleasing on the piece of land allocated for it.

He could hear Denise singing some random Barry Manilow song, and he smiled. How long was it since he had last heard her sing? She must now be feeling so much happier for having told him of her plans, and he had to admit to a feeling of lightness. He hadn't realised quite how dark and soulless his marriage had become; it was only now that he could see it.

He was looking through the plans when she came downstairs. She was wearing a smart navy trouser suit with a cream silk blouse, and she looked stunning.

'You've dressed to match the car,' he said with a laugh.

'I can't drive a Porsche wearing jogging bottoms and a hoodie, can I?'

'Well, you look amazing.'

'Thank you.' She glanced down at the paperwork. 'Plans for the new restaurant?'

'They are. I'd like to understand them back to front and upside down if necessary, so that I know what the architect is talking about at our next meeting. I've been staring at it for five minutes, and the headache is starting. I'm just glad I grow flowers and plants, and don't design buildings.'

'Both equally important,' Denise said, and walked across to take a bottle of water out of the fridge. She popped it into her bag along with her copy of the book they were discussing at the book group, and sat down opposite her husband. 'I'll leave in about ten minutes. You're sure you're okay with me taking the Porsche?'

'Of course I am. Just watch your speed. Apart from that, it's just like any other automatic.'

'I'll give you a ring when I'm leaving to come home, so you can open the garage for me. That okay?'

'It is, and it's pointing outwards at the exact right angle for driving up the road. That okay?' he said, grinning at her.

'You're a star. Listen, give Elle a ring. Reassure her we're fine. I know she's worrying, thinks her dad won't manage life without her mum, but we know different, don't we?'

'Well, it'll be a different sort of life for both of us, and you know if we ever divorce the division of money and property will be totally fair, but we're not looking at that, are we?'

She shook her head. 'No, I just want to be me.' She stood. 'And I need to go now. Ring Elle,' she repeated. 'She'll be waiting for your call.'

He watched from the kitchen window as she settled into his car, saw the lights come on as she worked out what switch worked which function, noted the hesitation before the car eventually pulled forward, then she stopped. No vehicles went past, and she pulled out of the gateway, turned left and disappeared from view.

'Enjoy,' he said quietly, 'and don't damage it.'

Elle cried when Ollie told her in a call. 'Dad, I've been so worried how you would take it, but Mum and I have spent so many hours talking about it, and then we found this flat.'

'There's no need for tears, honestly. There hasn't even been a raised voice, although she's had a bit of car trouble on the way down so has gone out in the Porsche. I'm not guaranteeing there won't be raised voices when she gets home. She's promised not a scratch on it.'

'It'll be fine, she's a good driver. She's gone to the book group?'

'She has. Immaculately dressed, no jeans in a Porsche. Your mum has an amazing ability to make me laugh.'

'Me too. You must come and see the flat. When Mum buys her new home, I'm going to be staying on in this one. It's perfect for me. I'm sorry I don't want to come back to Sheffield, Dad, but this has felt like home since the first day I arrived here, and while I don't know what comes next after I get my degree, it will involve Newcastle.'

'Whatever you do, sweetheart, it's fine with me. And Newcastle isn't the end of the world. I can soon drive up to see you.' He laughed. 'I have a Porsche.'

'Or I can drive down to see you. I have a Mini.' She giggled at the comparison.

They chatted for a short time longer then blew kisses down the phone before saying goodnight. After disconnecting he sat and stared at his phone. Life was changing. For the better? For worse? He wasn't sure, but it was definitely changing. And what did this mean for the fledgling relationship with Jess? The relationship that had been put on hold while they all watched the last few months of Chris's life fade away.

'Would you like a car like that?' Malcom's question told Jess exactly what he had been thinking about.

'The Carrera? Nah,' she said. 'I like a bit of luxury, it's why I bought the Lexus, but a Porsche is built for speed. In a country where the maximum speed limit is seventy miles an hour, that seems to me to be a bit silly. Did you enjoy going in it?'

'I did. Very much. So did Daisy. But don't worry, I won't be getting one.'

'Thank goodness for that. You cause me to worry far too much. I can't add a souped-up car to my list of worries.'

The sound of an engine caused her to stand and move to the window. 'Josh! What on earth is he doing here again? He can't keep away at the moment.'

But it wasn't Josh; it was Adam who climbed out of the

driver's seat of Josh's Land Rover. He waved when he saw Jess looking at him, and she quickly opened the front door for him.

'Adam? You're in the wrong car.'

He laughed. 'I know, and I'm not here. It's my designated day off, and I've been driving round a bit aimlessly, really. I ended up in Lincoln, did a bit of sightseeing and shopping, and decided it was really close to here, so here I am.'

'It's not your car.'

'You've noticed then?'

'Did you just take the one with the most petrol in it?'

'Partly that, but partly because mine is all loaded up with surfboards and wetsuits for tomorrow, so Josh said to take this. It's not the easiest car to drive, but I'm getting used to it. I'm only here for half an hour, then I'm heading home.'

Jess shook her head. 'To hear you and Josh talk, anyone would think that Devon was just round the corner. It's a hell of a journey, especially as it's starting to go dark. Can't you stay the night?'

'No, we're having a full morning of surfing tomorrow, then a 12-12 shift in the afternoon in the pub, so I've to go home. It's why I've only come for a flying visit, but I wanted to check you two were okay.'

'Well we are. And it's lovely to see you. You want food? A drink?'

'I'll grab a bottle of water to take back with me, if that's okay. I had a meal in Lincoln, so I'm okay, definitely not hungry.'

'Why Lincoln?'

'Memories really. Been a couple of times with Dad, haven't we?'

Jess nodded.

'He loved the cathedral. I spent an hour in it this afternoon. I'll go get my water, then I'll be on my way.'

Jess walked out to the car with him, and laughed. 'I'm going in a Land Rover tomorrow. Elsa is picking me up in hers, we're going to have a decadent latte in Costa.'

'What's she up to these days?'

'Busy, as you can probably guess. She has to pick her times, but she checks in with me. I think she had a proper soft spot for your dad, said he was the gentlest patient she had ever had. I get on really well with her, and she has tomorrow off so we're going to be ladies who take coffee mornings.'

Adam kissed his mum. 'Take care, old woman, and be good.'

'I'll try. Love to Josh, and let me know when you arrive. You know I worry when you travel between the frozen north and the balmier south.'

He hooted his horn as he pulled away, and she waved. Both boys, such a credit to her and Chris, with more than a little input from Malcolm.

CHAPTER TWENTY-ONE

Denise took all of thirty seconds to settle into the Carrera. By the time she'd reached the top of the hill she was itching to put her foot down and see what it was like to really test it. Ollie's words echoed around her head. 'Don't speed!' She was almost tempted to do it, knowing that if she was caught on any cameras it would be Oliver who got the speeding ticket, but he might be just a little bit miffed at her. At one time in their relationship he would have taken the points and the fine, but she doubted that would now be the case...

The right turn took her onto the darkness of a country road, Wood Lane, and her itchy right foot pressed down a little harder on the accelerator. It was only when she saw headlights behind her that she eased off, bringing her speed back down to the required forty miles an hour maximum on this quiet stretch. If it was a police car, she could allow it to pass her without fear of a speeding fine for Ollie.

The lights grew closer, but she couldn't see an indicator telling her it was about to pass her. So she continued at the steady pace she had set.

Then she felt the bump, and the Carrera's interior was

flooded with the main beam of the car that had just hit the rear end of it. Half a scream left her mouth. Then she felt a much harder bang and the Porsche shot forward. She wrestled with the steering wheel as the car seemed to want to leave the road altogether and travel into the wooded area on her left.

The next bang was huge, and Denise felt the pain caused by seat belt restriction; the Porsche left the road and smashed into a huge oak tree.

The car that had caused the damage pulled up, the driver exited, lit a small petrol bomb and threw it underneath the Carrera. Ten seconds later their vehicle left the scene.

The explosion was massive. The flames reached high into the oak tree, scorched a huge area of grass around the base of the tree and burnt for five minutes before a passing driver stopped and rang for emergency services.

Oliver's list of notes was growing with every thought and query that entered his head. He pushed the chair away from the table, needing to stretch his back for a few minutes.

He poured a glass of Coke, and drank deeply. The more he looked at the plans, the deeper his excitement grew at the idea of the restaurant. He wanted to give a new chef the start they needed in life; he didn't want a well-established one. And if this was to go ahead, he wanted that chef's input as well, so he would have to start making enquiries over the next few days.

He hadn't heard from Denise, so he assumed she had reached her book group at the library safely. He had been tempted to say, *Ring when you get there*. But he knew she would be offended that he didn't trust her to take his precious car and drive it carefully. She thought nothing of nipping up to

Newcastle whenever the fancy took her and she was a good driver. A confident driver.

But if he ended up with a speeding ticket, she'd be a regretful driver. He smiled to himself at that last thought.

He picked up the keys to Denise's car and went through to the garage. She said she had had trouble starting her car, and he thought he might just try it now, after it had been stood for a few hours.

He inserted the key, and turned the ignition on. Nothing. Totally dead. He sat and thought about it for a minute and decided he would jump start it once his own car came back home. If it started, then it meant it needed a new battery. He could then ring Colin at the garage and ask him to bring one out. Simple.

He took the key out, lifted the garage door with the fob, and left it open for when Denise returned from her book group. There was no danger of anyone stealing her car – it wouldn't even start.

He locked the door leading into the kitchen and returned to the table, where he pulled the paperwork towards him once again.

The peal of the camera doorbell sent him to the window. DI Will Stewart and DS Claire Landon. He opened the front door, but there was no smile on either of their faces.

'Oliver, can we come in?'

'Of course. Something's wrong?'

'There's been an accident, Oliver.'

He led them into the lounge and turned to face them. 'Accident? Where?'

'We've identified the vehicle as your Carrera.'

Oliver's legs buckled underneath him. 'Denise...'

'I'm afraid so. It left the road, although there is significant damage to the back of it so I'm sure forensics will confirm it was forced off the road, and it hit a tree. It burst into flames...'

Oliver was struggling to breathe. 'No...'

'The area is now cordoned off, and the car will be taken to our forensics department vehicle facility. We will find out what happened here, but I'm so very sorry that your wife didn't survive. She would have died very quickly, was possibly unconscious before the flames started. The pathologist is still on scene with Denise, but I can't let you go there. It is a crime scene. Is there anybody we can get for you? You shouldn't be alone.'

'My daughter, Elle, but I can't let you ring her. This is something I have to do.' Oliver's head dropped and he stared at the floor for a moment. 'They thought it was me, didn't they? That's only the second time my wife has driven my car, and she only drove it because hers is playing up. Whoever has killed her thought they were killing me.'

Will glanced at Claire, and Ollie saw Claire's reaction. 'I'm right, aren't I?'

'I don't know whether you're right or not; only the killer can confirm that when we catch them, but yes, it had occurred to us as well.'

'I offered to take her, and she said no. She wanted to drive it. Even wore smart clothes as befitting the driver of a Carrera, she said. If I'd been driving...'

'Then you would both probably have died. You have a daughter who is going to need you, Oliver. So don't think along the lines of you should have been driving it.'

'But I could possibly have handled the vehicle better.'

'Not necessarily. This was a hefty whack to the rear of the car from what I could see. I'm not sure even Lando Norris could have held that car on the road, and certainly she couldn't avoid the tree. That area is heavily wooded. If she hadn't hit that big oak, she would have hit some other tree. Tell me, Oliver, when your wife left here, did you watch her go?'

'I did, but only saw her go through the gates. I wasn't out there with her. I know it's stupid, but I thought she might think I considered her incapable, so I let her go on her own. I stayed in the kitchen.'

'Talk me through what you saw.'

'She got in the car and fiddled around the switches. As I said, it was only the second time of driving it. She drove it on the day I got it, and then today was the next time. She wasn't familiar with the light switches, Bluetooth and every other gadget that's in it, so she had a little play around. I saw the lights come on, then the indicators. She was quite happy with the automatic gearbox because her car is an automatic as well.'

'Okay. Which way did she go? I'm assuming left?'

'Yes. Her dipped lights were on, because I remember the sweep of them across the road as she pulled out to the left. She would have driven to the top of the hill, then turned right onto that dark, country...' His voice tailed away. 'Is that where it happened?'

'It is. About quarter of a mile on there. We believe she was maybe hit more than once, and it will show in tyre marks on the road, so we've closed the entire road off until forensics are satisfied they have every bit of evidence they need. But to go back to when Denise left here. Did you see any other vehicle follow her after she started on her journey up that road outside of your gates? Think carefully.'

Ollie kept his head down, almost as if the effort to hold it upright was simply too much for him. He closed his eyes, taking his memory back to the last sighting as his wife left their home.

Eventually he looked up. 'There was. About a minute, maybe not that long, after she left. The wall surrounding our home is quite high so I don't know what it was, but it wasn't anything like a Mini, or an Aygo. But I don't think it was a van either. Maybe something like a Jeep, but I'm not saying it was a Jeep. It was simply tall enough to show over the top of the wall. And its lights came on as it approached our gate. I remember the glow. For fuck's sake. Could it have been parked up further down the road waiting for me to go out?' He looked at DS Landon. 'Sorry, Claire, I don't normally swear.'

'Swear all you want, Oliver,' she said gently. 'That was nothing to what I hear at work.'

'I suspect that's exactly what happened, Oliver. They saw the car, not the driver. It's you this killer is after, so now we have to think what to do with you until we get them. And where is your daughter? We need to protect her as well.'

'She's at Newcastle University. I could go and stay with her until you tell me it's safe, but I have a business to run, some important meetings scheduled for this week, and they're on-site meetings, nothing I can do by Zoom. And to be honest, if they're determined to kill me, I don't want her to be anywhere near me.'

'Can you go to a hotel? Can you work from a hotel room and stay safe?'

'I suppose so. It's not ideal but it can't be forever, can it? What the hell does this person want, and why? What have the three of us done that can possibly have merited being killed for doing it? We played golf, and we were friends.'

'Off the record?'

Surprise showed on Oliver's face. 'Yes, of course.'

'I think the answer lies somewhere in Daniel Rubens' life. We believe he had an affair. We don't know who with but he referred to her as X, then suddenly it was over. It's the only thing out of character that we've come across. Did you know about it? Did either Chris Harcourt or Paul Browne ever mention anything about another woman to you?'

'Daniel? Another woman? If that is true, I'm well and truly

gobsmacked. I know this might sound odd, but the woman he divorced, Andi, was the love of his life. She wanted the split, not him. Do you know when he was with this other woman?'

Will shook his head. 'No, there were no dates in Daniel's little notebook, but it was kept in a locked drawer. So, I'm putting a car on your drive overnight with two uniforms in it. That will give you time to ring your daughter, and for you to arrange alternative accommodation that I need to know about, but nobody else. We don't know who this killer is, Ollie. It could be somebody you think is a friend, so keep your hotel secret. Okay?'

Ollie nodded. 'I'll ring as soon as I'm organised. Can I go and grieve for my wife now? And ring Elle?'

Claire softly touched his arm. 'You can. We're so sorry for your loss, Oliver. Ring us if you need us.'

CHAPTER TWENTY-TWO

It was the hardest telephone call Oliver would ever have to make. Elle sounded so happy when she answered the phone. 'Dad! We've already spoken! Twice in one evening is just too much.' She giggled, and he could tell she had been drinking.

'Put down the wine, babes,' he said. 'I have something to tell you.'

His next phone call was to the Mercure St Pauls, where he booked two rooms, stressing they must be adjoining. He didn't want Elle out of his sight until this nightmare was over. He figured that the largest and best hotel in Sheffield, which was always busy, would be the safest for them.

Elle was with him early Saturday morning. By just after nine they had said goodbye to the new team of uniformed officers still patiently sitting outside the house, and were driving to Sheffield City Centre. It felt strange to be driving Denise's car, but by nine it had been fitted with a new battery and pronounced fit and well again. They parked both cars and entered the hotel, with Oliver casting his eyes over everything. Having Elle by his side made everything scarier.

He checked in with DI Will Stewart, told him his room

number and that Elle was in an adjoining room. 'She's in a hell of a state, Will. She just can't take in what happened to Denise. I won't be more than ten feet away from her till all of this is over.'

'Good. I can't give you any more information because the Porsche is now in our forensic facility, but it is definite it was hit at least twice on the rear end. It was forced off the road.'

'It should have been me.' Oliver's voice was dulled.

'I believe you're the target, yes. And I believe the killer was sitting waiting patiently on the off-chance you left your home last night. Unfortunately, you have few neighbours for us to question but we have already spoken to the ones who live nearest to your home. Nobody saw a car that shouldn't have been there; nobody has seen a stranger over the last few days. In fact, it's a complete line of enquiry with absolutely no outcome at all. But I fully intend to find out who did this. I promise you.'

Ollie disconnected without further comment, but privately thinking that with three people already dead the police didn't seem to be too efficient at catching killers.

He desperately wanted to go to see Jess, to tell her face to face about the previous evening, but knew he couldn't leave the safety of the hotel. And definitely couldn't leave Elle. He glanced at his watch, saw it was after ten o'clock and decided to ring Jess.

She answered immediately. 'Oh, thank God it's you. I've just had a neighbour pop round telling me about a burnt-out Porsche on Wood Lane, and they knew one of my friends had a Porsche. I said it wasn't you, and thanked her, but I feel shaken now, because I didn't actually know.'

'It wasn't me,' he said carefully, 'but it was my car.'

'Stolen? Oh no!'

'Jess, sit down, love. I've stuff to tell you.' He heard movement.

She said, 'I'm in the library on the sofa. Talk to me.'

'It was my Porsche, as I said, but when Denise left Newcastle yesterday she had a hard time starting her car. So she took mine to go to her book group meeting last night.' He took a deep breath, and Jess didn't speak.

'She was forced off the road on Wood Lane and the car smashed into one of the big trees. It maybe wouldn't have been quite so disastrous if she'd been a little further along where the new saplings have been planted, but this was where the wood is at its thickest. The car burst into flames. Denise didn't stand a chance.'

His voice cracked.

'Where are you?' Jess asked. 'I'll come to you. Have you got Elle with you?'

'I have. She left Newcastle about 4am, and we've basically spent the morning in tears. And we're kind of in hiding. DI Stewart has sent me away. Like me, he believes the killer thought I was driving the Porsche. I offered to take Denise, Jess, but she said she wanted to drive the bloody Porsche, to show off a bit with it.'

'Oh God, Ollie, I simply don't have words. I realise I can't come to you if DI Stewart wants you hidden away, but I would if I could. But we can talk. You can ring me any time you want to. Do you want me to tell Andi and Naomi? They will want to know. We are all friends.'

'Thank you. I'm just holding it together, and it's been almost cathartic telling you, but I'm not sure I can keep repeating it to everybody. I have to concentrate on Elle now, get her through this.'

'I know. Leave it with me, I'll tell them as much as I know. I'm so sorry, Ollie, things just seem to be going from bad to worse. I'm here for you, any time, day or night. And give my love to Elle, I'm thinking about her.'

They disconnected and Jess immediately rang Elsa to postpone their coffee morning. She gave a brief summary of what had happened overnight, and they agreed to leave it for a couple of weeks. Elsa was shocked, it showed in her voice, and she was quick to say she was there for Jess if she needed her.

Then Malcolm came in, having heard Jess finish her call. He found her sitting on the sofa, crying.

'It's Denise. She's dead. Car accident last night.'

Jess let her father pull her to her feet and wrap his arms around her. 'No need to talk, my love,' he breathed into her hair. 'Not till you're ready. Then we will.'

Neither Oliver nor Elle wanted food: both seemed to be existing on water. Elle didn't want to talk, and every so often would disappear to her own room where he guessed she was speaking to her friends in Newcastle. Then she would return to his room as if needing human contact, before disappearing again half an hour later.

Ollie rearranged the meetings he had booked for the following week, and switched off his phone. He couldn't take any more; he needed time to think.

The more he talked, the more he realised that if Denise had agreed to him taking her to that bloody book group, they would probably both have been dead now, leaving behind an utterly lost daughter.

And the more he thought about Denise being in that burning car, the more he prayed that she had been unconscious and not aware of what was happening around her.

He lay back into the pillow and felt his eyes closing. The lack of sleep was now taking its toll, but he suddenly sat upright. He'd switched off his phone without thinking about the possibility of a call from the police. He switched it back on, feeling relieved there were no missed calls.

Ollie hoped Elle had finally given in to exhaustion, and fallen asleep. He made himself a coffee, then sat at his desk and opened his laptop. His inbox was overflowing with messages, and he couldn't handle it. Andi and Naomi had sent messages, both confirming that they had spoken to Jess, and both of them asking the same basic question: *What the hell is going on?*

He had no answer, but he replied to them telling them what he knew, which was very little. He promised to keep in touch, saying he hoped to know more by the end of the day.

He didn't know what to do. His headache was debilitating; he didn't want to disturb Elle in case she was asleep, but he sensed sleep would be out of the question for himself because his mind was a maelstrom of chaotic misery. He checked the room service menu then rang down to reception to ask if he could just have a couple of slices of toast and a pot of tea.

The food arrived almost immediately, and he forced himself to eat it. He washed a couple of paracetamols down with his tea, and within fifteen minutes was feeling more human, more willing to face the world. *Willing* was maybe the wrong word, but he was more prepared.

He picked up his phone and rang DI Will Stewart, who confirmed the road was still closed and the forensic teams were still searching for anything that would lead them to the killer. 'I'm at our vehicle forensic place at the moment,' Will said. 'I can't tell you I understand much of what they're saying and proving, but it seems the car didn't catch fire because of the impact when it smashed into the tree. They believe a petrol bomb, made with a dark green wine bottle, was lit and thrown underneath the Carrera. They have part of the bottle here, all to be logged into evidence. There are no fingerprints on the bottle. We couldn't be that lucky.'

THE HOUSE OF LIES

'You'll ring if anything else shows up? I'm feeling a bit shell-shocked by the thought that whoever is doing this to us has to be somebody who knows us, but I can't honestly get my head around the why. It makes no sense at all. We were simply a group of middle-aged men who got on together and used golf as an escape from our working lives. Now there's only me left, and that could have all changed last night.'

'You won't leave that hotel, will you? Whoever the killer is will be pissed off that it wasn't you driving the Porsche last night, and it's possible they have that information. It's on Facebook already, tentative guesses following on from the police statement that a female died in the traffic accident. You're protected in a locked room, so make sure you use the spyhole in the door if you have food delivered to your room.'

There was a moment of silence. 'I've just had some tea and toast delivered. Never even thought about it, just opened the door and took it. In my defence, nothing like this has ever occurred in my world before, it's all new to me. Good job I'm a fast learner. I'll talk to Elle about it when she wakes up. She's also not used to seeing danger in routine stuff, either.'

'It is a good job you're a fast learner. Take care, I'll ring if I have anything new to tell you. We have uniforms going door to door where you live, and now the much larger area, asking about strange vehicles being parked up, but no reports that anybody saw anything so far.'

They disconnected and Ollie refilled his teacup, lost in thought. A petrol bomb. Denise would probably have lived without that little addition. And the car that drove her off the road would have had to pull up to light and throw the glass bottle, completely without being seen. No other car had driven by for a few minutes, adding some luck to the killer's movements.

He heard a gentle tap on his door, followed by the sound of

a card being inserted into the handle. Elle looked inside. 'You're awake. Should we talk? You heard anything?'

'Little bits. Come in, sweetheart. Can I order you something to eat?'

'Maybe later,' she said. 'I just needed to be with you. I was crying when I woke up, couldn't stop, so I've showered and now I need a hug.'

He opened his arms. 'Any time, my love, any time.'

CHAPTER TWENTY-THREE

Saturday was proving to be a bit of a rubbish day for Jess. It started with a mild headache that became slightly heavier by the minute. So after putting in a wash load, she wandered into the library.

She reached up to get her replacement journal, and sat on the sofa to write down everything that was happening. Her hope that her journal would turn up had not been realised. And if it didn't turn up soon she would have a lot of transferring to do.

She chewed on the end of her pen while she considered what to put. She decided to write the bare minimum, and transfer more detail when the journal magically appeared. But it felt sickening to add the words *Denise died* to the bare minimum of *Daniel died* and *Paul died*. She had drawn a little heart around both the capital D of Daniel and the capital P of Paul, because in her way she had cared deeply for them. She hadn't slept with them because there had been love involved, but she had cared for them, and had enjoyed their company on the several jaunts they had had to assorted hotels.

Jess felt utmost relief that she wasn't having to draw a heart round a capital O for Ollie. But Denise was a friend; she had died and she had to be remembered as someone Jess cared about. She put two little stars in the centre of the capital D.

She thought back to her earlier conversations with Andi and Naomi. Naomi had been quite upset by it, but she was still feeling the loss of Paul only days earlier, and it had clearly compounded her grief. Andi had been less emotional – but Andi had never showed much emotion about anything. Not even the split from Daniel.

Jess began to write, and suddenly became immersed in the words.

She put down her thoughts and feelings, letting the grief wash over her as she thought of all the people she had lost in such a short time, and it was an hour later that she sat back, gave a huge sigh and walked across to Chris's whisky stash, to pour herself a small one. She needed it. One thing was for sure, nobody else must ever see her words; they were for her eyes only.

She poured a second small measure of whisky and went in search of her father. 'Dad,' she said, popping her head around the kitchen door. There was no response. She went back to the hallway, saw the dog lead was missing, and realised he had gone out for a walk. She had a vague memory of hearing Daisy bark, and of seeing Malcolm in the doorway of the library while she was writing. That must have been when he left.

She felt instant panic. He seemed to be so much better, but all week she had been going out with him, afraid of a sudden relapse with the blood pressure issue.

She took some deep breaths, and went back into the library so she could look out of the window, and down the road. She could see him in the distance chatting to one of their neighbours and the relief was overwhelming. She stayed watching him until he reached their garden gate, then went to open the front door.

'I thought you'd left home,' she said with a smile. She took the lead from him and unclipped Daisy. 'There's a whisky poured out for you on the coffee table in the library. You want anything to eat?'

'The whisky sounds like a good idea, but I'm not hungry. It was a good walk, and Daisy has inspected every other dog out there, I reckon. You feeling better?'

'I'm okay.'

'I saw you writing like a maniac, so I guessed you needed to get something out of your system. It's why I didn't disturb you by speaking to you. You sure you're okay?'

'I am. It's just been such a shock. I haven't told the boys about Denise yet. I know they've got a busy twelve hour shift at the pub, but I'll speak to them tomorrow.'

He sat down on the sofa and sighed. 'I'm getting old.'

'No, you're not. Drink that whisky, it'll give you an extra five years.'

'Is that a fact, or is it just your hare-brained theory?'

She shrugged. 'Might be my theory.' She reached across to pick up her notebook and replaced it in the Stephen King section of the bookshelf. 'That was pretty therapeutic,' she said. 'I'll be glad when I find my big journal though. I've still no idea where I put it.'

'When did you last see it?'

'I took a couple of photos out of the back of it on the day Chris died. I wanted to talk to him on my own, and I took the photos to show him, to remind him of our wedding day. When I went to put the photos back in the pocket, the journal wasn't there. It had been in the same old leather handbag since the day you gave it to me, the day before Chris and I married. It's annoying. My life is in that book.'

The doorbell chimed, and Jess moved towards the window, but spotted Elsa's Land Rover parked outside.

'It's Elsa,' she said, aware her dad had always been ambivalent about the carer.

'I'll leave you to it then,' he said, levering himself up out of the chair. I'll go watch the football for a bit.'

Elsa handed a huge bunch of flowers to Jess. 'I wanted to get you something that might let you know how sorry I am for all you're going through,' she explained. 'It just seems since Chris went it's been one thing after another, and it's got to be affecting you.'

'There have been a few tears,' Jess admitted. 'And I'm so sorry I couldn't meet you this morning, but Ollie's news completely flattened me. I'm trying to get my head around the death of Paul; and now there's Denise.'

'Have you heard any more from Oliver?'

Jess lied, and shook her head. 'No, he's with Elle, his daughter, but I don't know where he is, or what his plans are. He'll contact me when he needs to.' She turned to leave the room. 'I'll put these in water, and make us a cuppa. Make yourself comfortable, I'll not be long.'

She busied herself putting the flowers into one of her larger vases, and carried them through to the ever-tidy lounge, before returning to the library. 'They look lovely, but I've put them in the television room because it's cooler in there. They'll last longer. I'll make us a drink now. Coffee? Tea?'

'I'll have a tea, please. Had about three coffees already today, and I'll never sleep tonight. You want me to do it?'

Jess shook her head. 'No, I feel as though I need to keep busy, to stop me thinking. I've never known a period in my life quite as chaotic as these last few weeks have been, and I'm sure if I sit down and do nothing, I'll give in to it all and generally collapse. Do you ever feel like that?'

Elsa nodded. 'It's how I felt when Chris died. It all felt so unfair, and we're actually trained not to feel like that. But he was only young, relatively speaking, and he had all of you, a family that was so close, so loving. And I had lived here for five months, taking care of him, laughing with him at the beginning before he began to seriously deteriorate. It's not the first time I've felt like that, I've nursed younger people than Chris, but not always liked them. I liked all of you.'

'Thank you, you're a good friend, Elsa. I'll go and make our drinks, then we can relax.'

The relaxation period lasted well into the evening, with everyone, Malcolm included, opting for a takeaway because nobody felt like cooking. Chinese was the takeaway of choice, and when Elsa left to begin her journey back to her own home she said what a wonderful evening she had had, far better than the cheese on toast she probably would have made at home.

Malcolm and Jess, with Daisy standing by their feet, waved her off from the doorstep, and Malcolm waited until Jess had moved out of the way before carefully locking the door, and putting on the security chain. 'Can't be too careful,' he said. 'There's strange things happening at the moment, and I don't want to lose you.'

Jess hugged him. 'You'll not lose me, but thank you for caring.'

'Think we should have another whisky?'

She laughed. 'I think we might. For medicinal purposes, of course.'

They sat opposite each other and Jess placed the Glenmorangie on the coffee table. 'Don't get paralytic. I can't carry you upstairs.'

'I'll just have one,' he promised. 'When you get to my age you've learned all about alcohol limits, and mine is definitely one before bed. That's been a strange and unexpected evening.'

Jess nodded. 'I know, and I'm sorry if it took you away from anything you'd planned. It wouldn't have happened if I'd kept to my original arrangements and met Elsa for a coffee this morning, but after getting Ollie's news I couldn't go out and be sociable, so I cancelled. She was simply being nice, bringing me some flowers. It just dragged on a bit.'

'Hey, it's your home! I'm just a visitor. I suppose I've simply got used to being quiet in the evenings, reading, chatting to Daisy, and that's carried on while I've been here. Tonight was different.' He sipped at his whisky. 'I'm going to take this upstairs, get into bed and read. I've got the new Jack Reacher, so that'll keep me quiet for a bit.'

Daisy sensed what he was saying, and stood at the same time as he did. 'Come outside with me, Daisy, last wee time, then it's sleep time.'

Daisy gave a small bark in response, and Malcolm bent down to kiss the top of his daughter's head. 'I'm so sorry for all your losses, my love. I'm always here for you.'

'I know, Dad, now go to bed and settle down. Sleep well.'

She listened to five minutes of chat between Malcolm and Daisy as they gathered themselves together for the uphill climb to their bedroom, then peace descended.

And her brain started to revolve. She couldn't really ring Oliver – he would be with Elle – but she desperately needed to hear how he was coping. She picked up her phone and sent off a quick text saying she hoped they were both okay, and to ring if either of them needed anything. The response was swift and short.

> Will ring tomorrow xxx

She decided the best thing she could do was switch on the dishwasher, grab her Kindle and follow her dad's actions by escaping from the world, and reading. She checked everywhere was locked up, and headed up to her bedroom.

She knew tomorrow she would have to tell Josh and Adam about the death of Denise before they heard it on any news that it was definitely a suspicious death – she just hoped that part wasn't out there yet.

She was just dropping off to sleep when her phone pinged. She looked at the text – from Josh.

> Mum if you're awake, ring me. If not, early tomorrow. Seen news.

She sighed and replaced her phone on the bedside table. Tomorrow, then.

CHAPTER TWENTY-FOUR

Monday morning saw Malcolm being praised by his doctor for a complete sheet of blood pressure checks that confirmed the new strength of tablet seemed to be working. The GP wanted to see him again in three months, but earlier if he noticed a change in his readings. He was told to check his readings regularly, and dismissed.

Father and daughter called for a drink and a doughnut in Crystal Peaks to celebrate, then headed back to Jess's house. Malcolm packed up his few clothes and other bits and left for the ten minute walk back to his own home, backpack bulging, and Daisy trotting along by his side.

Jess felt suddenly lonely. The house was empty; she had rung Josh early Sunday, before eight, and he had said immediately that one of them would drive up. She stressed that wouldn't be a good idea. 'No, Josh. I'll keep you informed. I'm in touch with Ollie and Elle and they are safe. I don't want you two to put yourselves in any sort of danger by coming up to Sheffield.'

She had added, 'When DI Stewart has worked all this out, then come up, but please stay away for now. I'm fine, and your granddad is still here.' She didn't say he was going home the following day.

And now she really did feel lonely.

The briefing room was a busy hub of chatter which stopped as Will Stewart entered from his own office. The officers and staff waited, wondering if anything new had come in, if some miraculous fingerprints had arrived out of the blue, or if they were still at a standstill. That was how the weekend had felt. Standstill time.

'Okay, everybody, as most of you know, the death of Denise Newton is no accidental death. She was driving her husband's Porsche 911 Carrera on Friday night to go to a book group meeting. An important part of this is that her own car was having battery problems, so she took the Porsche to be sure she would be safe. This is a definite – the new battery was fitted early Saturday morning so Oliver Newton could drive to where we now have both Oliver and his daughter Elle safely stashed away. We have a signed statement for the files from the mechanic who came out to the Newton home very early on Saturday, after it had been explained to him why a new battery was now urgent. He confirmed the old battery was completely dead.

'Oliver and Elle are devastated by Denise Newton's death, as you can imagine, and Oliver does realise that what happened was probably meant to happen to him. We therefore have to look at Denise's death in conjunction with the deaths of Daniel Rubens and Paul Browne, not as an isolated road accident, because it definitely wasn't.'

He moved to the whiteboard where there was a picture of a Carrera, enlarged. He used his biro to point. 'The car was hit here, here, and here, with varying degrees of force. It was the third shunt that was powerful enough to send this rock solid piece of German engineering off the road, down a slight incline and into an oak tree.'

He paused before continuing. 'It wasn't hit by a Mini, or a Fiat 500, is what I'm saying. Whatever hit it had to be something hefty. Denise, although not a new driver in any way, was a new driver for this car. She drove it on the first day that Oliver got it, decided she was too scared of scraping it, and until Friday had never driven it again. She had only been driving for five minutes at the most when she was hit by the car that ultimately killed her. But it doesn't stop there.'

He pointed underneath the car picture, along the length of it between the front and back wheels of the driver's side.

'Whoever did this came prepared with a home-made petrol bomb that just required a lighter to ignite it. Forensics have proved that the car didn't explode on its own, the bomb was lit and thrown underneath it here.' He pointed to the stretch that had shown clear signs of initial burns. 'This means that car didn't simply speed off after the Carrera smashed into the tree. They stopped to see if it did explode, then got out of the car to ignite the bomb. We will never know if they realised at that point they were killing the wrong person. They will know now, of course. It is imperative we get this thug behind bars quickly.'

He looked around the room. 'Any questions to this point? I've taken time to explain it all because I realise the weekend has meant you could have missed bits of activity, so you now know as much as the Major Crimes Team does.'

'Small garages doing body work repairs?' somebody shouted from the back of the room.

'Got it in one,' Will said. 'Freya has produced a long list of them in this area, divided it into ten so you will have time to get round them all – time is becoming an issue. This has gone on for too long now. So I need ten of you out and about talking to them. We obviously don't know what vehicle we're looking for, but you can say it won't be a small one. Whatever it was, it took three bangs with it to get the Carrera off the road.'

There was general movement as the uniformed officers headed towards Freya, who was handing out the printouts. Will could hear her dishing out instructions, explaining the individual lists were in order of visiting, and if any garage objected to giving details to the police, they had to say they would get a warrant but it would specify a full search of the entire premises, not just looking at jobs done since Saturday morning. Will liked Freya.

Once the lists were sorted and swapped around to suit individuals, the office cleared remarkably fast. Claire finished a report and headed for Will's office. He had swivelled his chair around so that he was staring out of the window.

'You think the killer knew fog was coming?'

'I didn't. Did you?'

'No, and that's exactly what I was thinking. I got up and it was a real pea-souper. The sort that always lifts by lunchtime, but this time it didn't. In fact, I don't know when it lifted. It was still thick when we came away from the school, and that was after Paul Browne's body had been taken to the morgue.'

Claire smiled. 'You have our killer down as a meteorologist?'

'No, but not particularly a planner either. I believe, going by what Oliver said, that Daniel Rubens went to the golf course for an hour on his own, on the practice field. His body was found where the field meets the golf course, which confirms he was heading that way, and his clubs were with him. He could have been followed. The killer could have parked their vehicle on a side road and walked back across the road to the golf course. You can see into the bar from the golf club car park, but it clearly has CCTV on the cars, and if the killer spotted that, their car would be nowhere near the golf club. They just had to wait for Daniel to come out of the bar wheeling his golf clubs, alone, and bingo the killer has it handed to him on a plate. He follows up the field, makes sure nobody else is around and calls Daniel's name. Daniel turns round, and his throat is slashed. Quickest way of killing somebody. It had been raining, so it was highly unlikely anybody else would be on the practice field – very fortuitous for our killer. That's what I mean about not being a planner. I think the targets are planned, but the acts are... I don't know how to phrase this. Happy or unhappy accidents? Right place, right time for the killer, wrong place wrong time for the victim. You understand?'

Claire nodded. 'I've never heard you talk so much.'

'I know, but I've been awake most of the night thinking this through. I didn't want to say anything out there,' he nodded towards the briefing room, 'I just wanted an audience of one in case you thought I was daft. A killer who doesn't plan. Makes it twice as hard to catch them. It was the fog that really got me going.' He hesitated, sorting his thoughts into words that would make sense.

'It was impossible to plan a murder for that day, because it's British weather. Anything can happen if it's a killing that relies on the weather behaving itself. But fog, and fog that showed no sign of lifting, along with a teacher that tends to stay later than the kids at school to do marking, and lesson preparation. The killer could have known that, and let's face it, the killer must have known Daniel well enough to guess at his movements.' Will looked at Claire, watching her expressive face for signs that she thought he was losing the plot. She merely waited for him to continue.

'Again this is fortuitous for the killer, the murder of Paul, massively helped by no CCTV because the camera couldn't penetrate the fog. They simply had to hide near those bins, step out knife in hand as he bent over to put his stuff in the boot, then knife him – accurately I might add, it only took two stabs – followed by a quick push into his boot, again fortuitously a large boot.' He sighed and awaited comments.

'You really didn't sleep last night, did you?'

'No, and it's because I was following through on my thoughts about Denise Newton's death. I wouldn't mind betting the killer has been parked up somewhere close by Oliver's home, waiting for him to go out under the cover of darkness. If they had been there long enough, they would have seen Denise drive in and into the garage in her car, possibly have seen Oliver pull his car out of the garage as he got it ready for Denise to simply drive straight out of their gates, and bingo! They just had to watch for headlights, so possibly parked a bit further away. Fortuitous again. No real planning.' Will picked up his bottle of water, and took a drink before continuing.

'Unfortunately they didn't know about Denise's dodgy battery. She paid the price for whatever this killer thinks these three men have done. And really, their main link is the golf. I am absolutely bewildered by it. There's no suggestion that X is a connection. This was some woman Daniel had met, but he wasn't having an affair. He was a single man. The woman could have been the one having the affair if she was a married woman, but God knows how we find that out.'

Claire closed her eyes for a moment. 'You're right, it is bewildering. I got the impression Paul and Naomi were a happy couple, twin boys at uni, a shared life. Complete opposite to Andrea and Daniel, but even they jogged along together, more like flatmates of course. And there's no suggestion Oliver had somebody else. He seems happily married to Denise, with his daughter now in Newcastle. Unless we're not getting the full pictures with all of them.'

'But why would they hide something? Unless one of this

motley crew is the killer, but I reckon if we went down that route, we'd find everybody had an alibi. I know for a fact that Naomi couldn't have bumped Paul off, she was with her mother and her sister in Sheffield City Centre having a meal before heading off to the Lyceum. Or was it The Crucible? The theatre anyway.' He took a further sip of water.

Claire nodded. 'For the record, it was the Lyceum. But with Andi I don't think she cares enough to kill Daniel. I know that sounds odd, but they didn't share a life, just a house, and that system worked really well for them. And she's actually quite upset by his death, seems a little bit lost.'

'So now we're left with Oliver Newton. These three men have obviously caused some sort of upset with this killer, who by now will know the wrong person died.'

CHAPTER TWENTY-FIVE

Claire made two coffees, and took them back to Will's office. Although they had brainstormed everything that had been brainstormed before with the entire team, it had felt special to listen to how Will had clearly spent his non-sleeping hours thrashing out the ifs and buts of the case.

She now felt she could see it from a different angle, that it had all been pretty random, but that Oliver Newton was still in considerable danger. Could the X in Daniel's notebook be a woman who objected to being dumped? Claire wasn't convinced by that thought, because the feeling that came from the little notebook was that X had said goodbye to Daniel, not the other way round. Had she moved on to one of the others? To Paul, maybe?

And where did Christopher Harcourt fit into all of this? He seemed to be the trigger point for everything that had followed – the first of the golfing four to die. Just one of them was left alive, and that could change in an instant if Oliver was stupid enough to leave that hotel room maybe just for a short walk around the adjoining Winter Gardens, or a trip to the Central Library directly across the Theatreland Square... and would he be tempted if Elle suggested as they were within a minute's walk of both Lyceum and Crucible theatres that maybe they could take in a show?

She put the coffees down on the desk and looked at Will. 'You have to ring Ollie and stress he can't leave that room until we say we've got the killer. Both of them will be going stir-crazy anytime soon, and it's too easy in that hotel to get to any number of interesting places. And he would play the Big Daddy, knowing he would protect his little girl with his life. Which is exactly what may happen.'

'There you go, I knew you'd start to think like me,' said Will. 'While you've been making coffee and staring out of the window deep in thought, I've been ringing Ollie and laying it on the line. He's promised. No trips to anywhere. He's getting newspapers and magazines delivered to his room, and they've loaded up their Kindles. And we've had nothing rung into Freya yet re the garages, but she basically told me to butt out as most of them won't have got to their first visit yet. She said she will report the second we get a hit, but then said don't build your hopes up. The killer may not care about their vehicle, and not want it repairing. She's supposed to cheer me up, not shut me up.'

Claire laughed. 'She's so quiet, is Freya, but don't cross her. Her job is the most important thing in her life, and when you made her your tech support she was bouncing. Now it seems she's promoted herself to bossy boots. Love her.'

They sipped at their drinks and Will blinked several times.

'Tired?' Claire asked.

'Feels like a ton of grit is on my eyeballs. Bet I sleep tonight.'

'Unless we have to go out and arrest a killer, you mean.'

'If only. You know, I spent all that time on the theories I've just been going over with you, but I can't see anybody. You know what I mean?'

'I do. So let's talk about what we do know about the killer.'

They stared at each other, silent.

'Well that's helpful,' Claire eventually said. 'It's because we don't even know the gender, isn't it?'

Will leaned forward and opened up his laptop, pulling up the post-mortem report for Daniel Rubens. 'Okay, cause of death is exsanguination, but it is noted only one cut was made to the carotid artery, and death would have happened very quickly. It is suggested that medical knowledge may have been a factor in the killing.'

'There you go,' Claire said triumphantly. 'We haven't explored that either in the middle of the night or in the briefing room.'

'It says pretty much the same on the Paul Browne report, I believe. Hang on.' He opened the Browne report, read it quickly and looked up. 'The stab wounds were accurate and well-placed to expedite death. The victim would have died without the second cut being made.'

'Okay, what does Jessica Harcourt do for a living?' Claire said.

'Nothing. She worked in a charity shop, volunteer basis, until Chris's cancer was diagnosed, and she was told he wouldn't last longer than about nine months, so she left immediately and looked after him. I think that was the time frame she said. She definitely wasn't working for the NHS, anyway.' Will frowned as he tried to remember details.

'Right. Andrea Rubens. No idea what she does, but she works from home. She has a proper office set-up, and a legal background, pretty sure it's not a medical one. I did ask her if she worked for Daniel, but she said no; he was much smarter than her, and she didn't want the stress of working for him.' Claire dropped her head as she tried to recall if Andi had said anything else.

'Naomi Browne,' Will said. 'She doesn't work. She has an illness, MS – no, I'm wrong, it's ME. Some days she's fine, other days the pain is so bad she can't get out of bed. I remember asking her if she worked, and she said no employer ever understood ME and the way it attacks, and she happened to be in the fortunate position of not needing to work. As head of maths, Paul earned enough for them.'

'And that leaves us with Oliver, who I don't suppose has a medical background?' She grinned.

'He grows plants, very successfully so I'm told. So does that rule everybody out within the close circle surrounding our golfing foursome?'

'Well apart from Daniel and Andi who didn't have any, the other three families have kids. Unfortunately they're not here. Jess's boys are in Devon, Paul and Naomi's twins are in Manchester, and Elle, Oliver's daughter, is normally in Newcastle. So that little snippet from the post-mortem has led us precisely nowhere.'

Will nodded. 'Yeah, but keep it in your mind. And if anybody that we come across mentions they've been to the doctors, arrest them.' He finished his coffee and stood to stare out of the window. 'Have they all gone for their breakfast?'

'Nope. Stop mithering. There are loads of garages to visit, and only one can have possibly done the repair, if it's been done at all. If it was me, I'd bash it back with a hammer till it looked reasonable, then T-Cut the life out of it.'

'Think I dare wander over to Freya and just casually glance down at what she's doing?'

'Not if you value your reproductive system.'

He winced and gave a brief nod before returning to look out of the window.

Oliver didn't really like daytime television. Not even with the sound muted. In the end he switched it off, and picked up the crossword. Even that was bloody difficult today. His phone pinged and he read Elle's text message.

> Just woke from a nap. Can we eat in restaurant tonight? It's so boring not moving from our rooms.

Just for a moment he was tempted to say yes, but then he heard Will Stewart's voice inside his head. Oliver replied to his daughter:

> Sorry no. Room service only. We can have wine though!

He returned to the crossword, worked on it for five minutes then discarded that in favour of his Kindle. He had been hoping for a chat with his architect, but realistically knew that would happen later in the week. He hated this enforced idleness, and trying to squash the tears that threatened whenever he thought about the final moments of his wife's life.

He knew the end had come to their marriage, but it had been more than amicable, he had simply agreed with everything she had said. She would have been happy in Newcastle with Elle, much happier than in Sheffield with him. But now her dreams had gone, and he was left to help his much-loved daughter through the trauma.

And he couldn't even take Elle down to a bloody restaurant, just in case.

His thoughts had drifted away from the book he was attempting to read, and the Kindle had switched itself off.

He opened his laptop, and began to work on the websites for the individual GardenScenes. Some technical parts of his job he absolutely loved, and dealing with the websites was one of them.

He worked for an hour promoting the Christmas departments that were now in full swing in every one of his centres, and once again his thoughts drifted to Denise. She had loved Christmas passionately, had simply laughed at him when he complained how expensive Christmas was, and always ignored him, continuing to spend exactly what she wanted to spend.

It would be a very different Christmas for them this year. Maybe they should book into a hotel and go away for the festive period – or maybe Elle would want to stay up in Newcastle with her friends. He didn't think he would enjoy that.

And although he grumbled every year, it was always a source of great joy to pick out two trees to take home with him at the beginning of every December. One went in the hallway, and the larger one went in the lounge; Denise had loved that job. He knew he would do it this year. It wouldn't look quite as glamorous as in years past, but it would light up every corner of their downstairs. For Denise.

And he cried. Deep, heart wrenching sobs that he couldn't control, couldn't hold back; Denise had gone, and it should have been him. He knew that for a fact, the Porsche was instantly recognisable all over the place as his car, and she had paid the ultimate price for driving it.

He cried himself to sleep. Slowly the sobs faded and his eyes were raw, so he closed them and drifted off to sleep. He dreamed Elle had gone on holiday to France without him, and he woke feeling so scared that the dream had been real. He knew she couldn't go; the police had told him they needed to find the killer first. He truly panicked, and it was only when he rang Elle and heard her voice that his heart rate began to slow.

'You okay, Dad?'

'Had a nightmare. I dreamt you'd gone to France. Woke up in a bit of a panic, I can tell you. Shall we eat in here, or in your room?'

'Is yours tidy?'
'So-so.'
'Maybe we'll eat in yours then.' She laughed. 'I've been trying to do some work, and I've got papers everywhere. I'll come round now, and we can decide what to order. And which wine.'

'Okay. I'll be in the shower, I need to wake myself up. Give me quarter of an hour.'

Jess was still feeling lonely. She wanted to ring Ollie, but not knowing if Elle was close by, she couldn't do that. Malcolm had settled himself and Daisy back at home, and he was considering having a walk to pick up some fish and chips for his evening meal. She had been tempted to say make that two, simply because it was an easy option, but not being a lover of the delicacy decided to give it a miss.

Instead she opened a tin of soup and warmed it up, but couldn't face eating it so threw it away. She settled for a cup of hot chocolate and an early night, hoping she would feel better come Tuesday morning. At the moment life wasn't feeling too good.

CHAPTER TWENTY-SIX

It was raining. Every officer who walked in complained about it. Then they complained because they'd had to visit all those garages to find out that nobody had brought a vehicle in that wanted bodywork doing to the left front bumper.

'Told you,' Claire said. 'Bash it into shape with a hammer and T-Cut it.' She grinned at Will, who called her a smart arse.

He walked to the front and turned to face everybody. 'Thank you for all the work everybody put in yesterday. I know it's a thankless task, but if it had paid off we would have been arresting our killer by this morning. I trust everybody left contact details with every garage visited, just in case they get a job in later in the week?'

There was a general nodding of heads all around the room, and he began to fill everyone in on details that had emerged since they had left for their full day of garage visits.

'I now need to see filed reports of every visit. Please make them individual reports so that if a garage does contact us it will be easy to pull it off the system. We have three deaths, and one person that I believe is still a target. I don't want to hear of his death, so let's make everything as tight as we can make it from our end. In addition, I want you all to read the reports already filed by officers who have, and are, working this case. The post-mortem reports also need to be read, although we don't have one yet for Denise Newton. The pathologist is suggesting that the killer maybe has medical training – the knife attack was precise and in exactly the right place for both Daniel Rubens and Paul Browne. And if anyone can come up with a reason for the attacks on this pair of golf players, you'll earn yourself a gold star, believe me.'

'*Cherchez la femme*,' one of the uniforms suggested.

Will laughed. 'It may surprise you to know that your DI is pretty fluent in French, and actually agrees with that sentiment, despite it being a bit of a cliché that we use when we can't find a motive. We need to know who X is, and the general consensus is that X is a woman, not a man. Finding X could answer every other question, so yes, *cherchez la femme* indeed.'

He left the room and went back to his own office, closely followed by Claire. 'We going out today?' she asked.

He walked over to the window. 'I don't know. We have nothing, do you realise that?'

'I do. But something will break. And as long as we can keep Oliver Newton locked away, we're not going to lose him. That's the main thing. There aren't many criminals that let us know who their intended victims are, but it wasn't rocket science working this one out.'

'Have you been out to the scene of the crash?'

She shook her head. 'You want me to go?'

'We'll go together. I was there on the night it happened but I didn't stay long. It was such a busy scene, fire engines, ambulance, vehicle recovery, and there was nothing I could do. We knew it was a pathologist report that we would be seeing, but it was confirmed to me that it wasn't Oliver; it was a woman. I guessed it was his wife. They knew the car's owner pretty much straight away. That's why they called me out because Ollie was part of my investigation. I feel as if I should see it again.'

'I'll get my coat.'

The rain was truly torrential by the time they arrived at the still cordoned off site. The oak tree was badly burnt, and a dangerous tree sign had been placed on it. Will knew it meant the tree would be taken down as soon as the police gave the go-ahead, but first the site had to be released from its security cordon.

The two officers walked together across the grass after ducking underneath the tape. They stood silently surveying the scene – the intensely scorched grass, the scars encircling the tree trunk – and felt the atmosphere. Raindrops cascaded down from branches that bore very few leaves following a night of heavy rain and high winds, and it was definitely autumnal bordering on winter. There were some sprays of flowers by the side of the road, and Claire nodded towards them. 'I'll go and see who's left them,' she said, and walked away, pulling her hood tightly around her head in some sort of effort at protection from the rain.

Most of the sprays didn't have cards, but a couple did. She took several photographs, then walked back to Will.

'There's a feeling, isn't there?'

Will nodded. 'There is. It's perhaps because we know so much of the story surrounding this murder – because it definitely is murder – but it just feels so ominous. I've attended so many crime scenes over the years, but this one is strange. As I said, ominous, as though it's unfinished business. Did the flowers give out any clues?'

'Only two had cards attached. *Lily and Catherine*, and one was just an initial. *E*.'

'When we get back, find out who the uniforms are who've

been watching this place until they were released. They might have seen whoever brought those flowers. I'd just like to know who E is. And why only an initial. And what sort of car they drove.'

'Will do. I've taken pictures of the flowers in case we need them at some future time.'

'Come on,' Will said, 'now we've managed to get absolutely soaked let's go back and dry out. I think Ollie will want to come here at some point, probably him and his daughter. Let's hope it helps them, if they decide to do that. I only met Denise briefly, but I liked her. We have to find the evil bastard who is doing this, and we have to find them quickly. We can't hope to keep Ollie locked up for ever, and once he leaves the security of that hotel room, he'll be vulnerable to whoever is polishing them off.'

They climbed in the car, waited for the windscreen to demist, and headed back to the station.

It didn't take long for Claire to track down the officers who had been on guard at the crime scene over the several hours deemed necessary by the forensic team. There had been three teams of two, so she got the names of the six officers involved and attempted to find them.

She found four sat around one table in the canteen. They'd just finished eating, and were killing time before reporting back into work. Two had nearly empty cups of tea, and the other two had settled for cans of Coke.

She sat down with them. 'DS Claire Landon,' she said. 'I think you four are on my list of people to speak with.' She read out the names and one by one they nodded.

'You're in no bother,' she said with a smile. 'You were on security duty at a crime scene – the bad smash on Wood Lane. There's been some flowers delivered to the site, and I wondered if any of you noticed who brought them. Only two had cards.' She showed them the pictures on her phone.

'I remember two ladies bringing some flowers. They came together, said they were part of the book group that Mrs Newton had been travelling towards. They kept saying what a good driver she was, and they couldn't believe she had died in a road accident. Very talkative ladies. I can't say with any accuracy that they are Lily and Catherine – I was too busy stopping them going anywhere near that tree – but my guess is that they are their flowers. Did you see them, Dave?'

Claire checked that Dave had been on the same shift, and marked the information off on her list. 'I didn't see them. Craig was doing a sterling job of controlling them so I just moved a bit closer to the tree so they definitely got the message without us having to be nasty about it.'

'And the spray with simply an E instead of a name?'

All four shook their heads, and she thanked them for their time, before asking about the two remaining names on her list.

'On at four,' Dave said. 'Major Crimes have taken a lot of our uniforms, so we're working all sorts of strange shifts till we get them back. I'll still be here, so I'll ask them to come up to you if you want?'

'You're a star. Thank you. I'll probably be there till about six tonight.'

She returned to her own desk, and rang Oliver. He definitely didn't sound full of life, and she suspected he was doing a lot of napping to blot everything out.

'Oliver, did you know anybody in Denise's book group?'

'Not really. I knew a couple of names, but that's about it. I didn't know them as actual people. You want to throw some names at me?'

'I do. Lily and Catherine.'

'Ah, I can't say I know them, but I know they love to read psych thrillers and they're sisters. Does that help?'

'It does. Only two of the sprays had a card attached, and

that clears up one of them. The other one I don't expect you to be able to help with, it simply said E. Unless you know a group member with that initial?'

'I might have to think about that one. I don't think there's an Elizabeth in the group so that rules the most obvious name out. No Erica either. When I see Elle I'll ask her. The flowers aren't from her, by the way. We haven't moved from these rooms.'

'She's okay?'

'She keeps crying at odd moments, mainly when something happens that reminds her of her mum. We've shared more hugs in the last couple of days than we have in the last five years. I asked if she wanted to go to where her mum died, maybe take some flowers, because I felt sure one of you could facilitate that without getting us killed, but she doesn't want to go, not yet.'

'If you can wait, I would advise it. They're going to have to take the tree down, it was too badly burnt for it to survive, and now it's become dangerous, so wait until that has gone and the scene of crime tape removed.'

'And we can't see her? I don't really know why I'm asking that, because I expect identification has been done by her dental records in view of the scale of the fire, but it seems wrong that we can't say goodbye to her properly.'

'Remember her as she was. You understand?'

'I do, but it's all so bloody hard. She's my wife, Elle's mother. She drove down from Newcastle only three days ago, we talked about a new place she's renting up there so she can divide her time between here and there, and now there's nothing.'

'I'm so sorry. It's a huge loss for both of you, and this part of the process takes time to get it right, but we are determined to find who did this. We don't give up.'

There was a moment of silence, then Oliver said, 'Bye,' and disconnected.

Claire felt a little rattled, but went back to her computer to write the conversation with Oliver up as a report, as he had confirmed who Lily and Catherine were.

A few seconds later her phone rang again and she saw it was Oliver. 'Sorry to call you back, but I had a thought all at once about the possibility of the E. I can think of one person who knew Denise. Chris Harcourt had a nurse, a carer, for getting on for six months, I believe. Her name was Elsa. Denise met her a couple of times when we visited Chris in his last few weeks.'

CHAPTER TWENTY-SEVEN

Jess opened the door to the two detectives with a smile. 'I saw you pull up. Come in.' She led them through to the library. 'Can I get you a drink?'

Both Will and Claire shook their heads. 'No thanks, we're overloaded on caffeine today. We just came for a bit of information actually.' Will smiled as he spoke.

'Then I hope I can help. Please, sit down.'

'The investigation has ground to a bit of a standstill, so we're going back to the beginning and re-interviewing. We believe all of this began with your husband's death.'

A frown crossed Jess's face. 'With Chris? We had a terminal diagnosis seven months before Chris died. He got very poorly very quickly. They thought he might have nine months, but he didn't. How can that be connected to murder?'

'We don't know. And that's the truth of the matter, we don't know. The link is that Chris was one quarter of the golfing foursome, and now three of them are gone. If you've spoken to Oliver and Elle, you'll know we've got them tucked away for their safety. So we're going over once again what everybody has told us. Did Chris have a Macmillan nurse?'

'Not exactly, I hired a nurse privately, because I needed someone who could move in. We shared the care duties, but she tended to do most of the nights. Excellent help, I would highly recommend her. She left on the day Chris died, but I've remained friends with her. We shared a lot during the five months she lived here.'

Claire took out her notebook. 'Is this Elsa Manvers?'

'Yes, let me get her card, it's got her address and stuff on it. I know I've given it to you already on a scrappy bit of paper, but her card has email and everything on it.'

Jess moved to the bureau and fished around in a small drawer. She handed the card to Claire, who photographed it, checked the picture was clear, and handed it back.

'Thank you, we'll have a quick word with her, and leave her alone. We're simply crossing things off our list now. There is just one more thing. We would appreciate it if this doesn't become public knowledge, but Daniel Rubens was having an affair at one point. We don't have dates because he wrote little snippets about when they met in a small notebook, and when he was killed the affair did appear to be over, but he referred to her as X. Did you know about the affair, and do you know who X is?'

Claire's eyes never left Jess's face, and she noticed the reddening of her cheeks immediately.

Finally Jess spoke. 'An affair? But he wasn't married. You are aware of that? So really, you're saying he had a girlfriend. And what I'm saying is that it surprises me. Daniel was all about his work; possibly that was the real reason behind the split between him and Andi. But I don't know about X. I presume you've checked his laptop?'

'Our forensics department have checked it, it revealed nothing. The little book was locked in the drawer of his desk, and it reveals there was an X, but that is all. They met up several times, but we can't find anything else about her anywhere. So now we're questioning everybody connected with this case, just in case somebody suspected something was going on, or maybe they had seen Daniel out and about with her. We're hoping to only have to check his friends out, because asking around at his work would be a last resort. We don't want to have everybody talking about it. And they would if it was out of character.'

'But it is,' Jess said. 'Out of character, I mean. I feel a little shocked to be hearing it. Daniel was so quiet, lived for his garden, his business, his golf, and that was about it. He worked long hours, but even so Andi didn't stray either. They simply decided to split up, to still live in the same house, and it worked. Daniel was mainly in his office. If you've seen it, you'll realise it's very much like a lounge with the sofa and television, but believe me he worked in there as well.'

'You've been in it?'

'A couple of times. I'm not the world's best technical wizard, and Daniel was my go-to expert when I created havoc on my laptop. He used to come here before Chris began to deteriorate, but after that I took my laptop to him. Twice I think. I felt it was better to keep things as quiet as possible here.'

Claire made a couple of notes in her book, and then Will stood. 'Thank you for your help, Jess. Please ring, if anything else occurs to you. We'll have a quick word with your husband's carer, and then we can put it to bed.'

Jess escorted them to the door, watched as they drove away, then closed the door. She leaned against it, feeling slightly sick. X. How many times had they joked about his name for her being X? But she had no idea he had written it down.

'I think about my X when I'm in bed at night and needing her, when I am problem solving in the office and needing her, and when I feel as if I'm falling in love just a little bit with her,' he had said one day when they were sitting in his car, just before going their separate ways. But she had known then it had to end; she had to start to work on Paul. She hoped with all her heart that Paul hadn't written anything down anywhere.

'Was she lying?' Will asked.

'Too bloody right she was,' Claire said. 'Did you see the colour of her cheeks when we mentioned X? She's not going to admit he was her bit on the side, is she? We ladies have a special nose for spotting adultery, and although we might never get proof of it, and in the end it could be irrelevant, the point is she did lie about it. Possibly because it was over. She doesn't need to admit to it, if it's over.'

'That's how women justify adultery?'

'Too right it is. It's only adultery if it's current. But seriously, I get the impression that Jess is a forward thinking, strong-minded woman, and I wouldn't have said Daniel Rubens was her kind of man. Now Oliver Newton... he would definitely be on my radar, never mind hers, and Paul Browne would also be a possibility, but Daniel?'

'You mean he's too nice?'

'I would say so. Maybe she chased him, but if she did, why? And when? It had to be after Daniel and Andi split, because I don't think Daniel would see it as adultery, or would admit adultery into his life. Or are my glasses a little rose-tinted about him because he seems to have been a nice feller?'

'No idea. Let's go and see what Elsa Manvers has to tell us. Or shall we just assume she knows nothing as well?'

'We treating her gently?'

'Yes, unless she turns evil.'

'No problem. I can be nice,' Claire said, with a grin.

They walked up to the front door and pressed the doorbell. Elsa answered, dressed in her work uniform. 'Can I help?'

They held up their warrant cards and introduced themselves. 'Can we have a quick word, please. Ms Manvers?'

'What about? I'm just about to go to work. I have a long night in front of me.'

'It won't take long.'

Elsa reluctantly held open the door, and they stepped inside. She led them through to the kitchen and indicated they should sit at the table. She stood by the sink. 'I don't have time to make you a drink,' she said.

'That's fine, we're only here to ask you a couple of questions. What sort of car do you drive?'

'A Land Rover.'

'Where is it?'

'In my garage. If you'd arrived five minutes later it would have been on its way to my overnight job.'

'You recently nursed Christopher Harcourt, we understand.'

She visibly softened. 'I did. A truly lovely man. I hope I made his passing as easy as it could be made.'

'You met all his family and friends?'

'I did. His sons I met only a couple of times because they live in Devon, but obviously his wife and father-in-law were there most of the time. I am good friends with Jess now. I lived with them for Chris's final five months, and Jess and I shared the work that Chris's illness created.'

'And their friends? You met his three golfing partners?'

'I did. Four or five times at least during my time there. Their wives as well. It's so sad what's happened to them. Are you any nearer catching their killer?'

'We believe so,' Will said. He stood and waited for Claire to put away her notebook. 'One more thing to check. If you can just take us to your car, we'll leave you in peace.'

She took them through to the garage without saying another

word. Claire made a note of the registration, and Will bent down to look at the passenger side front bumper. It was damaged. He stood and turned to Elsa.

'When did the damage happen?'

'About three weeks ago. I hit the gate post as I drove into a new client's driveway. It didn't cause any damage to the stone gatepost, but my car is no longer pristine. I can't take it in to have it fixed yet because I need it for work, but hopefully next week I can get it in somewhere.'

'Address, please, of the gatepost that was hit.' Claire took out her notebook once more.

Elsa gave her the address, then said, 'It's where I'm going right now, so if you want to follow me you can check it out.'

'Thank you, we will,' Will said. He was beginning to find Elsa quite annoying. She was obviously not happy at having police officers in her home, interfering with her life. *Abrasive* was the word he would use to describe her. Very abrasive.

Claire and Will walked to their own vehicle, then waited for Elsa to exit her garage. She turned left and they followed close behind her.

'Do you believe her?' Claire asked.

Will shrugged. 'I don't know. There aren't any paint scuffs on that bumper, but it's definitely got some damage. And she seems really aggressive, to say she's in the caring business. If she was like that at the Harcourt home, I'm surprised Jess put up with it.'

Elsa only drove for just over five minutes before they saw her indicator lights come on. She turned into a driveway of a large house, and pulled high up on the left, leaving space for other vehicles.

Will and Claire parked on the road, and walked across to look at the gatepost. It was completely undamaged. Elsa left her own car and walked down to join them. 'I did tell you it didn't damage the gatepost, I guess metal is easier to bend than a stone post.'

She walked away without a backward glance, and Will and Claire looked at each other, trying desperately to hide their laughter.

'Consider yourself chastised, DI Stewart,' Claire said. 'She doesn't like us, does she? That could be because she thinks we're accusing her of killing people. Are we?'

Will sank into the driver's seat and turned to Claire. 'I have absolutely no damn idea, but one thing's for sure, I can't arrest her just because I don't like her. I would like forensics to take some scrapings off that bumper before she destroys any evidence there might be. Let's really upset her and get that sorted right now.'

They drove back to the station, and Will went to speak to the forensic people, while Claire went to her desk. She found the two uniformed officers who had been on duty at the Wood Lane site, but they confirmed they hadn't noticed who had brought the flowers. They were already there when they arrived for the last shift before the site was released.

CHAPTER TWENTY-EIGHT

Elsa couldn't have described to anyone how angry she felt. Two forensic people had knocked at the door of her client's home, to tell her they were going to take samples from her car. She then had to explain to Mrs Jacobs why there was a forensic van on their driveway, and also had to explain why she hadn't told Mrs Jacobs about hitting her gatepost.

'There was no damage at all except to my front bumper,' she explained. 'If there had been of course I would have told you. But it seems they would like me to be guilty of something else; I'm not sure what, but when do I get time to do anything even slightly illegal?'

Mrs Jacobs began to look slightly puzzled. 'They didn't say what they were looking for?'

'The DI is the one in charge of the murders of the men who were in a golfing team. I suppose they're questioning me because I knew them, but I only knew them because they were friends of my client, and came to see him regularly as he got nearer the end. I'm not sure I would even have recognised them out of the environment of that room where Chris Harcourt was.'

'Will they be here for long?'

'I'm sorry, I don't know. I didn't know they were coming. He didn't say they were, that horrible man. Can they just turn up out of the blue and do things like this?'

'It seems they can.' Karen Jacobs stared out of the window. 'It looks as though they're leaving. Click your fob now they're out of the car, then maybe they'll just go. I really don't like the police on my drive.'

Elsa did so, then turned her back on them and went to finish medicating her newest cancer patient. The driveway was clear of all vehicles except hers the next time she passed the window.

Wednesday morning saw the arrival of the post-mortem report for Denise Newton. It seemed the smoke inhalation was the cause of death, and Will Stewart couldn't help but feel relieved that she would have been dead before the flames reached her. The report suggested she would have been unconscious initially, so great had been the impact with the tree. The car had been embedded in its trunk.

Forensics also contacted him to report no paint scrapings on the Land Rover bumper, but they were surprised it hadn't done some damage, even if only minor, to the gatepost. The damaged area on the bumper had been washed, but as the whole car was relatively clean it was felt it had undergone a standard car wash since the accident that the owner had described. The report finished with *if further tests are required on this vehicle, it will necessitate bringing it into our facility.*

Will gave it some consideration. How quickly would petrol evaporate? If that home-made petrol bomb had been in the front of a car and some had spilt out, would it still register? Google was helpful only in that he knew it was too late. The petrol would already have evaporated after five days.

He knew he was clutching at straws – he needed a culprit, and for a small amount of time he thought that Elsa Manvers had fitted the bill, but he couldn't even bring her in for questioning on the flimsy evidence they had. A bump on the front of her car? Many cars on the roads sported some sort of minor bumps and marks. That wouldn't go down at all well with the CPS if he tried to charge her with anything. He needed much more than that. Especially as she was a member of the caring profession.

Harold Shipman was a doctor... Will's mind ran around in circles. He had to temporarily forget what Elsa did for a living, and look at her, the person. He hadn't liked her, that was for sure. She had exhibited aggression as soon as she opened her door, without even knowing who they were. Surely she wasn't like that with her clients, or even her clients' families?

Jess had said she was now a friend of Elsa, and they had stayed touch after Chris had died. Was he seeing a different person to the one who had clearly wormed her way into Jess's affections? Or was it more that Jess was still vulnerable after the death of Chris, and the carer was the link with her husband that she didn't want to give up.

Will checked his watch and decided to go out to Belthorpe. They hadn't visited the school since Paul Browne's body had been found in his car, and he hoped the children had received their counselling, along with any members of staff who might have needed it, especially the lovely secretary, Christa, who had been so helpful, if a little tearful.

He walked towards Claire's desk and she looked up at him.

'You okay?'

'Sick of thinking about that horrible woman yesterday. If ever I'm ill, don't let anybody organise her to take care of me.'

Claire laughed. 'I promise.'

'You doing anything that can't wait?'

'Reading through all the reports that have been uploaded so far, just in case something now jumps out at us that didn't before. I'm always surprised by the number of people who are spoken to at the beginning of any investigation. We're at the point now where it's slowed down a bit. You want me to do something?'

'I'm think of a trip out to Belthorpe, see how the school is acclimatising to losing their head of maths, and really making sure we don't need to do anything to help the kids come to terms with it. Christa said he was their most popular teacher, so it's bound to have affected them. And so far, we haven't spoken to anybody, haven't got much of a feel for what Paul was like outside his home environment. I know there was no marital problem with Naomi, unlike Daniel and Oliver...'

'Oliver? He had a marital problem?'

'I'm possibly reading more into it than I should without actually asking the questions, but Denise Newton had just taken on the rental of a flat in Newcastle for her and Elle. Does that sound as though she was happily married? I'm guessing it was turning into a similar situation as the Rubens' marriage – they've simply grown out of the relationship. A bit like my own marriage really.' He looked pensive. 'Such a bloody shame when it happens.'

Claire closed her laptop. 'Hey, don't go all maudlin on me, boss. Let's go to school, see if they can teach us anything.'

The sun that crept slowly from behind clouds was shining on the front of the school when they arrived. The gates were opened after they had shown their warrant cards to the camera, and they drove up to the small car park designated for visitors and staff.

Christa appeared on the steps leading to the front door, and smiled warmly at them. 'I guessed you would be returning at some point. Unfortunately our head isn't here today – a conference on school safety would you believe – so you'll have to speak with me.'

'That's fine. We're really here to check the children have adjusted to the news, and hopefully that the staff have as well. It's been chaotic for us...'

Christa held up a hand. 'I realise that. The newspapers have linked the RTA on Wood Lane to Paul's death and also his friend Daniel's death. So you now have three murders to solve?'

'We do. I think we have some naïve copper with a big mouth who passed the information on, but this moves the investigation into serial killer territory which tends to put everyone on their guard, so maybe it's not such a bad outcome that the papers have got hold of it.'

Christa passed them a coffee each and sat down. 'So what can I do for you to make life a little easier. Just so you know, I couldn't do your job, not ever. Blood absolutely freaks me out.'

'And yet you called the police when you saw the blood on Browne's car?'

'I knew. Not because I expected him to be dead – to be honest I thought he'd maybe run off with his other woman – but it was his car, and it was still at school. And there was blood underneath it in a puddle. I legged it back inside, too scared to even look in the car, or try the boot lid, and rang 999.'

Claire had her notebook open on the desk, and she held up her pen. 'Hang on, let's backtrack a bit. Other woman?'

'Oh dear. Maybe I'm being a bit unkind. We actually thought he'd seen the error of his ways and had finished it with her, because nobody had seen her for a while. So really I shouldn't have thought like that when Naomi rang to say she wasn't getting an answer from him. But I thought like that, because there genuinely had been somebody else in his life. If I was to hazard a guess, I'd say it lasted four or five months, but then fizzled out. Pretty woman, maybe a little younger than he was, but that's guesswork because I didn't know who she was. I think she was blonde, but that's all I can say, really.'

Claire was writing furiously. 'How long ago do you think it finished?'

Christa frowned, trying to remember. 'Maybe nine months. I'm not sure. There was a change in him; he started doing more hours at school, as he did the night he was killed. He didn't use his fob to exit the school till five o'clock. He doesn't need to be here till that time. Maybe he didn't want to be at home, I don't know.'

'His wife wasn't at home that night. She was at the theatre with her mother and her sister, and at the time he was killed, which was as he returned to his car at five, the three of them were in a restaurant in the city centre having a pre-theatre meal and drinks. We didn't get the chance to ask this at the time, but is there a separate gate for people to access the school who don't drive here in a car?'

'There is. It's unlocked every day from three o'clock until the cleaners have finished around six o'clock. They use a fob to lock it as they go home. The children exit via that gate to get to their parents, or to walk home.'

'And that's how our killer got in, aided and abetted by the dense fog. They probably hid close by Paul's car, and simply waited. They must have been really pissed off that he didn't finish for the day until five.'

'But why?' Christa asked. 'Paul was a lovely man, so why kill him?'

'You're not the first person to ask that,' Claire said with a smile. 'And the short answer is, we don't know. The more we hear about this case, the more we hear how nice they all were.'

They finished their drinks and stood. 'The children are okay?' Will asked.

Christa nodded. 'Kids are resilient; they were all upset on

the Monday they came back into school, but we had help in place for them. If there's anything else I can help with, either ring or email me.' She handed her card to Claire. 'Or simply call in for a cuppa.'

The two police officers left, their heads buzzing with the information that not only had Daniel Rubens been playing away from home, but so had Paul Browne. Was the link locking everything together... adultery?

CHAPTER TWENTY-NINE

Thursday morning was definitely wintry. The clouds were dark grey, and it almost felt as if it would snow.

Elsa was definitely feeling disgruntled, as well as cold. At first she had blamed Jess for passing her address on to the police, but then she realised Jess wouldn't have had a choice. Even if Jess had pretended she didn't know it, they could have found it out because they were the police and they could do what the hell they liked.

As a result of the two visits to her driveway – in full view of her neighbours – Mrs Jacobs had requested a change of carer. She told the agency, 'I don't like the police turning up at my home because the carer has some issue with them.'

Then, of course, Elsa had been called into the agency where she had to try and explain what the police wanted with her. Fortunately they had accepted her explanation that Christopher Harcourt was linked to the present police investigation into three murders. 'They were interviewing me just as contact,' she said. They had booked her a new job to go to, but it was five miles away, not just around the corner, as the Jacobs' home had been.

Hence the disgruntlement. And more than a smattering of anger.

Elsa zipped her jacket, picked up her bag and went outside to her car. The garage had agreed to fit it in for the minor repair to the bumper during her unexpected three days off work.

She didn't notice the small black car parked a little higher up the road, nor did she notice Claire Landon inside it. She also didn't see the camera Claire was pointing directly at her.

Claire took three quick snapshots, then watched as Elsa drove away from her. She started her own engine and drove to her next destination.

Jess opened the door. Her normal welcoming smile wasn't there, and Claire briefly wondered if it was because Will wasn't standing on the doorstep seeking admission.

'Claire. You needed something?'

'Just a welfare check, Jess. I'm visiting everybody to make sure they're okay, and don't have any worries about what is going on.'

'I see. Do you need to come in?'

Claire felt definitely unwelcome. 'Yes, please. Just for a minute. If you've any questions about what's happening, I can try to answer them.'

Jess held open the door, and Claire waited in the hallway to see what Jess would do next. It felt as though it was a different woman to the one who had made her and Will feel welcome on their earlier visits.

'I'm sorry if I seem a bit out of sorts,' Jess said. 'I'm worrying all the time about Dad. He came here for a week so I could set him on the straight and narrow with blood pressure checks and new medication. He's gone back home now, but says that his blood pressure is fine at the moment, so he's stopped the new medication. He admitted it this morning, and if I could strangle him, I would.'

'I feel for you,' Claire said with a smile. 'I've got a mum. She was diagnosed with an under-active thyroid, but because she didn't feel ill, didn't bother with the medication. By the time we realised, she really was ill. And you know what, Jess? They get worse as they get older.'

'Don't say that,' was Jess's fervent response. 'Shall we have a cup of tea?'

'I'd love one, please. I wanted to thank you for yesterday, for handing over Elsa's details to us. It saved us time, which at the moment is the one thing we're short of. And I also wanted to check everybody is okay who is in some way connected to this case. I know you and Chris were close friends of Daniel, Paul and Denise, and to lose all three so soon after losing Chris has to have affected you. I'll be moving on to see Naomi after I leave here, then Andi if she's home. She was staying at her mum's.'

'Sit down, I'm sorry I was so unwelcoming, it's not like me, but I'd just finished speaking to Dad. Is it a life sentence if you throw your Dad off a cliff?'

'Afraid so. We don't recommend it.'

'I'll make the tea. It might calm me down.' She left to go into the kitchen, and Claire took her camera out of her bag. She walked over to the bookcase where there was a picture of Jess with Chris, and took two shots of it. She slipped the camera back in her bag, and sat on the sofa.

Jess returned with a tray, and said the tea needed to mash. They chatted about life without Chris, life without her boys, and life with her Dad, then she poured out the tea.

It was clear Jess was angry with her dad, but she did admit to not wanting him to stay full time with her. 'I need a little bit of time to myself after the horrors of the past year, following

Chris's diagnosis,' she said. 'I don't know what I would have done without Elsa. She was my absolute rock for five months, didn't intrude, beavered away in the background, and allowed me to rest during the nights when Chris was at his worst. I haven't heard from her since you called yesterday. Was she home?'

'She was, but I don't think she approved of our visit. As a matter of routine, we asked to see her car. In fact, as a matter of routine I checked your Lexus out as I came in. Whoever killed Denise has got to have a sizeable dent in the left front bumper. Unfortunately, Elsa did. We had no option but to call in forensics for them to check if there were any paint deposits inside the mangled metal. She took offence, but of course we had no choice but to do it.'

'I'll give her a ring later, check she's okay now.' Jess gave a slight laugh. 'I really don't see her as the killer, though.'

'Neither do I, but we have to check everything.' Claire sipped at her tea, and looked around. 'I do love this room. You read a lot?'

'Constantly. Have a couple of favourite authors, but honestly, I read anything. Hence this room. I remember Chris's face when we first moved here, and I said I wanted to make this room a library. He was horrified that it wouldn't have a television in it, but he came to love the ambience of it, and this became our most used room. Everybody comes in here; the other room is used mainly at Christmas, or if there's something on television we need to see. And of course we used it for Chris for his end of life care, because the room next door was free to be made into a bedroom for Elsa.'

Claire nodded. 'I'm glad Chris could pass at home. He was surrounded by all of you, would have felt your love almost to the very end. That must give you some comfort.'

'Oh it did,' she said. 'I was able to tell him everything I

needed to tell him, everything was sorted that had to be sorted, and he simply slipped peacefully away after he'd had his last visit from Daniel, Paul and Ollie, and spent some time with Josh and Adam. I hope I got it all right.'

'I'm sure you did.' The detective put down her empty cup and stood. 'I'll not disturb you any longer, I'm off to see Naomi and Andrea now.'

'Please,' Jess said, 'give them my love and remind them I'm here if they should need me.'

Naomi was emptying her car as the DS pulled up. Claire took a couple of the carrier bags, and waited for Naomi to lock the car before following her into the house.

'With everything that's happened,' Naomi said, 'I found I had precious little in, in the way of stuff like milk and bread, so I went shopping. I've cried most of the way round Tesco because I kept bumping into nice people who wanted to tell me how sorry they were to hear of Paul's death.'

'It's a tragedy, Naomi, it really is. He was so well regarded at Belthorpe, and they've had some very weepy children who didn't really comprehend what it meant, that it was forever that they'd lost their favourite teacher. With that age range, eleven to eighteen year olds, many of the younger ones haven't experienced death. We were there yesterday, doing follow up work, and there's a silence about the school, considering how busy it must normally be.'

Naomi began to fill her fridge. 'Can I get you a drink, Claire?'

'No, I'm fine thanks. I've just had a tea at Jess's and I'll be spending the rest of the day seeking out toilets. Am I okay to use yours?'

'Of course. First right at the top of stairs. Can you pop these in the bedroom opposite for me please? Save my legs...' She handed some new make-up to Claire. 'Just stick it on the bed, I'll sort it later.'

Claire went upstairs, and into the bedroom first. There was a large photograph on the wall of Naomi and Paul – she had hoped for a small one, but the large one was definitely a bonus. She took a couple of shots of it, used the toilet then went back downstairs.

'Lovely picture of you and Paul on the bedroom wall,' she said.

'It is, isn't it? It was our Christmas present from the boys last year. They've taken themselves off to the library today, to do some research. I didn't ask what into, just took it they knew what they were doing. I can't seem to get my head around anything.'

'Can we sit down?'

'Of course! Forgive me, I'm turning into a moron, I think. Let's go in the lounge; it'll be warm in there.'

They sat side by side on the long sofa, and Naomi spoke first. 'What's wrong? What have you come to tell me?'

'Nothing to tell you; the investigation is ongoing and we are treating it as a triple murder. Denise was, we believe, killed by the same person who killed Daniel, then Paul. I do need to ask you something that may be a little sensitive.'

'Go ahead. I'm a big girl.'

'Did you ever feel that Paul was seeing another woman?'

There was a moment of silence, and that silence told Claire what she wanted to know.

'I suspected. I don't believe he was when he died, I think it was over by then, but some time ago I felt there was something wrong. We've always had a healthy sex life, but it seemed to grind to a halt. He was going out more, having meals out, that sort of thing, then suddenly he became himself again. Although I never asked him about it, deep inside me I knew he'd lost me. I realised if he'd done it once he could easily do it again. I never knew who it was, guessed it might be a teacher at school, or even Christa, the school secretary, but I didn't think he would mix work and pleasure. So no, I didn't know, I just knew when it was over.'

'Thank you for being honest,' Claire said softly. 'I was dreading asking you. I didn't want to make everything worse.'

Claire stood. 'I'll leave you alone now, but if you need me for anything, ring.' She handed Naomi her card. Naomi escorted her to the door, and gave the police officer a hug.

'Thank you. I think I needed you today without realising it. And, Claire, you really couldn't make anything worse than it already is.'

CHAPTER THIRTY

To Claire's surprise, Andi was in. If being in the garden can be called being in, then Andi was in. She looked up as Claire stopped her car out on the road. Her frown cleared when she realised who her visitor was. 'It's DS Landon, isn't it?'

'It is. Well done for remembering. It's just a courtesy call really, to make sure you're okay and to apologise for having to cancel our promised visit for Saturday morning. We were dealing with the Denise Newton's death. I didn't expect to find you here, but decided to try. I thought you might still be at your mum's.'

'Strictly speaking, I am. But I have houseplants, so I came home for a couple of hours to check my mail, water the plants, and see if anything in the garden needs sorting. The garden seems okay, it's had plenty of rain, but the indoor plants looked a bit sorry for themselves. I've watered them all as a matter of urgency, and given them a good talking to.'

Claire laughed. 'I talk to my plants. My mum told me to do it when I was little and I had been given my first cactus, so I've always done it, no matter what the plant. And I still have that first cactus, so it must work. It's a lot bigger now!'

'Come in and meet mine. Don't expect them to talk back to you, though. I've not trained them to do that. Shall we have a drink?'

Claire hesitated, then decided as she didn't really know Andi Rubens, maybe she should take time to have a drink, and talk to her a bit more in depth. She'd deal with the potential urgency for a toilet when she returned to the station. 'Thank you, that would be nice.'

Andi rubbed her hands down her leggings to get rid of any soil clinging to her fingers and led the way into the kitchen. All her plants had been brought a bit nearer the water source and placed on the work surfaces.

'These are my babies,' she said. 'Until I come back here to live again, this is where they'll stay. For the moment I'm remaining with Mum, probably until after Daniel's funeral, and we've been given no information when we can have that. I don't suppose...'

'Sorry, no, we don't get to hear such details, but when I get back I'll see what I can find out.'

'Coffee or tea?'

'Tea, please. Milk, no sugar. This is a lovely kitchen, even with all these plants taking over.'

'Dan and I designed it together. The house was a wreck when we bought it, but I love how it turned out. Dan felt the same, which was the main reason behind us continuing to live together after we called an end to our marriage. We agreed that if one of us met someone else, then they would be the one to leave the marital home.' She paused. 'That's not going to be an issue now though, is it?'

'Did you ever think Daniel might have met someone else?'

She laughed. 'I know Daniel was a highly intelligent, super-smart guy, but he didn't have a deal of confidence. I can't imagine for a minute that he would know how to approach another woman. I had to chase him when our relationship started. It was really funny, he had to have it spelled out when we became a regular item, I had to actually say the words boyfriend and girlfriend. So in answer to your question, if he had met someone else, I'm not sure he would have known it.' Again she paused while she thought through what she had been asked. 'Is there something you know that I don't know?'

'We believe that when he died there was nobody else, but there had been prior to that. We have no idea of dates, his notes on the affair were very sporadic, but we're pretty sure he did have someone else. We only know he referred to her as X. If it was a her.'

Finally Andi allowed herself to relax. 'I can assure you he never expressed any interest in men. No, it would have been a woman, but I'm still in shock that he had anyone, man or woman. I had no idea.'

'I hope it hasn't upset you.'

'It's more surprised me than shocked me.' She poured the tea from the teapot into two mugs, and handed one to Claire.

Claire looked at the picture on the cup. The gods were on her side. It was a snapshot of Andi and Daniel on a beach, with a date from three years earlier imprinted below it. She just needed to get a photo of it.

And she did. Andi had three small plant cuttings that were doing very well despite their water deprivation, and she disappeared into the utility room to get a plastic carrier bag to put one in for Claire to take home with her.

Claire grabbed her camera, snapped the picture and replaced the camera just as she heard Andi returning.

'Don't forget, it's a coleus, and don't overwater it. Once a week is enough.'

'That's lovely. I'm going to keep it on my desk at work. And speaking of work, I'd better be getting back. We've got a briefing in an hour, and I've got stuff to prepare. Thank you for the drink,' she said, draining her cup, 'and I promise to try to find out if there's a release date for Daniel's body. I'll let you know, even if there's no news yet.'

Andi walked with Claire to her car. 'It's been horrific,' she said quietly. 'I wake up every morning hoping it's not true. And then it hits me that it is. I loved him deeply once, and that will never leave me.'

Claire couldn't help but hug her. 'I'll be in touch,' she said, and got into her car. She watched through her rear-view mirror as she drove away. Andi stood there until Claire turned left at the bottom of the road.

She turned on her radio just as the midday news started, only to hear that the police had nothing further to report on the serial killer who seemed to be stalking Sheffield.

She slammed her hand on the steering wheel and swore. Loudly. What the fuck did some tinpot little Hitler in the newsroom know about what the police knew; how bloody hard they worked; and how distressing it was interacting with relatives of the victims?

She had just about calmed down by the time she got back to the station. She placed her new little plant on her desk, and stood to admire it for a moment. 'Grow on, little plant, I'll think of a name for you soon.'

She opened her computer, connected her camera and downloaded all the photographs she had taken that morning. She added all of them to the same file – Elsa Manvers, Jessica Harcourt, Naomi Browne, and Andrea Rubens – then added the picture of Denise Newton, taken from the whiteboard. She had considered trying to get a photo of Elle Newton, but decided against it because Elle was in Newcastle most of the time, and a little young to be having an affair with any of the golfing group.

She emailed Christa at Belthorpe, and asked her to look at the file containing five photographs, and to see if any of them resembled the woman she had seen with Paul Browne. She didn't supply names, merely numbered them.

Claire popped her head around Will's door and he waved her in, finger to his lips. She sat opposite him, waiting until he finished the phone call explaining why they still hadn't arrested the killer of their three victims.

He disconnected, said bugger off, and looked at Claire. 'Did it pay off?'

She nodded. 'Good morning's work. I caught everybody either in, or available to me without them knowing they were available.'

He laughed. 'You're telling me you managed to get a photograph of Elsa Manvers without her knowing you were taking it?'

'She was on her way out. Don't want to hold her up if she was on her way to work, did I?' Claire grinned. 'I really don't like that woman. Can you tell?'

'I'd never have guessed. And the others?'

'Jess was a bit snappy when I got there, but I took a shot of a picture of her and Chris, the one in the library on the bookcase, while she was out making us a drink. I've had that many drinks this morning, I'll spend all afternoon peeing.'

'Hazard of the job,' he said.

'I went to Naomi Browne after that, helped her in with her shopping. She'd guessed Paul had got somebody else, but she felt it was over pretty quickly, so she let it go.' Claire shook her head. 'I don't understand wives who just accept adultery, but really I suppose they just switch off the love and continue their life with absolutely no respect for their husband.'

'Ouch. That's a bit harsh. You could be right though. And I

guess you managed to get a picture. Was Andrea Rubens at home?'

'She was. Gave me a plant for my desk. She didn't know about X, couldn't really believe it because she said Daniel had no confidence. She had to chase him when they met. I like Andi. I had to get my picture from a mug that I had my drink in.'

'You got them all?'

'I did. Enjoyed it actually. They're different when it's just me they're talking to. I reckon they all go starry-eyed when you're there.'

'I'm sure they do.' He burst out laughing. 'I've never had anybody be starry-eyed over me before.'

Claire smiled but didn't respond. She reckoned if she tried a bit harder she could go all starry-eyed over him... 'Anyway, the result of all this gadding about and much use of my petrol tank gave me five photographs which I have now numbered. No names. I've emailed the file I've created to Christa at Belthorpe, and I'm hoping she gets back to me pretty quickly.'

'Well done, Claire. When you rang last night and suggested you do this, I was a bit sceptical. Turns out I was wrong: even Andi Rubens cooperated by being there.'

'Must admit I left her till the last. I thought she wouldn't be home, but it seems she cares about her houseplants, so popped home to water them.' She stood. 'I'll let you know when I hear from Christa. You are prepared for it not being any of these five, aren't you?'

'Nope. You convinced me one of them is a serial adulterer. The only thing is, why? I'm baffled. Does one of these women have to sleep with everybody she sees?'

Claire walked to the door. 'Well, if Christa identifies the woman she's seen several times with Paul, we can get her in an interview room and ask her.'

She headed back to her desk, and picked up the little plant.

'I'll call you Elsie. I always loved my Aunty Elsie and she'd be dead chuffed to have a plant in her name.' She replaced it and sat at her desk, opening up her computer once more. Still no email from Christa, but she couldn't expect her to be sat at her computer simply waiting on the off-chance she would get an interesting message.

She set her notifications to ping loudly for an incoming email, and went over to the whiteboard. She stared at all the pictures, feeling sad that so many had died. And they still had no clue why. Nice men, nice women, nice families. And a total of four dead including Chris Harcourt.

Ping.

She almost ran back to her computer.

The response was short and sweet. Christa began by apologising for the delay in replying – she had been out most of the day on a school trip. She said she knew Naomi Browne, image number three, anyway; had known her for several years, but the woman she had seen with Paul was definitely image number two.

CHAPTER THIRTY-ONE

Jess wasn't even awake when she heard the loud banging on her door heralding the dawning of Friday. Her immediate thought was that there was a problem with her boys, and she ran downstairs frantically trying to put on her dressing gown.

Two uniformed officers, one male one female, stood on her doorstep. They held up warrant cards. 'Mrs Harcourt? We've come to take you to the station for questioning.'

Her brain told her to shut her open mouth. 'What?' she spluttered. 'What the hell time is it?'

'It's seven o'clock, ma'am. Would you like to quickly slip some clothes on, or we'll have to take you as you are,' the female officer said.

'Why?'

'I'm sure DI Stewart will explain when we get you there. We've simply been asked to pick you up and deliver you to the station.'

'Wait there,' Jess said, and tried to close the door. She was utterly unsuccessful.

'I'll wait in the hall,' said the male officer. 'My colleague will escort you while you dress.'

Jess stomped off angrily, wondering what the hell was going on. The female officer said nothing, simply walked behind her as they headed for the bedroom. Jess tried to close the door behind her, but the officer pushed it open. 'I don't need to be present while you dress, but I do need you to leave this door open,' she said.

Jess pulled out clean underwear, jeans and a thick woolly jumper, ran a hairbrush through her hair and walked out onto the landing.

They headed back downstairs where the male uniform waited patiently.

'Thank you for cooperating,' he said quietly. 'The inspector is waiting for you, so maybe you won't be too long.'

'I'd better not be,' Jess said angrily.

They placed her in the back seat of the squad car, and set off for the short trip to the police station. She didn't speak on the journey; she felt her brain hadn't really woken up, but she knew she hadn't broken any laws. Hadn't killed anyone, hadn't even knowingly driven her car a bit too fast, so why this early morning debacle? And what on earth would her neighbours think?

They pulled into the car park and all three of them got out of the car.

'You're going to behave?' the male officer asked.

'What? What the hell are you talking about?'

'If you don't, we will need to use handcuffs. They are uncomfortable, and can hurt, so I'd advise you to just do as you're told and wait to speak until DI Stewart interviews you.'

Suddenly fear tumbled from the early morning clouds and descended onto her head. She'd read about wrongful arrests, inventive crimes and suchlike, and she was now in a situation she had never imagined she would ever be in.

She didn't deign to answer, simply stood there and awaited

further instructions. They led her up the steps and into the reception area, where she was booked in and then transferred to an interview room. She had been carrying her house keys and her phone, the only things she had brought with her, and they had been taken off her after the booking in was completed. Her anger had now dissipated. Now she was simply scared, and it was completely fear of the unknown. She didn't know why this was happening, and was fearful of what she was about to find out.

She was alone for what seemed forever, then the door opened and the female who had brought her to the station arrived, and handed her a bottle of water. 'It suddenly occurred to me we hadn't given you a chance to have a drink. I don't think it will be long before DI Stewart is ready.'

'Thank you. Do you know why I'm here?'

'No, sorry,' she said with a smile. 'Enjoy your water.'

Jess did think she would have more enjoyed a bacon sandwich and a coffee, but she opened the water and drank deeply. She really had been thirsty. It was a further half hour before the door opened once again and Will and Claire walked into the room.

Claire spoke all their names into the recorder, and the two police officers sat opposite Jess.

'Jessica Harcourt, you do not have to say anything, but it may harm your defence if you do not mention, when questioned, something which you later rely on in court. Anything you do say may be given in evidence.' Claire spoke the words, and both of them watched the last dregs of colour fade from Jess's face.

'What?' she finally said. 'What's going on? Are you accusing me of something?'

'Not necessarily,' Will said, 'but you are being interviewed under caution in case we do have to end up in court using your answers. That can't happen if you haven't been cautioned. It's a formality, but a necessary one. So, is it okay if we call you Jess?'

'You always have,' Jess responded. 'All three of us have met several times already.'

'Thank you,' Will Stewart said. 'Jess, you knew all four members of the golf foursome who met at least twice a week to play a round of golf together. Is that correct?'

'Yes.'

'Can you repeat their names for the record, please?'

'My late husband, Christopher Harcourt, the late Paul Browne, the late Daniel Rubens and Oliver Newton.'

'Thank you.' Will looked down at his notes, and Claire held her breath. They had decided on shock tactics, so she knew what was coming next. Jess didn't.

'Jess, how many of the four have you slept with?'

For Jess, what had started out as a bad day suddenly became so much worse. 'I...'

'Just a number from one to four will do, Jess.' Will deliberately kept his tone light, a little bit facetious.

'Four.'

'Thank you. How many other people in your life since you were sixteen and legally old enough to have sex, have you slept with?'

Jess dropped her head. Had they really got her in their sights as the killer of the men she had made love to? She took a deep breath.

'Zero.'

Will glanced at Claire. The answers were starting to come a little closer, the motive hopefully a little more obvious. 'For the tape and for clarity, you have only slept with four men in your life?'

'That's right. And as far as I'm aware, it may be immoral, but it's not a crime.'

'That's true. It isn't a crime. Killing them is.'

She jumped up. Claire waved a hand at her to tell her to sit back down. 'Histrionics don't work in here, Jess,' she said.

Jess slid back down onto what had become the most uncomfortable chair in the universe. 'I could never kill anybody. I feel as if I've been crying forever, with one man after another dying. And then Denise is almost the final straw. It should have been Oliver, shouldn't it?'

'We think so,' said Will. 'And I don't doubt you're in touch with Oliver, despite our taking him out of circulation.'

'Just keep him alive for me,' she said. 'I didn't sleep with Paul and Daniel because I loved them. I cared about them, both as friends and lovers, but I deliberately took them as lovers. It was calculated. But Oliver and I – we've become close, very close. Just keep him safe for me.'

There was a brief period of silence then Jess spoke again. 'Do I need a solicitor? I know I've not been charged with anything, but am I likely to be? You have my full cooperation, although I'm not sure what you want to know, but I'm happy to tell you anything that will find the killer of my friends.'

'Thank you,' Will said. 'And no, I don't think you need a solicitor, so don't waste your money. I never thought you'd done the actual killings, but I think you're maybe the key to whoever did. And there was no way you would ever have confessed to sleeping with anybody while we were simply popping in for a cup of tea and quick chat; I had to formalise the situation. For that I apologise, but we need full disclosure of what the hell you've been playing at.'

'Ouch,' Jess said. 'I can tell you part of the story, the part that I know, but I promise you I have absolutely no idea who is killing my friends, or why. You're Major Crimes, and it doesn't get more major than a serial killer, but even though I am in the thick of it, I have no clue about what is happening. I can only tell you what led up to me sleeping with Paul, Daniel and Oliver. You're on your own when it comes to solving who did what in this one, but I could no more have stabbed Daniel and Paul than fly to the moon. And as for killing Oliver...'

She looked at Will and Claire. 'Never in a million years would I harm one hair of that man's head. And I think it's quite possible now that Denise is gone, that I may have lost him. He is a good, decent man, and he will think only of getting Elle through this, I know that for a fact. I think we will both realise it can't happen, the two of us, because he is honourable. Yes, we slept together, but he rarely saw Denise. She was in Newcastle more than Sheffield, and last time I spoke to her she told me in confidence that she was going to be moving there permanently, not divorcing unless that was what Oliver wanted, but definitely splitting up. And I had hopes we would be able to be together, but her death has taken that future away, I believe.'

Jess waved the empty plastic bottle around. 'If you're not going to arrest me, could I have more water please?'

Will smiled. This interview was going exactly where he wanted it to go, and he could afford to slow it down, calm his interviewee down a little, and they could all enjoy a hot drink. He was getting answers that had seemed impossible to achieve, and he seriously thought there was much more to come from Jess, even if she didn't realise it. He glanced at his watch. 'It's almost ten, let's have a break, a hot drink and we might be able to find a few biscuits, then return to your story. Hold it there in your mind, Jess, but unless you actually confess to murdering all these people, you aren't going to be arrested for anything. I just think you know stuff that is relevant, that you don't realise is part of this criminal investigation, and we need to tease it out of you.'

They logged themselves out, and Claire went to get refreshments for them. Will smiled at Jess. 'You okay?'

'I am now we've reached some sort of understanding that the most I'm guilty of is sleeping with men other than my husband. God bless his soul,' she added somewhat drily.

He laughed. 'I'm not holding it against you that you've slept with other men. Good grief, I'm two years younger than you and I've had more partners than four in my lifetime. No, Claire and I talked through what would happen today, and we can see you're a private person, so decided we had to use up-front, quite blatant tactics, and not give you chance to wriggle out of answering. You have single-handedly opened up this investigation from stalled to active. For that I thank you, so we'll have a drink, some biscuits if Claire has managed to find some, and relax for a few minutes, before delving back into your mind for other things that you think are irrelevant, that turn out to hold even more keys to all these locked boxes.'

CHAPTER THIRTY-TWO

They had a bit of a picnic. Claire managed to persuade the duty sergeant to get them a pot of coffee and a pot of tea, milk, sugar, and digestive biscuits. 'No custard creams then?' he said, his eyes twinkling.

'Stop it, you'll spoil us,' she laughed, 'but if you've got them...'

And he had.

Once the refreshments arrived, the atmosphere changed. They didn't talk about the case while they were on the break time, but spoke of Josh and Adam, how they had come by their pub in Devon, their surfing skills, and their general love of the whole south west of England.

'Presumably they're very close, your boys?'

'Fifteen months apart in age, but Josh is definitely the older brother and I don't just mean in years. He watched over his little brother almost from birth, and even now they're as close as close can be. When I tell them about what's happened today – and I will – one or other of them will be here within a couple of days. They may even arrive together. I love it when that happens, they bring light into my home. My dad adores them.

They would have got a sizeable inheritance on Dad's death, but he gave it to them instantly when they said they were looking to raise money on a mortgage to buy the pub. He rings them at least three times a week, kind of taken on the father figure as well as granddad role in their lives.'

They finished their drinks and Claire cleared away the debris before she logged them back in.

'We're going to continue recording, Jess, because as I've explained earlier, you may say something that is minor to you, but is so much bigger to us. If it's on record we won't lose it.'

Jess nodded. 'Just do what you have to do. I've lost so much, I just want to get to where we find who's doing it. Because I'll be brutally frank, I don't know anybody in my life who is capable of murder. But there must be somebody, according to you two.'

'Okay, let's start as early in your life as you need this to start, so we get the full picture.'

Jess nodded. 'Okay, then we have to go back to my wedding day in April 1997. I married for love, and I thought Chris was the same. At our wedding reception I saw him dancing with my best friend who was my chief bridesmaid, and I knew. I could see there was something big between them. But Chris being Chris, he thought he could have his cake and eat it, so he did.'

Jess took a drink before continuing. 'I had almost decided to leave him, because I knew he was still seeing her, when I discovered I was pregnant with Josh. Chris seemed to change and I decided I could maybe put it all behind me, have our baby and be the happy loving couple I had always envisaged.'

Josh was only about six months old when I realised I was pregnant again, so I settled for that life. But I knew Chris was still seeing her, Katie. Dad bought me a beautiful leather journal as a little wedding gift, and I wrote everything down in that, all my hopes for my marriage, every time I knew he was out with her, absolutely everything about me, about my feelings.'

'And then Katie met somebody else who was free to marry her, so Chris spent a couple of nights as a farewell screw in a posh hotel with her, and she emigrated to Australia with this new love. I followed them to the hotel and took photographs. He didn't know I even suspected. But that was when I decided that when my boys left home I would confront Chris with all the evidence. And I would leave him.'

She took a deep breath.

'Take your time,' Claire said. She could see distress building in Jess.

'I will. Then golf became part of Chris's life, and I was introduced to Daniel and Andi, Paul and Naomi, and Oliver and Denise. We became friends, but still I wasn't close enough to any one of them to talk about Chris and his other women. So I planned for the day I would leave him. There would be truly magnificent retribution. As I have already said, I have never had sex with anyone other than my husband, but I set about seducing his three friends. I was with Daniel first and we were together for about three months, then I pleaded that I felt guilty about Chris, and we had to finish. He wasn't happy, I think he saw a long term thing between us. I asked him not to tell the others: I didn't want it to get to Chris.

'I moved on to Paul. Again, we had a good thing going, with the same result. In the meantime everything was being written in my journal. And then I moved on to Oliver.'

She shuddered. 'I'm sorry, this next part is so hard, because then Chris became ill, in a lot of pain. We thought initially he had hurt himself playing golf, because most of the pain was in his back, but of course by the time the pain had developed to that extent the cancer was rampant.'

'I met Oliver the day after Chris's diagnosis. We talked for hours. By this time we had fallen for each other. Denise had basically moved to Newcastle: she preferred her life up there near to Elle, and they had lived separate lives for years. Very similar to Daniel's strange lifestyle.' She hesitated for a moment, and took a deep breath. The memories were getting harder to handle.

'I gave Oliver up to nurse my husband, and everything was okay. It was hard staying awake for so many hours and I was scared I would fall asleep and miss the fact he needed some pain relief during the night or something, so I went to the agency and Elsa moved into my life. We shared the care of Chris. My journal entries changed.'

'You can show us this journal?' Will was fascinated by her story. She had clearly held a grudge against her husband for over twenty-five years, and had planned for the denouement that she had slept with his best friends on the day she walked away from their marriage, but then he had thwarted her by dying.

'I wish I could. It wouldn't bother me to show it to you, but the day after Chris died, it disappeared. For twenty-seven years I have kept it in an old leather handbag that used to belong to my mum. I treasured the bag because of that. On the day that Chris died I had taken four photographs out of the back pocket of the journal, and the following day went to put them back in. The journal had gone.'

But Claire was two steps in front of Will. 'Did you tell Chris? Did your revenge work?' Suddenly this nice woman wasn't so nice.

'When Elsa came to us I told her then that if Chris got near the end, I would need to know in case we needed to change any requests for the boys, or anybody else for that matter. When that day came, I sent Elsa out for a couple of hours, and I sat with Chris. Josh and Adam were on their way from Devon, and I knew I didn't have long. You see, two weeks earlier, Chris had asked me to let Katie know. Up to that point I wasn't sure I could go through with my plan, but he clearly hadn't forgotten her. So, in his final hours, with just me and him in the house, I showed him the pictures from the back of my journal of him and Katie going to the hotel in Newark. Then I began to tell him about Daniel, about Paul and about Oliver. I also told him I loved one of them. I didn't tell him which one.'

'What if they had called to see him?' Will sounded horrified at the thought.

'They had been earlier to say their goodbyes. Emotional, to say the least. At this point, after I'd told him everything, especially about me knowing about Katie from the start, he switched off from me. Then Elsa returned and Josh and Adam arrived, more or less altogether, and Josh and Adam went to sit with their father for a good hour. They eventually came through to the kitchen, because it was time for pain relief. Dad popped his head around the door, stayed about five minutes knowing it would be his last time of seeing Chris conscious, then Elsa dealt with Chris and his needs. His eyes were closed. He never opened them again.'

'So somebody knows about these three men and your activities with them. That's pretty clear.'

'But nobody knows other than me, the three men involved, and my late husband. This has gone round and round in my mind ever since Daniel was killed.'

'What about your father? Did you ever tell him your plans?'

'He was well aware of my husband's philandering ways, but nobody knew of my life plan. Dad tried desperately to stop me marrying Chris, without telling me why. Kept saying I could do better. But we produced two handsome young men who are doing very well in their own lives, and we had a good life. Dad has only recently found out about my journal. He didn't know I started to use it right at the beginning, when he first gave it to me. In truth, he was quite shocked to hear I'd actually used it.

But twenty-seven years of my life is in it. I just can't find it, and it's like a huge part of me is missing.'

'Can we talk about Elsa?'

'You're calling the shots.'

'Was she fond of your husband?'

'I'm sure she was. I know she kissed him. Adam told me. He'd looked through the front window to see if his Dad was awake, and Elsa was bent over the bed kissing him.'

'You didn't say anything?'

'No. He was probably asleep anyway. And don't forget, I didn't love Chris, not at all. He could have had a whole harem of women, and I wouldn't have cared enough for it to bother me. You can school your mind to accept any situation, you know. I believe he loved Katie, so I simply cancelled our love. Elsa was genuinely grieving for Chris when he died. She had nursed him for five months as a live-in carer. And she keeps in touch, not really able to leave us, even now.'

'Okay, think carefully about this, Jess. After you had told your husband about your affairs, was he still aware of his surroundings?'

'Yes, he was. The boys had a chat with him, although I suspect they spoke more than he did, and Elsa certainly had a conversation with him because she would need to know the depths of his pain and where it was worst. She's an exceptional nurse. She predicted he would slip away before morning. His breathing was getting more spaced out and lighter.'

'And you still say only you and the men involved knew of your affairs, and they didn't know you had slept with all three of them. Have I got that right?' Will's tone had hardened slightly, as he followed her long story.

Jess nodded before saying yes, and accepted the bottle of water he handed to her.

'Have this, that's a lot of talking. Has it occurred to you, Jess, that there may be others who know of your extra-marital affairs?'

'Like who?'

'A secretary at Paul's school picked you out of a series of photographs. She saw you with Paul on a couple of occasions. That's why you're here at the moment, because of that identification.'

Jess waited, sipping at the water. She actually was starting to feel physically sick.

'And your husband, inconveniently for you, spoke with at least three people after you had bared your soul to him with details that you knew would hurt him. I believe you gave him the ammunition to kill the three men. What you couldn't have known was that Denise would lose her life because of your revenge.'

CHAPTER THIRTY-THREE

'At least three people?'

'Possibly four. Your two sons, Elsa Manvers and your father.'

They could tell from the expression on Jess's face that her mind was racing, that she was trying to deny what they had just pointed out. Could Chris have told Elsa? Or her boys? He definitely wouldn't have told Malcolm.

She didn't need to think about Josh and Adam; they couldn't kill. And Elsa was a nurse, a member of the caring profession. Her dad? Maybe he could have bumped Chris off at the start of her marriage thanks to the protection he afforded his only child, but over the years he had built a relationship with Chris that had become marginally closer than at the beginning of their marriage. No, none of them were killers.

'What if one of the wives knew?' Jess said.

'You're clutching at straws,' Will said.

'I went to see the wives, both Andi and Naomi, yesterday. They are just very sad people at the moment, with no idea why their husbands and partners are dead. Talk to me about Elsa,' Claire said.

'I'm not sure what to say. I know very little about her as a person, but as a carer I can only sing her praises. She put Chris first. She went without sleep to make sure he was cared for, and although it wasn't a cheap option to have a live-in carer, it was what I needed. She was really upset when he died. I think they had lots of chats about everything while his mind was still functioning properly, and she kept him pain-free for most of the time. I believe she was married at one point, but that only lasted a couple of years. I gathered she suffered a degree of domestic violence, so walked away. She devoted herself to nursing, then moved on to what she seems to specialise in, end-of-life care. Could she kill?'

'Could she?' Will asked.

'I would say no, but who knows when it comes down to it? When I followed Chris that night to Newark, when I knew what he was about to do with Katie, could I have killed? I think the answer is yes for me. But as we get older, we mellow. Surely murder is the ultimate answer for any problem? A younger person than Elsa might consider it, but Elsa is as old as me, and I know this sounds ridiculous, but murder is simply too much trouble.'

Will stood, and Claire logged them out. 'We'll be back in a bit, Jess.'

Jess watched as they left the room, and thoughtfully sipped at her bottle of water. They seemed focused on Elsa, and she was starting to feel concerned that maybe Elsa had focused on Chris. All this focusing wasn't good for anyone, she decided. One thing she was sure of, they could hold her here all day, but they couldn't charge her with anything at all, as she simply hadn't done anything. She hoped her belief in the British justice system was justified.

'Let's go up to my office,' Will said. 'We need to talk away from Jess.'

Claire nodded, and followed him. She pulled out the chair across from his, and sat. 'If we're going to make a habit of discussing things in here, I want you to apply for a new chair. I'm going to end up on the floor one day, it's that rickety.'

'Really? I didn't know; never sit on it myself. I'll sort it when we catch this bloody killer. Agreed?'

She sighed. 'Well, the way it's going, I'll end up on the floor then.'

'Negative Nellie,' Will said. 'We're almost there. We learned a lot, didn't we? We certainly found out about how far a woman will go to get revenge. Scares me a bit.'

'And it does seem to be a woman thing,' Claire admitted. 'I've a couple of women friends who've taken the revenge thing a bit far. Not known anybody do it after twenty-five years, but in Jess's case it was clearly a matter of putting her kids before retribution; but that would have happened anyway. The retribution, I mean. She would eventually have walked away, then told him what she had done with his friends. It was only the cancer that changed everything. She saw his life out to the very end, but couldn't resist that last little twist of the knife. Certainly backfired, didn't it?'

'It did. Chris got his own back in what were possibly the last words he would ever speak. Tangled webs and all that. So, we bring Elsa Manvers in? If we don't get cast-iron alibis for the murder times, I think the CPS will say charge her. That kiss she was seen bestowing on Chris Harcourt could be her kiss of death. Any reasonable prosecution chap could get that through as her having feelings for her long-term patient.'

'You think she did it?' Claire asked.

'I do. And let's not forget that bump on the car. Even the

forensics chap said it should have made some sort of mark on the stone gatepost, if her story was true. But it didn't. It's starting to add up, so the next step is to get her in here. Can you contact the nursing agency and find out where she is today?'

'What about Jess's boys?'

'Last resort. They may have known, but I'm not sure. Would a father put that onto his sons at the point of death? And they're only early twenties, adultery and suchlike probably haven't touched them yet. I don't see them going on a killing spree to satisfy their dead father, do you? And certainly not from Devon. I can just sense it now. Where were you at 5.03pm on such and such a day? Devon. Nah, they're definitely on the back burner. It would have been good to see this journal, though. Do you keep one?'

'I do. Ten minutes a night just filling it in for how the day has gone, and if I've done something really special I stick pictures and receipts and suchlike in as well. Been keeping journals for years, but from the way Jess spoke, it seems like it's an undated one that you write the date in, and just annotate as much as you want. I buy a new one every year. Part journal, part diary. She must be feeling sick that she's lost hers.'

'Or somebody took it. You see, it doesn't have to be Chris finding the strength to speak to Elsa or the boys. What if Malcolm has the journal? What if he's read it, realised just how unhappy his only daughter has been, and he's done something about removing all the men in her life. Would he do that?'

'My gut feeling,' Claire said slowly, 'is no, he wouldn't. He would have hurt Chris, but the journal didn't go missing until the day of Chris's death, so that doesn't fit. My guess is he might actually have felt grateful to them for giving some joy into her life. It seems he never really approved of Chris and Jess's marriage.'

Will nodded. 'I suspect you're right on that one. He is in his late seventies, bit elderly to be doing anything that requires a degree of strength and medical skill, and according to our pathologist there was some medical knowledge used. I don't see Malcolm being under that banner, but we have to work through everybody. So, we bring Elsa in?'

'Definitely. And we lead gently up to the possibility she could have killed three people. Let's try and get her talking about Chris first, find out if there were feelings between them, or if it was just in her mind. I know this kiss was seen, but what if he wasn't a willing participant? What if he was in a morphine-induced sleep? We need to suggest things, rather than ask the direct questions. You think?'

'I think. I also think she'll believe she can wriggle out of anything, but we can keep her for twenty-four hours without charging her, and she'll not like that little fact, will she? And she's not getting custard creams.'

'I think we ate them all. So, now we have to decide what to do about Jess.' Claire paused, deep in thought. 'Have we got absolutely everything from her that we need? She didn't hold back, told us what we wanted to know. She obviously hadn't realised that her journal was potentially part of the crime, was quite open about it. She's clearly miffed that it's gone missing, so when we get a search warrant for Elsa's home, my guess is we'll find it. And we'll be able to tell Jess she can have it returned to her eventually. After the court case, and when all her secrets have been revealed to the world. Think I might go home right now and destroy all mine. I've got six years of back journals and there's lots of things in them I wouldn't want to be public knowledge.'

'Really?'

'Really. Darkest secrets, horrible things said to us, travels,

McDonalds receipts – anything that means something goes in mine, but it's definitely for my eyes only.'

He laughed. 'Shall we have a coffee and leave her to sweat a bit longer? It won't hurt. And I think she'll be so fed up when we get back down there, that she'll actually feel grateful to us for releasing her. At this moment she's probably plotting to have us sacked.'

Their trip back downstairs to the interview room was via the reception instead of the back stairs, so that Will could request Jess's belongings be brought to the desk ready for her release. Sitting on one of the benches reading a book was Malcolm Johnson.

'Mr Johnson?' Claire said, leaving Will to sort out the paperwork. 'Can we help?' Daisy gave a growl as she approached them.

'Release my daughter. I've been here most of the day, and I need to take her home with me. One of the neighbours rang me to tell me she had been taken off in a police car.'

'We're just going in to officially release her,' Claire said. 'I'm sorry we had to bring her in, but we had questions. People don't realise they know stuff when they're in their own home, so we bring them in to question them. She's absolutely in no trouble, and I'm sure you'll see her in about ten minutes. She has been most cooperative, a truly helpful lady.'

'Of course,' Malcolm said. 'She's my daughter. We don't kill, we don't steal, we don't do anything except live peaceably. Now, I've missed one lot of medication and two blood pressure checks already while I've been sat here, so if you can bring her out in five minutes, I might just not die.'

Claire knew chastisement when she heard it. 'We'll just go and get her, finalise it all officially, and I'll bring her out to you. Treat her gently, she's had a rough day, with a lot of stirred-up memories, but she has opened our investigation for us.

Tomorrow will be a busy day for us, even though it's Saturday, and that's thanks to your daughter being honest.'

'Well that's all right for you,' Malcolm said, 'but wait while she finds out I've missed two blood pressure checks and medication,' he grumbled. 'My life might take a sudden dip.'

CHAPTER THIRTY-FOUR

Saturday was a grey day, and it had rained most of the night, leaving puddles dotted around the car parks and roads. The same two officers who had been despatched to get Jessica Harcourt now found themselves on a similar mission to collect Elsa Manvers.

Elsa wasn't happy. She had tried to ring Jess the previous night, but Jess's phone kept going to voicemail.

Elsa was hoping to reinstate the cancelled coffee morning from the previous week. She had an unexpected day off due to the earlier than estimated death of her client. But it could only happen if Jess answered her phone.

She'd left messages for Jess to ring her, but she hadn't done so. She also tried Malcolm's phone in case Jess was with him, but that too went to voicemail.

Malcolm, Jess and Daisy had driven directly to his home from the police station, picked up his medications and nipped around to Jess's home for a couple of spare pairs of knickers and a nightie, and headed off to a Derbyshire hotel for an overnight stay. Jess had one brief conversation with Oliver, then both phones were switched off.

They didn't even think to inform Elsa of their plans. They simply told Josh and Adam they were going away for a couple of days. No reasons given, just a little holiday. Both boys thought nothing of it: said have a lovely time, ring when you're home to let us know you're safe.

So Saturday morning dawned with an out-of-sorts Elsa making plans to drive around to Jess's home and find out what was going on. Until somebody knocked on her door. A loud knock.

She initially thought it might be Jess. It wasn't. It was a male and a female police officer holding up warrant cards and speaking their names; they asked if she was Ms Elsa Manvers.

'So? What if I am?'

'We're here to take you into the station to be questioned.'

'About?'

'We don't have that information. We just follow instructions, and our instructions are to take you in. Please get a coat, and we'll transport you there.'

'I'll take my own car.'

'I don't think you understand, Ms Manvers. We're here to take you in. There is no option for you to drive yourself. Now, if you need a coat, then please get it.'

Anger washed over Elsa. Just who did these upstarts think they were speaking to? 'No, I need to know why before I go anywhere.'

'You're going in for questioning. We've already explained that. You have only seconds to comply before we place you under arrest and take you in with handcuffs.'

Elsa laughed at them. 'Don't be ridiculous.'

She found herself spun around and handcuffs placed on her wrists. The female officer led her outside, opened the back door of the car and placed a hand on her head to make her bend down to get inside. Elsa had stopped speaking.

The male officer secured her home and took the key to a second car that was patiently waiting for confirmation that the prisoner had been collected for transport.

'Hey,' Elsa shouted to him. 'That's my key!'

The male officer returned to his own car and got into the driving seat. 'The key will be handed in at reception as soon as they have finished. They have a warrant signed by a judge to search your premises. Your car will be collected shortly and taken to our forensics facility where it will be thoroughly searched.'

He switched on the engine and glanced in his rear-view mirror. Elsa's mouth was open as if she was in the middle of speaking. No words were coming out.

It wasn't a long drive; it was the only thing Elsa was grateful for. She was uncomfortable with her hands behind her back, and assumed, wrongly, that the handcuffs would be removed as soon as she was out of the car.

They were finally taken off as she reached the interview room.

Will and Claire had watched her arrival into the car park from the rather grubby window in Will's office.

'They've had to cuff her.' Will sounded shocked.

'Not surprised,' Claire said. 'I suspect she's got a bit of a temper, which probably means she refused to go with them. She'll be livid that we're searching her house. How long are we waiting to go down?'

'Let's let her sit for an hour. Build the temper up a bit more. They always say too much when they're pissed off with us.' Will turned away from the window. 'It could be a long day, but I don't think it was advisable to leave her over the weekend. I believe Oliver Newton is still at risk, so if we can take her off the streets now, he can go back home.'

'Let's play it safe, leave him in that hotel until Monday. What if...'

'What if what?' Will looked at his DS, wondering what she was thinking.

'What if we're wrong. What if it's not Manvers. What if she's got alibis for when the killings happened. Don't let Oliver go yet, it could still be dangerous for him.'

And Will nodded. 'You're right. I'm jumping the gun. Or the knife. Let's have a cup of tea to calm the nerves, then we'll go down and get things moving.'

Claire felt strangely nervous as they headed downstairs to the interview rooms. They walked through the door and Elsa looked up. Anger flashed across her face.

'About bloody time,' she said.

'Sorry,' Will said apologetically, trying not to let a smile attach itself to his face. 'It was our tea break so we had a cuppa before heading down to you.'

She simply stared at them both.

Claire logged them in and then read Elsa her rights, repeating the words so recently delivered to Jess.

'What am I supposed to have done?' Elsa demanded.

'Why don't you tell us, Elsa?' Will said. 'Let's start with a Saturday a couple of weeks ago, and man named Daniel Rubens. Does that ring a bell?'

'Of course it does. I knew Daniel. He was my client's friend.'

'Okay, two weeks ago today Daniel was attacked on the golf course where he was hoping to go on the practice field. He never reached that field. His throat was cut before he even took a club out of his bag.'

Elsa felt cold. She shivered, and stared at the two officers in front of her. 'That's nothing to do with me.'

'Okay, let's move on five days to the Wednesday of the following week. Do you know a man called Paul Browne?'

'You know I do.' Her tone was sullen. 'Are you trying to set me up for their murders?'

'Of course not. We're police officers. We don't set people up; we search for the truth. Let's go back a step. Where were you on the day Daniel Rubens died?'

'At home. Christopher Harcourt's death had been harrowing, and I tried to carry on working straight after but ended up taking a few days holiday. I know I was at home that weekend because when I heard about it I went round to Jessica Harcourt's to express my condolences on the Sunday. We were all upset by it.'

'And where were you on the day Paul Browne died, stabbed in the back in his school car park? That was the day of the big fog, if your memory needs jogging.'

'I didn't go out that day. I rang in sick because fog scares me. I stayed home all day.'

'And did you stay home two days later on the Friday. Friday evening to be more precise? Because I'm assuming you also know Oliver Newton. It's a shame you didn't realise it wasn't him driving his Carrera, but his wife. Was it easy to make the petrol bomb?'

There was a gasp. 'Of course I didn't make a petrol bomb! I wouldn't know how.'

'So where were you on the Friday night. At home again? You don't seem to have worked much over the last couple of weeks. Just how close was Chris Harcourt to you? Did he tell you about his wife sleeping with his best friends – all three of them – and you decided to avenge him?'

All colour had drained from her face. She looked ill. 'I haven't killed anybody! And yes, Chris and I grew close, but only because his wife didn't care about him. I just made sure his last few months were pleasant. I knew nothing about her sleeping with his friends; she never spoke to me about it.'

'But Chris found out on the last afternoon of his life. Did he ask you to go after his so-called friends, to get his own revenge on his wife who had achieved her own retribution by telling him what she had done? Is that what this is all about? Retribution and revenge par excellence? Did you love Chris Harcourt, Elsa?'

'Yes, yes I did,' Elsa sobbed, 'but you've got it all wrong. I haven't killed anybody except Chris, and that was only because he begged me to up the morphine dose.'

Claire sat immobile. Will was taking no prisoners. And now it seemed the murder count was increasing. Although heaven only knew how they would prove an overdose of morphine with only an urn of ashes, no body. Thankfully the recorder had been on.

Elsa was now openly crying, and Claire raised her eyebrows towards her boss. He stood. 'We'll leave it there, but we'll be back. I'll arrange for a tea for you.'

Claire logged them out and followed Will outside the room.

'I never saw that coming,' she said. 'And there's not an alibi in sight for any of the deaths. Let's hope they find that journal at her place, because that would be proof that she knew all about these men and their dalliances with Jess.'

'We've not heard anything yet?'

'Not yet, but I told them to be thorough.' She turned as the door from reception opened. 'Speak of the devil,' she said.

The uniformed officer held up an evidence bag. 'Will this do?' he asked.

Inside the evidence bag was a knife, with blood on its handle.

'Got her,' Will said. 'Where was it? Is that soil on it?'

'It is, there are two large plant pots either side of her front door with some sort of plants in them. Not sure what they are but I took a photo so I can research it for my report. I moved the plant pots to look underneath them because you said to look everywhere, and I could see the end of the handle between the soil and the edge of the plot. It had been stuffed down out of the way, but it's slightly longer than the depth of the soil. A bit more soil in it and I wouldn't have seen it.'

'You've made my day,' Will said. 'Sign this over to me, and I'll make sure it goes to forensics to get the blood checked. I need to show this to Ms Manvers for her comments.'

Claire held out her hand. 'Show me the picture of the plants. I may be able to help.' He brought up his pictures file and passed it to her. She glanced at the picture and handed it back. 'Ornamental bay trees with a corkscrew stem. Quite expensive, hope you haven't killed it.'

'I think that's the least of this lady's worries,' he said with a smile. He handed a receipt note to Will. 'Chain of evidence receipt. Don't take the knife out of that bag, but I don't need to tell you that, do I?'

'You don't. Believe me, I'll take good care of this. This is her stay in jail for free card. You didn't find a large brown leather journal then?'

'No, boss, and we've turned that property inside out. There's a wood burning stove in the lounge, she could very easily have burnt it once she'd got the information she needed.'

Will nodded. 'Thanks for a job well done. Now we'll see what she has to say.'

CHAPTER THIRTY-FIVE

Elsa was shaken. 'Where did you find that?' She stared in horror at the plastic bag containing the long knife.

'Can't you remember where you hid it?' Will asked.

'Don't be ridiculous. I've never seen it before, and one thing's for sure, you'll not find my fingerprints on it.'

'You wore gloves? You're a nurse, it's automatic to wear gloves, isn't it? And I bet you always have them somewhere close.'

'No I didn't wear bloody gloves! I keep telling you I haven't done anything.'

'Tell me about the bang to your car. I understand it's been mended now. That's convenient for you. How many times did you have to ram the Carrera to get it off the road and wrapped around a tree? And were you careful with the petrol bomb? They're looking for petrol spillage in the passenger footwell of your car, or even in a cupholder.' He hoped she didn't understand about petrol evaporation, but she didn't flinch.

'I've already told you I have no idea how to make a petrol bomb. And I didn't ram his damn Porsche. Maybe he did it himself so he could get rid of the wife and have his fancy bit.'

'The fault with that theory is that he didn't have a car. His wife was in his car because her car had a dead battery. So we know your thoughts are slightly skewed, because he couldn't have done it.'

Elsa Manvers seemed to fold in on herself. 'I haven't killed anybody.'

Will picked up the knife, placed it in his briefcase and stood. 'Elsa, you're now going to be taken to our charge officer who will complete the formalities.' He logged them out, and he held the door open for Claire to pass through in front of him.

They stood at the glass looking into the interview room and watched Elsa. She seemed to be in shock, unmoving, but suddenly she reared up and slammed her fists down on to the table. 'Bastards,' she screamed. 'I haven't killed anybody.'

They stared at her, knowing the knife recovered from her plant pot would hold two sets of blood, Daniel's and Paul's.

'I want this sealed up so tightly she'll go away for life with no chance of parole. Little miss nursey thought she'd got away with it. We can now give Oliver and Elle their lives back, but thank God they found that knife.' Will spoke quietly, knowing that careful digging and more than a little bit of luck had given them the answer. 'Let's go tell the team we have a result.'

EPILOGUE
EIGHT MONTHS LATER

Elsa Manvers became known as the Retribution Killer in the newspapers. She denied she had any involvement in the deaths of the two men and one woman, although admitted to an overdose in the last medication she ever gave to Christopher Harcourt.

Hearing it said in open court when the prosecution played the interview words sealed her fate on that one alone, but the jury was constantly told that she had no alibis for any of the three murders.

The motive, of course, was the feelings she had for Chris, and with his voice fading fast he had repeated to her what his wife had told him an hour earlier. The press were all over it; the motive was clear, the carer had fallen for the patient with disastrous consequences.

Jess tried to maintain contact with Oliver, even eye contact would have been something, but she knew she had lost Oliver completely when he wouldn't answer her calls or even look in her direction.

The jury returned a unanimous verdict of guilty and the judge was scathing in his comments towards Elsa Manvers, sentencing her to life in prison on each count, to run concurrently, and she must serve a minimum of thirty-seven years before applying for parole.

Naomi was the spokesperson on behalf of herself, Andi and Oliver, on the steps outside court, and she thanked the police for finally taking a serial killer off the streets of Sheffield. Everyone could now sleep easier at night. They would never forget Daniel, Paul and Denise, and Chris would always hold a special place in their hearts. Four people gone, she said, because of one woman who was now paying the price.

Jess had avoided the others in court; she saw this as being her fault entirely. If she hadn't carried out her twenty-seven year plan, none of this would have happened, but she also recognised that Chris had used the affection of his lonely carer to point her in the direction of murder.

Oliver and Elle had been in court every day, but he hadn't even looked at Jess; she would have given everything for just a smile.

Andi and Naomi, along with her twin sons Alex and Harry, had arrived every day together, but they hadn't spoken to her either. Jess was so relieved when the court case finished and she could continue with her plans for her and Malcolm to leave Sheffield.

There was nothing here for her now. She had bought a small cottage about a mile from Josh and Adam's pub, and she was moving there with Malcolm and Daisy. The house in Sheffield was in the final stages of being sold, and she looked forward to the next part of her life. Chris's ashes had been scattered in the rose bed, albeit earlier than he had requested because she wouldn't be at this home in August when the roses were at their glorious best. She knew that was to make sure she left him behind; she didn't want him on this new journey.

Malcolm had reluctantly put his house on the market, but over the months had seen that it could be a positive, moving to the coast in Devon. He would see so much more of his grandsons, and Daisy would love beach walks. He didn't think he would ever recover from the discovery of what Jess had done with Chris in his last hours of life; this wasn't the daughter he had loved unconditionally all his life. If somebody had asked him to describe her, vengeful would not have been on the list at all.

So come Saturday morning they would be loading up a big removals van with furniture they would need in the cottage, and heading off to pastures new.

Josh and Adam had taken the night off. They had spent the day at Jess's new cottage, giving it a thorough clean and had arranged for evening staff in the pub so they could chill out upstairs.

'You looking forward to Mum and Granddad coming down?' Josh stared into the fire, sipping on a small whisky.

'I am. It'll certainly save on petrol; it's a long journey to Sheffield.'

'It was sometimes hard doing it in one day, must admit.'

The fire crackled and Josh pushed his chair a little further away from it. 'We didn't need a fire, it's warm.'

'I like lighting a fire,' Adam said. 'It's comforting. And it might be June, but it's not exactly flaming.'

'Wonder if it's cold in a prison cell?' Josh said quietly.

'You're thinking about Elsa, aren't you?'

'I think about her a lot. Don't you?'

Adam shrugged. 'I do. I can't imagine having a thirty-seven year sentence, and that's only a minimum. She may never get out.'

Josh stared at the flames. 'And you know, I don't think it's totally fair that they counted Dad's death into it; he asked for that, he asked us to do it and we didn't have the guts. She did, and she knew how much to give him to make it an easy passing. She cared that much about him.'

'Josh, I saw her kiss him. Properly, on the lips, and he brought his arm up and around her, so he wasn't asleep. He knew what she was doing. Nurses shouldn't do that.'

Josh sat up. 'I thought you only saw her kiss him. I didn't know he knew what was happening.'

'I didn't tell anybody. I thought why shouldn't he have a bit of fun, but it was only later I realised how wrong it was. At that time I thought him and mum loved each other.'

'Well we know different about that, don't we?'

'The whole fucking world knows about their fake life. And it was, wasn't it?' Adam spoke angrily.

'Don't get uptight about it, and we have to put the whole sorry story behind us. We have to remember our childhood when cancer didn't come into it, and Mum and Dad behaved in front of us like normal loving parents. We have to forget what we heard in court, what we saw in the papers, what we read in that bloody journal.'

'Should we do it now?'

'What?'

'Burn it. We always said we couldn't give it back to her because it would kill her if she thought we'd read it, but we've had it all this time she's been looking for it, so we can't hand it back now. We have to burn it, and we have a fire. We've two days, half tonight and half tomorrow, then put the leather cover in a bin bag and bury it in the bin. Even that will disappear on

Monday in the bin collection.' Adam stared at his brother, waiting for a decision.

'Yes,' Josh said. 'Go and get it.'

One page at a time they destroyed their mother's words. They burnt them all that night, all twenty-seven years of memories. They stayed up till three o'clock, simply burning page after page. Then they fetched a black bin liner and put the exquisitely hand-tooled leather cover in it. Adam carried it outside, rummaged around until it was covered by other rubbish, and headed back upstairs.

The clean-up took longer; ash was everywhere and with their cleaner expected the next morning they wanted to leave no evidence of a strange activity. Vacuuming helped, washing-up liquid and water did the rest. Eventually they stood back. It didn't exactly look pristine, but if the cleaner said something they could just say they were burning old pub paperwork from the previous owners. Josh and Adam had discovered the art of telling lies.

'Can I go to bed now?' Adam said. 'I'm knackered.'

'We can. That's almost the last thing we had to do to make Dad proud. And he would have been proud; we've managed this lot perfectly, followed his final instructions to the letter.'

'Almost the last thing?' Adam stared at his older brother. Didn't three deaths count as perfection, plus a wrong imprisonment for Elsa Manvers because Adam had rammed the bloodied knife used on Paul Browne and Daniel Rubens in a plant pot?

'Dad gave us three names. We got two right, slipped up on the third one. He'll only be truly proud when Oliver Newton is dead.'

THE END

ALSO BY ANITA WALLER

Psychological thrillers

Beautiful

Angel

34 Days

Strategy

Captor

Game Players

Malignant

Liars (co-written with Patricia Dixon)

Gamble

Epitaph

Nine Lives

One Hot Summer

The Family at No. 12

The Couple across the Street

The Missing Ones

Kat and Mouse series

Murder Undeniable (Book 1)

Murder Unexpected (Book 2)

Murder Unearthed (Book 3)

Murder Untimely (Book 4)

Epitaph

Murder Unjoyful (Book 5)

Supernatural

Winterscroft

The Connection Trilogy

Blood Red

Code Blue

Mortal Green

The Forrester Detective Agency Series

Fatal Secrets

Fatal Lies

Fatal Endings

ACKNOWLEDGEMENTS

My grateful thanks go in the first place to the amazing company that is Bloodhound Books. This is my 21st book with them, and is the first one not to be in for the deadline day because I fell down the stairs and did a considerable amount of damage! But it ended up only being two days late, and I hope the little wait was worth it. Thank you Betsy and Fred for welcoming me back into the fold, and to all the rest of the team who will speed this book on its way.

Thank you also to my family who have encouraged me as I start a new part of my writing journey, and have laughed at me as I tremble at the thought of writing a synopsis. A book? No problem. A synopsis? Runs away screaming.

As always I have cheerleaders Judith Baker and Valerie Keogh to thank for their never-ending encouragement. Thank you ladies, stars both of you.

And a massive thank you to my readers, who keep my books high in the charts. That makes me smile!

Much love,
Anita
Sheffield UK

A NOTE FROM THE PUBLISHER

Thank you for reading this book. If you enjoyed it please do consider leaving a review on Amazon to help others find it too.

We hate typos. All of our books have been rigorously edited and proofread, but sometimes mistakes do slip through. If you have spotted a typo, please do let us know and we can get it amended within hours.

info@bloodhoundbooks.com

www.ingramcontent.com/pod-product-compliance
Ingram Content Group UK Ltd.
Pitfield, Milton Keynes, MK11 3LW, UK
UKHW041125040825
7210UKWH00034B/334